DECCIE MUST DIE

MCM INVESTIGATIONS – BOOK 2

CAIMH MCDONNELL

Caimh McDonnell

Visit my website at www.WhiteHairedirishman.com

ISBN: 978-1-912897-39-1

AUTHOR'S NOTE

Hello Dear Reader,

And thank you, as always, for buying/borrowing/stealing my book. Your continued patronage/appropriating/larceny is much appreciated.

Previously, I have used these author's notes to prepare North Americans for the trauma of seeing things spelled correctly, or to explain how a prequel can have a sequel. I've possibly even just rambled on about my dogs, which I would do twenty-four-seven, if allowed. This time though, I wish to discuss with you the nature of time and in particular, the effect of its passing on characters.

You may have read Angels in the Moonlight, the prequel to the Increasingly Inaccurately Titled Dublin Trilogy, or indeed, one of the two sequels (so far) to that prequel. All of which feature a YOUNG Deccie Fadden. I emphasise the word young there. Those books take place in 1999/2000. This book, however, takes place in 'modern times', and yes, I made all of us feel horribly old there, but it had to be done. It's 2022, or later, and we're all going to have to deal with it. At the time of writing, the dreaded pandemic is in the tricky the-worst-is-over/lull-between-the-worst-bits/pre-zombie stage and Deccie

Fadden is a full-grown man. I point that out as, if you the reader, go into this still thinking he's the little fella standing on a sideline beside Bunny, the opening chapter is transformed from an amusing introduction to a rip-roaring tale of high adventure, to the reason you will be burning me in effigy as a monster.

Again, he's a full-grown man. As anyone who has met a man will know, that doesn't mean he's matured, but he's allowed to drink, drive (not at the same time – that's a no, no, for everybody), join an army, see RoboCop in the cinema and do 'other things'.

Consider yourself duly warned.

1

SAY MY NAME

Deccie Fadden stared hard at the ceiling and racked his brain. Yvonne? Yvette? Lynette? No, none of those seemed right. The woman asleep beside him must have a name, and Deccie, as he had solemnly sworn to his dearly departed grandmother, was not the type of man to sleep with a woman without knowing her name. She hadn't made him swear to that precisely, more that he would stick to a general gentlemanly code of conduct. You know, hold doors open, don't make lewd remarks, don't tell tales out of school, don't get caught in the Tesco car park shagging that strumpet from the deli counter in the back of a Ford Cortina.

That last one related specifically to Mr Harper from across the road. Deccie's granny had been great friends with Mrs Harper. Being good Irish Catholics, the Harpers didn't divorce after the incident; instead, they stayed together and provided an invaluable revenue stream for the Irish crockery-manufacturing industry – every couple of weeks the neighbourhood would listen in as the wronged woman hurled plates at the right man.

Pam? Was she a Pam? Was anyone called Pam these days? Oh God, now he was losing faith in the theory he'd developed over the last hour that her name contained a Y and an E. He was screwed in every sense of the word.

In his defence, he'd been drunk. As soon as that justification occurred to him, however, Deccie unhelpfully remembered his grandmother's face as she did her knitting and listened to Mr Harper shouting that very same excuse while ducking airborne items of crockery. It didn't make it any less true, though – both Deccie and [insert name here] had been drunk. Very drunk. Free-bar drunk. He'd been invited to one of those celebrity things – the opening of something or other – which had been held in a nightclub-type place. Come to think of it, it might have been the opening of the nightclub. Over the last few months, he'd been to several of these events, and they were beginning to blend into one. He was drinking a fair bit, but not because of an alcohol problem, rather because of a holy-shit-this-is-free problem. He realised that he'd better cop himself on before he drank himself into an early, albeit freely acquired, grave.

He could remember thinking the girl's name was quite unusual; not unusual enough to stick in the mind, but unusual enough that you wouldn't be able to risk a Fiona or a Helen and have any shot at being accidentally right. Hang on, how could he remember thinking that her name was unusual but couldn't remember what it was? The human mind was an incredible thing, and not in a good way. Deccie's brain might be exacting its revenge for all the grey matter recently sacrificed at the altar of a complimentary bar.

His life was changing quickly and in a multitude of ways. This was his first one-night stand. Technically, it wasn't a one-night stand yet. It might be the start of something more. Maybe he and [insert name here] were destined to be together for ever? Soul mates? Admittedly, the name thing wasn't the greatest of omens. On second thoughts, while they were "at it" earlier on, she had, ironically, kept asking him to call her all manner of names, most of which he felt very uncomfortable uttering.

Why did people get so excited at being told they were naughty? In his less than illustrious academic career, Deccie had been sent to the principal's office countless times, and at no point had it made him horny. As luck would have it, he had been part of one of the first generations of Irish schoolchildren the staff weren't allowed to slap, no matter how annoying the kids were. He knew that for a fact as Mr Dempsey, his ex-headmaster, had spent a great deal of time wistfully explaining it to him while they waited for Deccie's grandad to arrive for yet another "little chat".

Mr Dempsey and Granda had an understanding that it should be Granda, and him alone, who dealt with Deccie's run-ins with the authorities. The one time his granny had shown up, she had instigated a one-woman attempt on behalf of legions of Irish schoolchildren to redress the balance in the smacking stakes. Mr Doyle, the bastard of a religion teacher, had dared to suggest that Deccie was going to end up in prison, and Granny had lost it. She had gone for him as if he were on fire and only she could put him out.

He had wanted to press charges until Dempsey had talked him out of it. Doyle already hated his nickname of Sprinkler, bestowed upon him as a result of his propensity to spit profusely. They could only imagine what his new one would be if it became widely known that a grandmother had bitch-slapped him. Children can be so cruel – especially to those who are cruel to them.

The thing was, Deccie only ever got into trouble for talking. Teachers give out about kids not listening but, in his experience, they got even more annoyed if you did listen and asked a few questions as a result.

So no, the odds of this "romantic coming-together" with [insert name here] being the start of a long-term relationship weren't great.

Deccie glanced to his left at the woman who was asleep on his arm and drooling on his pillow. As if on cue, she spoke in her sleep.

"Disneyland."

Her breath was of the kind several free cocktails thrown into an empty stomach will leave you with. What grown woman dreamed of Disneyland?

Another memory from last night popped into Deccie's head – Bono! Had he really met Bono? Not only that, had he kissed him? Before last night, Deccie, like everyone else in Ireland, had slagged off

Bono. *Damn bleeding-heart do-gooder. Tax-dodging so-and-so. He didn't do enough; he did too much. The new music was shite; the old music was shite. The new way they played the old music was shite.* Say what you wanted about the fella, he provided an invaluable service in being somebody everybody could hate, even if it was for reasons that were diametrically opposed.

While the idea of the man was one thing, the reality was something else. The experience was akin to turning around to find the Sydney Opera House standing beside you at the bar – he was an historical landmark, a cultural touchstone. He was one of the most recognisable people on the planet, even if the recognition was often accompanied by a stream of emphatically-delivered expletives. And Deccie had slapped a big kiss on him? He must have imagined that. It must have been a bloke who looked like Bono. Jesus, that was worse. If there was one thing worse than Bono, it was someone trying to be Bono.

Deccie's memory moved on to a vague recollection of Bono and a giant gorilla. That couldn't be right. While these launch events were always trying to outdo each other in the publicity-stunt stakes, you couldn't have a real gorilla making an appearance. There were rules – actual laws – and there was every chance Bono had campaigned for them to be passed.

The only reason Deccie hadn't dismissed out of hand the idea of it having happened was that recently his life had become all kinds of weird. He was now a "celebrity". People shouted things at him in the street – not always very complimentary things, but still, it beat being ignored. He had been ignored his entire life, and now, suddenly, people were paying attention. Case in point – he was in bed with a girl he was pretty sure was a model and whose name he couldn't remember.

If his gran could see him now. Not right now, obviously. In fact, any other time but now. If she were to see him now, she would drag him out of bed and hose him down like a new inmate in a prison movie. There was nothing hypothetical about that scenario, though. She'd done it before – when she'd discovered him intensely perusing the ladies' underwear section of a mail-order catalogue when he was fourteen.

He was a grown man now – thirty-three years of age. Same as Jesus when he'd reached his grand finale. Much like Jesus, Deccie had found fame in his thirties, and was dividing opinion in a similar fashion – with some people loving him, others not so much. Deccie had kept that comparison to himself, obviously, as even he knew people would take it the wrong way. He had considered trying to grow a beard, though.

Deccie looked around the bedroom. The girl's purse was over on the dressing table. There had to be some ID in it, didn't there? He wrote off the idea almost immediately. Not being able to remember somebody's name while you were waking them up to usher them out of your apartment because you had a busy day ahead was bad; them waking up to find you going through their purse was way worse. Judging by her snoring, the girl was a heavy sleeper, but Deccie still wasn't prepared to take that chance. She might come to suddenly when one of the rides on her imaginary trip to Disneyland became too exciting.

She spoke again. "That's not a walrus."

Deccie agreed. He was pretty sure they didn't have walruses at Disneyland.

A thought struck him. "Hello," he whispered softly. No reaction. "What is your name?"

The girl stirred slightly, smacking her dry lips.

He tried again, leaning in to murmur in her ear. "What is your name?"

She turned her head and moved her face as if she were definitely about to speak.

Deccie held his breath.

"That wasn't offside, Lou Diamond Phillips."

Deccie had no idea what that meant, other than it was entirely useless to him.

As the dawn light peeked through the curtains, he had a brainwave. The venue would have taken pictures of everybody at the party last night and, by now, those images would be all over their social media accounts. He would check Twitter and Instagram, find a picture of the woman currently in his bed, and that would hopefully give him her name. It made perfect sense and he was rather pleased with himself for coming up with it. Now, where was his phone? He must have left it out in the living room, along with most of his clothes.

He slid his arm out from under the girl and tried to get out of bed without disturbing her. Despite his best efforts, she turned over in her sleep and said in a loud and clear voice, "Bastard donkey chiropodist."

Deccie really, really wanted to know what kind of dream this was. Maybe he would ask [insert name here] when he woke her up with breakfast, and her name.

He walked towards the bedroom door, stifling a yelp as he skewered his bare foot on what must've been a piece of jewellery hastily discarded in the throes of passion. He bit down on his lip and, in an act of true bravery that tragically would go unappreciated, managed not to scream. He limped out the door and closed it behind him.

The living room was in near-total darkness, thanks to the fancy blackout blinds he'd installed to maximise the effect of the massive TV he'd bought on hire purchase. He might be famous now, but because Oliver Dandridge, his agent, kept turning down contract offers as he thought they could get a better deal, the reality was that Deccie had little money.

Still, it didn't matter if everyone kept giving him stuff for free. The swish apartment was free, and it was the fanciest place he'd ever set foot in. Lansdowne Towers – fourteen storeys of luxurious existence. Deccie appeared in the marketing brochure as part of the deal. They'd even hired someone to airbrush his image, so he looked less like a tubby chancer who would normally never end up in such opulent surroundings unless he were there to unblock the toilet.

The only light in the room came from the clock on the oven as it flashed 00:00 because he'd never figured out how to set it. It was also the only use he'd got out of the oven so far.

Deccie turned and did let out a yelp this time as the outline of an enormous figure reared up in front of him. He flailed about and eventually found the light switch. The downlights illuminated the spectacle of a huge gorilla in the middle of his lounge, wearing a pair of oversized sunglasses and holding a cocktail. It wasn't real in the sense that it was alive or had been formerly alive, but it was about six feet tall and was also wearing a pair of women's knickers on its head.

Had he stolen or won the large not-real gorilla? Were those Bono's sunglasses? Deccie shook his head. His life was becoming weirder than he ever could have dreamed possible. Speaking of which, he still needed to find out the name of the woman in his bed, and for that, he needed his phone.

He moved around the gorilla – Charlie, his name was Charlie! How could he remember that and not [insert name here]'s name? Unbelievable! He ducked under Charlie's arm – the one holding the cocktail glass – and scanned the coffee table for any sign of his phone. As he did so, his eyes were drawn to what the estate agent had described as the feature wall of the living room.

This time, he screamed. Properly screamed.

A few seconds later, the bedroom door flew open and his guest appeared there, entirely naked save for a concerned expression on her face. "What happened?"

He didn't answer. Instead, he pointed a trembling finger at the wall upon which three words were scrawled in large red letters: *DECCIE MUST DIE!!!*

Three exclamation marks too – the surest sign of an unhinged mind.

"Oh my God," exclaimed [insert name here]. "Who's Deccie?"

He turned to look at her. Honestly – the nerve of some people!

2

THE DISTRESSING THINGS PEOPLE DO FOR DISTRESSED WOOD

Brigit threw herself onto the couch. "OK, where do you want to start?"

"Well," said Dr Megan Wright, "you could start by explaining why you're here."

Brigit took a deep breath. "That's a very broad question, isn't it? I mean, I know it's part of the whole therapist shtick – you ask a wide-open question, and the way I, the patient, interpret said question tells you a great deal about my state of mind. Do I go for the existential crisis 'why are any of us here?' approach, or should I go for a more specific reason like I'm here to discuss my relationship with my father, or why am I having weird dreams where I'm drowning in treacle, or, I dunno, being chased by giant penises."

"Fine. While I am intrigued by the giant-wangs thing, let me be considerably more specific. What the hell are you doing in my office?"

Brigit didn't even look over to where Dr Wright was seated behind her desk. Instead, she stared up and was infuriated to see there was still a picture of an adorable kitten taped to the ceiling. If Brigit had any choice in the matter, which she didn't, she would have gone to see a therapist, any therapist, who didn't possess some inexplicable belief in the healing power of cute felines. The irony was Dr Wright was not the cutesy type. Brigit knew for a fact that her romantic history compared unfavourably with that of a praying mantis.

"Our deal was that I got twenty sessions with you, as part of your divorce settlement, and seeing as I have only used nineteen, I have one session left."

"Given that I never bothered my ass to keep records, I'm forced to take your word for it. However, we had the other nineteen two years ago, and what you definitely do not have is an appointment."

"I know. Lucky for me, your assistant was away from her desk and you were alone in your office."

"That very much depends on your definition of the word 'alone'."

"What's that supposed to—" For the first time, Brigit looked in Dr Wright's direction.

The good doctor turned her laptop around and a nervous-looking, round-faced, auburn-haired woman on the screen gave an awkward wave.

Brigit cringed and sat upright. "Oh my God, I'm really sorry."

"Yes. Before you barged in, we were very close to a breakthrough in relation to Katie's feelings that people are ignoring her."

"Actually," said the nervous-looking woman, "my name is Karen."

"Exactly," said Dr Wright, glaring at Brigit. "Well, the hour was nearly up anyway, so apologies for the interruption. We'll pick this up next week."

"But we were only fifteen minutes into—"

The rest of the sentence was lost as Dr Wright slammed her laptop shut.

Brigit lay back down on the couch. "You really are a terrible therapist."

"You say that, yet I have people literally barging into my office demanding my time."

"I thought that now the pandemic is ... well, sort of over, people would have gone back to in-person sessions?"

Dr Wright pushed back her chair, put her feet up on the desk and pulled out a vape from somewhere. "Mostly, but some people got used to the Zoom thing and they prefer it. One of my male clients seems to be trying to get change out of his pocket offscreen all the time he's talking to me."

Brigit wrinkled her nose. "You don't mean …"

"Yes, I do."

"That is disgusting. Is there someone you can report him to?"

"No, but I do charge him triple. He's paying for all the new doors in my house."

"You are despicable."

Dr Wright blew a plume of scented smoke into the air. "That's as may be, but I got me some bitchin' distressed oak doors. Now, at the risk of repeating myself, what the hell are you doing in my office?"

"I need to talk to somebody."

"Haven't you got friends for this kind of thing? I mean, I can see how you're not the easiest person in the world to get along with, but somebody must have managed it?"

"I have lots of friends actually," responded Brigit tartly. "Probably because I've never slept with any of their husbands."

Dr Wright flopped back in her chair and pulled a face at the ceiling. "Bleugh! That was one time – three times, tops. What exactly is the difference between you and a stalker?"

"Mainly that I, or rather my private investigation agency, was hired by your then husband to follow you because he suspected – correctly, I might add – that you were cheating on him."

"How is it you can't let that go? Terence has."

"Good for him." A thought struck Brigit. She lifted her head off the couch and craned her neck to look over at Dr Wright. "You're not …"

"I'm not what?"

Brigit studied the other woman's face. She was always so infuriatingly well-put-together. Perfect hair. Long eyelashes. Teeth you could see your reflection in. Dr Megan Wright looked like she was made for TV, which she had been until one of her affairs – with a TV producer on that occasion – had scuppered that particular career.

"Oh my God, you're banging your ex-husband, aren't you?"

Dr Wright shifted her gaze and shrugged. "We were in lockdown. It was very hard to meet new people."

"Unbelievable! MCM Investigations is going down the toilet because 2020 was the year philandering arseholes started sleeping with their own spouses, and my therapist is the one person who bucked the trend."

"Let's not pretend I'm your therapist. I'm someone you come to mostly to argue with for twenty sessions – nineteen of which happened a couple of years ago – and I thought we'd both happily moved on with our lives until you came charging into my office in the middle of someone else's appointment."

"Sorry again about that."

"Yeah. Anyway, this might just be the Stockholm syndrome talking, but can we get to the reason for this unhappy reunion? Have you and lover boy broken up again or something?"

"No. If you must know, Paul and I are engaged."

"Congratulations. If you're here to invite me to the wedding, I'm afraid it's a hard pass."

"Really?" said Brigit. "I always assumed you love weddings. You've had enough of them."

Dr Wright laughed. "Good one."

"Thank you."

"If you're looking for a dress, I think I still have a couple of my old ones somewhere. You could staple them together."

Brigit gave a subtle nod. "Touché."

It was fair to say Dr Wright and Brigit's relationship was rather unusual. Almost the entire time the two of them had been in a room together had been spent throwing verbal jabs at each other. It was pretty messed-up, but it served a purpose. Brigit's job – hell, her entire life – felt as if it were taken up with trying to manage other people and make sure everyone else was happy. She was the one who made everything tick along nicely. Dr Megan Wright, Canada's one-woman gift to divorce lawyers everywhere, was somebody Brigit didn't even have to pretend to get on with.

"So," said Dr Wright, "is this pre-wedding nerves?"

"No. We haven't set a date. In fact, we haven't even told anybody. We were about to, then my father announced he was getting remarried and I didn't want to steal his thunder."

A groan came from the other side of the room.

"What?" asked Brigit.

"Sorry. It's just that I've already had two daddy-issues sessions this morning and I'm really not in the mood for a third."

"I do not have daddy issues."

"Now, where have I already heard that twice today?"

"I'm delighted he's getting remarried. Delighted. Admittedly, if I'd have known it was going to be postponed so many times, thereby delaying my own wedding, I might not have held off saying anything, but I'm committed to it now. And again – absolutely delighted."

"The lady doth protest too much, methinks."

"Oh, shut up. That isn't the problem I'm here about. Paul and I are fine. Well, fine-ish. I mean, he's not fine. I broke his leg in three places."

"What? You broke his leg?"

"No," said Brigit. "I said he broke his leg in three places."

Dr Wright leaned forward. "Paging Dr Freud. That's not what you said. You said, and I quote, 'I broke his leg in three places.'"

"I didn't. I mean – OK, I was holding the ladder, but it wasn't my fault."

"Neither I nor your subconscious believes you."

"OK. Obviously, I feel bad about it. I answered a phone call and I shouldn't have. But in my defence, we're trying to run a business while setting up our new office-cum-home and I was multitasking while he was trying to find a leak. But yes, I let him down ... Unfortunately, from about twenty feet."

Dr Wright sucked in air through her teeth.

"I know. It was horrible."

"Does he blame you?"

"No," said Brigit. "At least, he says he doesn't."

"That's good, then." Dr Wright delivered the three words in such a way that made it clear that not only did she not believe them, but nobody else involved did either. "So, if he's fine with the GBH," she continued, "what exactly is the problem?"

"Well, if you must know—"

"It seems you feel I must."

Brigit ignored the interruption. "Everything was going great. The business was expanding, so we bought ourselves a magnificent building up in Christchurch. The idea was that the first two floors could be our offices, and the third and fourth ones would be our living space. When you think about it, buying a home together is a much bigger commitment than getting married."

"I've had more marriages than houses," conceded Dr Wright. "In fact, it was because of the last marriage that I lost the last house. Thanks again for that."

"Stop having sex with people you are not married to."

"Do you think it's this judgemental attitude that makes you such an unhappy person, Brigit?"

"No. It's mainly because I went a bit crazy, and to overcompensate for the wedding I was unable to have, I convinced my partner that we could afford to buy a building we probably couldn't, and then there was a bloody pandemic."

"Weren't there furlough schemes and payment holidays, and all sorts of other stuff to cover that kind of crap?"

Brigit raised an eyebrow in the doctor's direction.

"What? I don't know. I'm a therapist – we were making money hand over fist through the whole thing. People were trapped in their houses with their families. I'm about to even out the number of houses and weddings."

"Well, that's great for you," said Brigit, with zero sincerity. "Meanwhile, over here in the real world, we furloughed the limited staff we had and shut up shop. The building we bought was a fixer-upper so Paul decided to do all the building work himself while I answered the call and went back into nursing for the year."

"What was that like?"

Brigit said nothing but gave the doctor a very long and very hard look.

Dr Wright shrugged apologetically. "Yeah, that was probably a stupid question."

"Agreed. I went back to the hospice where I used to work, so in a way, I was spared the worst of it. The people on the front line of that thing all deserve medals or to have songs written about them or, at the very least, a pay rise that is not derisory."

"Didn't people clap on their doorsteps or something?"

"No," said Brigit firmly. "That was in Britain. Thankfully, the Irish government didn't patronise people who have been underpaid for decades by encouraging the public to give them a round of applause. They're highly skilled medical professionals, not kids in a nativity play." She picked up a cushion and hugged it, which helped her relax a little. "I'm sure a lot of the people clapping probably meant well."

"So now you're back in the detective business?" asked Dr Wright. Brigit guessed she was keen to move the conversation on.

"We're trying to be. Paul is out of action as the full-leg cast means he's in a wheelchair."

"Which he definitely doesn't blame you for?"

"In my defence, I said that we needed to hire someone to answer the phones."

"You picked a hell of a way to prove your point."

Brigit glared at her. "I am trying to get to the key problem."

"You broke a man and that really isn't the key problem?"

"I wish! I've not told him because he's struggling with being cooped up as it is, but we're broke."

"Completely?"

"Well, the mortgage payments restart with a vengeance next month and we don't have any money for that, let alone for any other bills. So, yeah – we're broke."

"Why haven't you told him?"

"Because," snapped Brigit, "I started lying about it, and now I've dug myself into a hole I don't know how to get out of. Paul, thanks to his start in life, is ludicrously tight with money. It's so bad it's a mental issue, and I spent months talking him round and convincing him everything would be fine."

"Ah, I see. And you're worried that Paul will leave you when he finds out?"

Brigit gawped at Dr Wright. "Well, I wasn't until you said that."

The doctor shrugged. "Hey, look on the bright side. Sounds as if he's going to find it really hard to go anywhere."

"It'll be fine. All I need to do is find one or two – three, tops – really well-paid jobs and we'll be OK-ish." Brigit placed the cushion over her face and screamed into it.

"Alright," said Dr Wright once Brigit had emerged from her primal scream into soft furnishings. "It was 2020/2021. Nobody did well out of it."

"You did."

Dr Wright laughed. "I really did. I'm seriously considering buying a sports car."

Brigit gave Dr Wright a withering glare that would cause most right-minded people to burst into flames out of sheer shame. Of course, for that to happen, the recipient would have to have the requisite capacity to feel any kind of shame.

"Do you wanna see pictures of the two cars I've narrowed it down to? I could really use a second opinion."

"Read. The. Room."

"Alright. My point was, apart from me, do you know anybody else who has thrived in the last year?"

"Well," said Brigit, "as it happens, I know one other person. Our receptionist, the person who, ironically, was supposed to be answering our phones. The guy I hired only because he was an old school friend of Paul's. He found himself a new career. Turns out his annoying compulsion to have an opinion on absolutely everything, which made him the world's worst receptionist, works out pretty well on the radio. For some inexplicable reason, Deccie's become a sensation."

"Oh my God," said Dr Wright, sounding genuinely excited. "Deccie Fadden? You know Deccie Fadden?"

Brigit rolled her eyes. "Please don't start."

"It's just, I'm a big fan of his show and I've been chasing his producer. I think he could have me on as an occasional guest presenter. He and I would work great together."

"Doesn't the show already have a female co-host?"

Dr Wright batted away the question. "Could you introduce me?"

"No, I could not. Deccie is Paul's friend, not mine. To be honest, my only connection to him any more is that I have to interview people to be his replacement. I say replacement, but we got way fewer complaints and way more business the week he accidentally sent the switchboard straight to voicemail. You could literally throw a rock and find somebody better for the job. Seriously – a person who is partially concussed and pissed off *after being hit by a rock* would still do a better job answering our phones."

"Couldn't Paul answer the phones?"

"No."

"Why—" Dr Wright stopped and slowly began to nod. "Ahhhh, because you haven't told him the company is in trouble and you don't want to, so you're going to hire somebody you can't afford instead."

"You have a really unhelpful way of phrasing things."

"It's called the truth. Hey – I'm not judging." She gave Brigit a broad smile. "I've lied to my partner in the past."

"This is different."

"Sure it is."

"Stop smiling at me. I'm hiring somebody on a trial basis – they just don't know that the trial is more about whether we'll make it through than they will." Brigit stopped talking, looked down at her watch and gasped. "Oh shit!" She leaped to her feet. "I'm supposed to be doing the interviews right now. What the hell am I doing here?"

"This does kind of feel like where we came in," offered Dr Wright. "I would mention that from now on you'll have to pay for sessions, but given what you've told me, it's an unnecessary cheap shot."

"Thanks for nothing," said Brigit as she threw open the door and strode out of the room.

"Although," shouted Dr Wright after her, "if you get me a meeting with Deccie's people ..."

"No!"

3

PLEASE LEAVE A MESSAGE

Brigit did not consider herself a "bargy" person. She had been raised properly, with an appreciation of the importance of knocking, queueing and waiting your turn. When she first started working as a nurse, she'd been taken under the wing of Dolores Stone, a matronly matron from Wexford. Sister Stone had a great many theories on a great many things – chief among them was manners. She had worked in England for many years and had noticed a difference between the Irish and the English. In her opinion, the English were more likely to be lacking in the manners arena.

This belief was not based on any lazy xenophobic stereotypes, but on geography. Sister Stone believed Irish people benefited from coming from a smaller country. In practice, this meant she believed that most Irish people lived with a nagging little voice in the back of their head that suggested they were being watched by somebody they knew at all times. She called it the "someone from the village" theory.

It was nothing to do with the ridiculous notion some foreigners have that Ireland is a small enough country that everybody knows everybody else, but it is small enough that somebody somewhere nearby *might* know you or somebody from your family, or be the friend of a friend. Her theory also explained why people from Dublin had fewer manners than people from the country, and this might have been why Brigit found it so credible.

So, in general, she prided herself on being a very polite person, yet here she was, barging into her second room of the day, and it wasn't even 11am. In her defence, the door she was now barging through was one she owned. It was the front door of the new MCM Investigations offices, although the sight of the woman standing behind the reception desk caused Brigit to do a double-take.

The building was currently in a "state of flux", which was a very kind way of putting it. Paul was no DIY expert and, unfortunately, before he could get around to finishing any of the things he'd started, the ladder incident had happened. Now he was a mess and their office/home was too. Phil Nellis, Paul's oldest friend and MCM Investigation's sometime employee, had assisted Brigit in moving the fridge up to the top floor. That way, Paul could at least reach some food and pop it into the microwave.

Previously, the reception area hadn't looked too bad, but somehow, the glamorous woman behind the desk holding a phone to her ear while taking down notes made it appear shabbier, if only by contrast. She was in her early forties, with long black hair that fell around her shoulders. She wore a burgundy designer suit that accentuated her impressive figure and was living proof that some people had avoided piling on the "pandemic pounds". She flashed Brigit a bright apologetic smile as she held up one finger in the internationally accepted sign language for "please just give me a minute" while she spoke into the receiver in a silky-smooth telephone voice.

"OK," the woman purred. "I understand the urgency of the situation, and don't worry, I guarantee someone will get back to you as soon as possible. You have my word." She listened for another couple of seconds then nodded. "Absolutely. We will be in contact imminently. Bye-bye, then." She put down the phone, finished the note she was writing on the pad and looked up at Brigit. "Sorry about that. Are you here for the interviews?"

"Yes," said Brigit, because in a way she was, although this other woman seemed so confident that Brigit wondered if she had walked into the wrong offices.

"I am really sorry," said the woman, "but due to a last-minute development in a case, the person who was supposed to be doing the interviews has been unavoidably detained. If you have the time, you're welcome to wait and I can grab you a cup of coffee?"

Brigit looked in the corner at the expensive coffee machine she had bought the company as a moving-in gift, and which she had been meaning to send back. The bloody thing didn't work. All it did was make a sound that reminded her of one of her uncle George's more expansive attempts at clearing his throat, before the machine spat out boiling-hot water in alarmingly random directions. She pointed at the out-of-order sign she had hung on it after the guy who had come in to fix the broadband had almost come to blows with the thing.

"I don't think it works."

"It didn't," said the woman, "but I fixed it. Again, we are so sorry for the inconvenience. If you can't wait, could you give me your name and number? I guarantee somebody will ring you back and reschedule your interview for a time that suits you."

"Actually," said Brigit, "I'm the idiot who was supposed to be doing the interviews."

The woman dropped the pen she had been holding and blushed. "Oh my God, I'm so sorry."

"Why are you apologising?"

The woman looked slightly flustered. "It's just, I got here and the door was open but no one was about, so I sat down to wait, and then the phone rang and I answered it because, well, a phone was ringing, and while I was doing so another lady came in for an interview, so I ended up taking her details because she thought I was ..." She looked down, realised where she was standing, and moved away from her position behind the reception desk as if she had just been informed it was about to burst into flames. "I'm so sorry."

"Stop apologising. I'm the one who should be apologising. I got delayed."

"These things happen," said the other woman diplomatically.

"They really shouldn't," countered Brigit. "Which is why, as you can see, we desperately need an excellent office manager."

"Right. Oh, speaking of which, you had a call from the assistant of Oliver Dandridge from the Dandridge Talent Agency. He is really keen to speak to you ASAP. She emphasised several times how important it was. All the details are on the pad there."

"I'll phone him back after I'm done bringing our new office manager up to speed."

The woman's face dropped and she lowered her gaze to her shoes. "Good. Of course. Excellent."

"By which I mean you," added Brigit. "I mean, assuming you're willing to take the job on?"

The woman beamed a perfect smile at Brigit. "Absolutely."

Brigit returned the smile and held out her hand. "Excellent. I'm Brigit Conroy by the way."

The woman accepted the handshake. "Cynthia Marsh. Delighted to make your acquaintance."

"Cynthia? I read your CV last night. To be honest, I assumed you'd sent it in by mistake. Didn't you work for the fund management company up in the IFSC?"

"I did."

"What makes you want to leave there to come here?" Brigit winced at the tone of disbelief in her own voice.

Cynthia blushed. "I just fancied a change of scenery."

"Not that I'm trying to talk you out of it, but you know our salary won't be as good as it is there?"

She shrugged. "Money isn't everything."

Something in Brigit found anybody who said that kind of thing inherently untrustworthy. She'd made a snap decision, and while she wasn't regretting it, one of those pesky little tickles was creeping into the back of her mind, like something wasn't quite right. What was she missing?

"Wouldn't you need to work your notice?" she asked.

"Not in the circumstances."

"Right," said Brigit with a nod. She paused for a second, then her deeply ingrained need to know everything made its presence felt. "When you say 'the circumstances'..."

Cynthia gave a curt bob of her head. "Last Friday, I punched the CEO in the face."

"Hard?"

"Not hard enough. I should probably explain."

Brigit shook her head. "No, you shouldn't. When I left nursing, I'd just tattooed a doctor, and not in a way he wanted to be. So really – no explanation is necessary. Besides, you made the coffee machine work. Anything short of manslaughter and the job would always have been yours. Actually ..." She licked her lips nervously. "Yeah. Look, Cynthia – I need to be honest with you. We really need an office manager, but also, you should know we're not in great shape financially."

"Right," said Cynthia slowly.

"I mean, we were. Before ..."

"The thing."

"Exactly. The thing. The global shitshow thing. And we hope to be again soon. But I can't make any guarantees about how good a long-term prospect we are."

"OK." Cynthia looked around. "I appreciate your honesty. I do need a job, but I also want to work somewhere that's fun, and I reckon this might be it. So I'm willing to take the chance."

"Brilliant!" said Brigit.

A thumping noise from upstairs stopped their conversation from going any further.

Cynthia pointed towards the ceiling. "That's been happening a lot, but I wasn't sure what it was."

"Don't worry about it." While Brigit felt better for being honest, explaining how the noise was a cry for attention from her partner whom she had accidentally and temporarily crippled felt like too much honesty.

Cynthia gave her a relieved smile. "Cup of coffee?"

Brigit let out a deep sigh. "Thanks, but no, thanks. I'd better go see if I can score us a job."

4

THE SACRED ART OF LESBIAN JUGGLING

Brigit had returned the call she'd missed from the Dandridge Talent Agency and was informed that Oliver Dandridge himself needed to speak with her immediately and in person. The woman on the other end of the phone delivered the "in person" bit in an awed whisper, as if Brigit had just been granted an audience with the pope. Brigit consulted with her new office manager and, without being briefed, Cynthia had fake-checked Brigit's diary and come up with some imaginary meetings she could move around if absolutely necessary. Brigit could tell she was going to be invaluable. Fingers crossed they'd land the kind of whale clients they desperately needed so that MCM Investigations could actually pay her at some point.

The offices of the Dandridge Talent Agency were located just off Baggot Street and demonstrated the kind of wealth that Brigit was in the market for. There was an awful lot of white-on-white decor that called to mind the set of a toothpaste commercial – an expensive one. She also observed that the place was staffed exclusively by stick-thin women in their early twenties.

Brigit knew it was wrong to judge people by their looks, so she held off doing so right until the point at which three of the women drew lots to see who would have to take out the bin. The brunette lost and Brigit watched on as she turned the process into the opening act of an opera while the other two shouted encouragement from behind the reception desk as if it were the bunker of a nuclear testing facility. When Brigit had been their age, she had been dealing with bedpans, many of which were still being used at the time. The three women took turns asking Brigit if she fancied a beverage, although each one seemed surprised when she said yes to a cup of coffee and promptly ignored her request.

It turned out that in the world of the Dandridge Agency, "immediately" didn't carry the same meaning as it did in Brigit's world. She'd been waiting for over an hour when she caught herself fantasising about ripping the sign that read "be kind" off the wall and beating the receptionist to death with it. The only reason she held back was the mental image of a poor cleaner having to spend their evening trying to get all the blood out of the white carpet, because there was no way the two remaining staff would do it. Just as she was about to consider leaving, or at least pop out to get her own coffee, the receptionist rushed over and hurried Brigit to her feet and through a door to meet the man himself.

Oliver Dandridge's office was decorated in the same overly white colour scheme as the reception. He sat behind a desk the size of a snooker table, but unfortunately, the room itself was not much bigger than a snooker table. Brigit squeezed into the guest chair as directed by the woman who was still recovering from taking the bin out. She was beginning to realise why the staff were so thin – they had to be in order to manoeuvre around his furniture.

Dandridge's mop of blonde hair fell over a face that had been nipped, tucked and plucked so much that he looked more like a latex puppet than a human being. Guessing his age was an impossible task, although "old enough to know better" seemed a safe bet. Even amid the whiteness of the room, his teeth stood out, bleached so bright as to be painful to look at. His garish paisley shirt at least went some way towards camouflaging the stains from the breakfast roll he was wolfing down with one hand while holding a phone to his ear with the other.

To avoid watching the spectacle of a middle-aged man angrily masticating his way through a meal while making unhappy grunting noises into a phone, Brigit pretended to be inexplicably interested in her own fingernails. She jumped as Dandridge abruptly hurled half of the breakfast roll across the room and it collided with the wall just beside and above her head.

He spat out several large chunks of his meal as he screamed, "Damn it, Tina! You're supposed to be my charity pimp. Don't you screw me on this."

Brigit watched the breakfast roll slide down the wall beside her and into a bin whose position suggested this was not the first time such an event had taken place.

Dandridge, paying Brigit no attention, scratched his nuts furiously as he spoke. "And you know how much my client loves charity. He lives for charity. He eats, shits and breathes charity, but it's my job to make sure that you do your job so that he can keep doing his job. He is not doing an appeal about intestinal diseases. No client of mine is going to be the face of bloody stools. Do you understand me?

"The last time we worked with you, you put him with his arm around a young woman in a bathing suit. I don't care if she'd just become the first whatever to swim the Irish Sea. We both know Twitter had a field day at his expense. They pick the one picture where it looks like his eyes are looking somewhere they shouldn't and suddenly, he's no longer presenting the Irish Plumbing Awards. He had that gig for eight years. I'd already asked my comedy guy to do up five sheets of plumbing jokes. Do you know how much comedians cost? Actually – fuck all, but that's not the point. What am I supposed to do with those sheets now, Tina? Do you want me to email them over? Maybe you can repurpose them as jokes about the large intestine?"

Dandridge raised his fist as if he was going to knock the desk out if it started to move. "Pet neutering? Are you trying to kill me? The man is going through a divorce, owing to some totally unfounded allegations which, unfortunately, they have video footage of. Do I need to draw you a picture of how easy it'll be for them to edit that together with the neutering appeal?"

"For God's sake, the *Sunday Bastard* has him on camera showing his you-know-what to you-know-who. If you don't know who, buy a newspaper – his pixelated scrotum is receiving that much press exposure, I'm thinking of getting it to run for a seat in the next election. What we need here is some misdirection. We need one of the big boys. I'm talking cancer – he's either going to have to have it or cure it. Give me something I can work with, Tina. We're trying to save lives here. Quite possibly yours."

Tina said something. As far as Brigit was concerned, the second word of it should have been "off", but Tina's voice sounded depressingly placatory.

Dandridge got to his feet, sending various pieces of his breakfast tumbling to the floor, and roared into the phone, "To quote my client, 'Yes, it's hard, and what are you going to do about it?'" He slammed the phone into its cradle and slumped back into his chair. After a moment, he remembered Brigit was there.

"And you are?"

"Brigit Conroy."

"Right. Lesbian juggling troupe. Nice. Empowerment, sexual tension, objects being thrown around – there's a lot there to love. Afraid you are shit out of luck, though. I found out this morning that bastard Eddie Warring just signed a disabled juggling troupe. You haven't got a hope against that. The whole lesbian thing is sexy, but it's not disabled sexy."

Brigit nodded. "I've been in this room barely two minutes and I can confidently say you are the worst human being I have ever met, and I've previously encountered an actual serial killer and a bona fide war criminal." She hadn't expected to say this, but it turned out that, despite her overwhelming need to secure a client, everyone has their breaking point, and a splodge of unapologetic breakfast roll on the shoulder of her jacket was hers.

Dandridge seemed entirely unconcerned with her assessment of him. "While you're not the first person to say that, I can name two people who are worse than me, one of whom I represent. You're not even the first juggler to insult me this week. Look at my face – do I seem concerned?"

"You've had so much done, it's impossible to tell."

As Dandridge was drawing in breath to return fire, the intercom on his desk beeped and the receptionist's voice came through quickly. "She's not the lesbian juggler lady."

He threw out his arms in disgust and shouted at the ceiling, "Who the hell is she, then?"

"I'm the MCM Investigations woman," supplied Brigit. "And you can speak to me directly. I'm not deaf."

"Pity," said Dandridge. "If you were and you could juggle, then we might have something."

"What is the obsession with juggling?" Despite herself, Brigit really wanted to know.

Dandridge jabbed his finger at the table. "We've already found everybody on the planet who can sing, dance, bake, do all those things at the same time, or do any of those things having also previously presented the weather forecast, competed in the Olympics or been in a soap opera. That stuff has been done. Juggling is the new frontier. The gold rush. Well, that and other circus skills, really." Dandridge jumped to his feet again and yelled, "Marcy – ring Tommy Bowe and tell him we're sending him to clown college."

He settled back down in his chair, looking inexplicably pleased with himself, then pointed across the table at Brigit. "I've decided I like you."

"Cool. If it's all the same to you, I'm going to stick with my initial assessment of you being a massive arsehole."

"I am." He attempted what might, several operations ago, have been a smile. "It pretty much comes with the job. My redeeming feature is that at least I know it."

"There is absolutely nothing redemptive about that. If anything, it makes your arseholery even worse."

Dandridge nodded. "I do find myself drawn to you. Are you single?"

"Are you joking?"

"Dinner. I'll pay. How's your schedule looking?"

Brigit paused to consider the offer. "I think I have a gap just after hell freezes over. Why would you want to go out with somebody who has already called you the worst human being they've ever met?"

Dandridge shrugged. "It's kind of my thing. All my ex-wives hate me. I believe they still meet up for lunch on alternate Thursdays to discuss precisely how much." He leaned forward. "Don't tell me you've never had angry sex with someone you loathe? There's nothing quite like it."

Brigit winced. "I'd throw up right now, but I think your staff would need to call in the UN to handle the clean-up operation. Thanks for thinking of me, but I'd rather jump in front of a bullet."

Dandridge clapped his hands together. "Actually, that kinda works out perfectly. That's what I needed to talk to you about."

"Excuse me?"

"Our mutual friend, not to mention my number-one client, Deccie Fadden, finds himself in need of protection, and he has directed me to hire you, or at least your agency or whatever, to do it."

"Deccie? Why does Deccie need protection?"

"He received a death threat."

Brigit opened her mouth to dismiss the idea, but stopped herself. She was pretty sure she had personally threatened to kill Deccie on at least three separate occasions, the last time being when he had confused her sister-in-law with a client and had informed her that her husband had been having an affair with a truck driver.

"Exactly how did he receive this threat?"

"Written in blood on the wall of his apartment."

"Blood?" she echoed.

"Well, blood-red paint." Dandridge looked oddly disappointed at having to make this admission. "Still a death threat, though. Why is it this world always tries to take the great ones young – Lennon, Cobain, Tupac, Deccie ..."

"You are kidding?"

"Do I look like I'm kidding?"

"Again, with apologies to your plastic surgeon, it is literally impossible to tell."

"While you're sitting here flirting with me, Miss ..."

"Conroy," offered the disembodied voice through the intercom.

"Right now, your client, the national treasure that is Deccie Fadden, is defenceless and in fear of his life."

"OK," said Brigit. "Pretty much every element of that last sentence was incorrect, but let's focus on the big parts. First things first, why would somebody be trying to kill Deccie?"

Dandridge threw up his arms. "How do I know? You're the detective. The man has a lot of enemies."

"How?" asked Brigit. "From that radio show thing he's on?"

Despite its limitations, Dandridge's face gave looking shocked a good go. "That radio show thing?" he repeated. "The man is a sensation. He's currently the hottest property in town, which is why we don't want this getting out and messing up his contract negotiations. No police either. I want people focused on one thing and one thing only – Deccie Fadden, in media terms, is the second coming."

"Alright," scoffed Brigit. "I know it's your job, but let's dial down the bullshit a few notches, OK?"

"Have you heard the show?"

Brigit shrugged. "I'm more into podcasts."

"It's also the most popular podcast in Ireland."

"Really? To be honest, if I was that keen to listen to Deccie's opinions, he'd still be our receptionist."

Brigit had in fact been avoiding hearing or reading anything about Deccie's media career. The last contact they'd had was when he'd emailed her to announce he was leaving his position as manager of MCM Investigations to pursue a career in the media. Paul had stopped her from writing back to inform him he'd never been the manager and had barely been the receptionist. She had hired him only as a favour to Paul and had instantly regretted her decision from day one. Having Deccie sitting in their office, supposedly answering the phones, was like witnessing the comments section of a newspaper article come to life.

Dandridge shook his head. "Unbelievable." He raised his voice. "Ethan – Deccie presentation."

An expectant pause followed. Dandridge raised a finger. "Give it a second."

The lights dimmed and, with a whirring noise, a projector descended from the ceiling above Brigit's head.

"What the actual ..."

An image of Deccie, looking as mysterious and brooding as a tubby Dublin lad in his mid-thirties could manage, appeared on the wall behind Oliver Dandridge's head.

He pointed up at it. "Who is Deccie Fadden?"

"I know who ..."

"Shush," hissed Dandridge. "I'm doing this presentation for ITV tomorrow. You're a good dry run."

The picture changed to Deccie giving a cheeky grin. He'd either had his teeth done or somebody knew their way around Photoshop.

"In just eighteen months, how do you go from being a caller to a late-night phone-in show to becoming the presenter of the highest-rated radio show in Ireland?"

"Really?" Brigit had heard from Paul that Deccie was doing well, but still.

"Oh, yeah," said Dandridge. "He owns drive time. Caint FM's third-highest-rated show is a repeat of his show they broadcast at midnight."

"But ..." The world had finally gone mad.

Dandridge gestured in an overly showy manner, like he'd practised this presentation one too many times. "I could tell you about it, but why don't I show you?"

He raised one hand and brought it down in a chopping motion.

Nothing happened.

"Why don't I show you?" he repeated, before doing the hand chop again.

"Are you OK?"

"Shut up," he snapped. "There's a sensor thing. The guy swore to me it was fixed. Useless piece of—"

Dandridge was interrupted by a female voice from a concealed speaker somewhere in the room.

Today on the show –

"Finally!" said Dandridge.

– we're going to be discussing whether gay people should serve in the military, following comments by the departing head of the Irish Armed Forces.

The voice stopped and Dandridge pointed at the ceiling. "There, gentleman ..."

"Excuse me?" said Brigit.

"The ITV people are all men," barked Dandridge. "There, gentlemen," he continued, "is the start of a debate that's been had thousands of times on shows all over the world – where liberals and conservatives do battle again and again. It plays out the same way every time – unless ..."

He performed the chopping motion repeatedly until the female voice came back. *Before we go to the phones, let's get the thoughts of my co-host. What do you reckon, Deccie?*

I'll tell you what, Rhona – I don't care.

Dandridge gawped with faux surprise.

I don't know why we have an army at all. Pointless. I'd just have a load of guns, and if we get into a war, we just give them out to the toughest fifty people in Ireland and let them handle it.

The lights went up and Oliver Dandridge spread his arms wide in a ta-da-type motion, which Brigit felt was entirely unwarranted.

"I don't get it," she said.

"You don't get it?" repeated Dandridge, looking genuinely surprised. "The toughest-fifty-people-in-Ireland bit has been running for a month. It made the papers. They've had people ringing in non-stop to argue who should make the list. So far, they've got two-thirds of the Irish rugby team, those two female boxers, Roy Keane ..."

"Obviously."

"Obviously. That MMA guy, Martin Regan, threatened to knock

Deccie out because he's not on the list. I mean, it was mentioned in front of the world's press at a weigh-in in Las Vegas, baby." Dandridge actually hugged himself with delight. "Meanwhile, the ratings for Deccie's show continue to rise."

Brigit was incredulous. "Because of that one bit?"

"No," said Dandridge. "That's just one example from many. All right, it's the best one. There were even questions asked in the Dáil last week because the rugby team has agreed to take on the Irish Army in a charity paintball tournament, but the army is refusing. The public has pledged a quarter of a million euros to the children's hospital if they go ahead with it. But again, just one example. People who had never heard of Caint FM – a station that was failing spectacularly, by the way – are now avid listeners. People love him."

"Apart from those who want to kill him."

Dandridge flapped a hand dismissively. "People love him or they hate him. The point is – he inspires genuine emotion in people. You can't put a price on that, although, seeing as his contract runs out next month, I will be doing so." He pointed a finger in Brigit's direction. "And that's why we're hiring you to protect him and find out who's behind these threats."

"Hang on – threats, plural?"

Dandridge flapped a hand about. "He's received threatening letters. Who hasn't?"

"From who?"

"That's what I'm paying you to find out. Actually, the station is – I got them to agree to fund any security costs as part of the year-long contract the idiots put him on after he'd finished his six-month's probation. I need you to investigate and, y'know, protect Deccie in the meantime. I'd never forgive myself if anything happened to him."

As he said that last bit, Brigit could actually see the euro signs in his eyes.

"Right," she said, cursing herself for feeling the need to be honest. "Thing is, we don't do protection work. That's pretty specialised."

"I know. It's why you're perfect. As part of the thing with that MMA fella, Deccie didn't put him on the list, but he did put the guy's bodyguard on it. Said his bodyguard must be tougher, as real men don't need bodyguards."

"Ahhhh," said Brigit.

Dandridge nodded. "Precisely. You can protect him and we can pretend you're his temporary personal assistant. Apparently, Shauna, his actual assistant, needs a holiday."

"I bet she does."

"So, if anyone asks, you're one of his hangers-on, and he's giving you some work because he's such a generous guy."

"No way."

"Oh, please, save me the wounded pride. You go through people's bins for a living. What's your daily rate for twenty-four-hour protection?"

Brigit locked eyes with the agent. She settled on the highest number she could say while keeping a straight face. "A thousand euros a day."

"Absolutely not."

She stood up to leave. "Final offer."

"It'll be two grand, and if anyone asks, I talked you down from three. I'm not having a client of mine protected for so little."

"But ..."

"No buts. If you want to thank me, let me take you to dinner."

"I will never be that thankful."

Dandridge reached his hand across the desk. "Shake on it?"

"I'm not touching you." She turned to leave, which was an ungraceful operation thanks to the confined space. "Have one of your staff email me the details, and have the other two check to see if she managed to do it correctly."

Brigit pushed through the door to find the three female members of staff standing there, glaring at her.

"Hi again, girls." She pointed over her shoulder. "The big baby tossed his food again. You might need to call in a specialist to clean it up. And by the way, I never got that cup of coffee."

5

SACRILICIOUS

Jimmy Stewart opened the cardboard box and looked inside. "Ah, Phil, you really shouldn't have. It's a cake. This is so unexpected."

He stared at the face of Phil Nellis across the kitchen table from him and, despite being wholly familiar with the man's inability to grasp playful sarcasm, a part of him was still disappointed to see the blank expression beaming back at him.

"Of course it is a cake. It's in a cake box. I deliver cakes for a living."

Jimmy sighed. "I know, Phil. I was only pulling your leg."

"My wife makes the cakes. I deliver the cakes. We've been doing this for a year and a half now. Do you need to take one of those tests? Maybe old age has made you go loopy? It happens. Mrs Byrne from across the road keeps getting her jubblies out. It's very upsetting, to tell you the truth. One of the young fellas from the estate burst into tears. He's not been the same since. Seeing your first pair of boobs is a big deal for a young man. The last thing he wants them to be is eighty-six years old and belonging to a woman screaming about the bin men stealing her rubbish."

Jimmy paused. It happened a lot during conversations with Phil

Nellis. There was something oddly hypnotic about listening to the way the man saw the world.

"Relax, Phil. It was a joke."

"You shouldn't make jokes about Mrs Byrne. It's not her fault. The doctor said it was the medication."

"I wasn't. You were the one who brought her up. I was just making a joke because you come here every week, and every time you bring a cake."

"Do you not like the cakes?"

"I love the cakes."

"Da Xin makes a great cake. You should see our online reviews. We've got four drivers now, and she's taking on another couple of staff."

"She makes a fantastic cake," said Jimmy, both to reassure Phil and because it also happened to be the truth.

Da Xin was that rarest of things – a Covid success story. Everybody and their auntie had got into baking when the first lockdown hit, but only she had turned her skills into a thriving business. The Little Cake Lady had become nothing short of a phenomenon. As the company expanded, Jimmy had watched in wonder. The biggest threat to its rise had been the great flour shortage of 2020. Phil had mentioned it to him a couple of times and then it had been mysteriously resolved.

Jimmy had decided not to ask questions. His and Phil's relationship had got off to what could kindly be described as a very rocky start. It had begun with Jimmy informing Phil that he had been the arresting officer when Phil's uncle had been sent to jail, and then Jimmy had accidentally played a role in getting Phil arrested too. True, he'd also helped to fix that mess, and had even broken the habit of a lifetime and called in a favour to help Phil secure his private investigator's licence despite his criminal record. Still, their friendship was based on a tacit agreement not to discuss certain things – such as who Phil's auntie may or may not know who could get hold of a large quantity of flour, no questions asked, when your competitors are boxing you out.

Jimmy looked down at the cake and back up at Phil. He hesitated before speaking. "Now, to be clear, Phil – as previously stated, I love the cakes."

"Noted."

"But can I ask, why has this one got a picture of the Virgin Mary on it?"

Phil looked away. "I don't want to talk about it."

"Right."

Jimmy nodded then picked up a knife and let it hover over the picture. Phil had explained that it was now possible to print a photo onto a cake. He had forgotten the how and didn't want to ask again, as it had been one of Phil's longer explanations.

He tried to catch Phil's eye. "I mean, is it technically sacrilegious to eat the Virgin Mary?"

"You told me you were an atheist."

"I am," confirmed Jimmy, turning his attention back to the cake. "But there's atheism and there's atheism."

"Come to think of it, if this is a new line you're starting, you could call it Sacrilicious." Jimmy was pleased with the pun. Sadly, wordplay, like sarcasm, was wasted on Phil Nellis.

"We're not. It was a one-off."

"Right."

"If it makes you feel better, that's not the Virgin Mary. That's Our Lady of Lourdes."

Jimmy put down the knife. "But isn't Our Lady of Lourdes the Virgin Mary?"

"Ah," said Phil. "No, she isn't, actually. She's the ghost of the Virgin Mary who appeared to some girl and told her to drink the water in Lourdes to cure her whatever. I Wikipediaed it. Da Xin wasn't sure about doing it either, but I said it was OK as it wasn't the Virgin Mary herself. It's like a hologram of her."

"Right. I see." Jimmy didn't see at all, but he had become better at recognising a potential Nellisian logic sinkhole and he wasn't going to spend the next hour swirling around this one. "That makes sense."

"That's what I said. Then the woman this morning hit the roof at me."

"Was she very religious?"

"No. She'd wanted a cake for her daughter's birthday. Apparently, there's a pop star called Lorde and Da Xin's cousin took the message down wrong."

"Oh."

"Yeah," said Phil, puffing out his cheeks. "I bleedin' hate dealing with people. She was all, 'I want to speak to your manager. This is an outrage.' I mean, calm down. It's a cake. No outrage is delicious. That's just a fact."

"Amen." Jimmy sliced into the cake and cut them each a generous piece. "By the way, how's Maggie the dog getting on in fat camp?"

"They don't call it that."

"That's what it is, though."

"I know," said Phil. "I mean, she's not technically my dog. She's Paul's. Really, she's her own dog but I do feel bad about it. She was staying with us when she put on all the weight. Da Xin should not have let her help so much when she was developing those dog-friendly cakes."

"Well," said Jimmy, "I'm sure she'll have fun at the camp."

"You reckon? She's got a problem with authority – I'm not sure I'd want to be the person trying to get her to go jogging and eat carrots or whatever. Do you reckon they'll let her have a drink?"

Jimmy looked up from serving up the cake slices. "Like a drink drink?"

"Yeah."

"I seriously doubt it."

Phil sucked his teeth. "I said this was a terrible idea, but nobody listens to me."

Jimmy handed him a cake-laden plate. "I'm retired. Nobody ever listens to me either. Cheers."

Phil looked down at his slice. "I think it was comfort eating. Maggie got bored because there was nothing to do."

"Except be a dog," said Jimmy.

"Well, yeah. But she isn't a big fan of that. She enjoyed chasing villains, being useful."

"Didn't we all."

"Do you miss it?" asked Phil.

Jimmy's first forkful of cake paused in mid-air. One of the other things about Phil Nellis was his alarming lack of subtlety.

"I mean," he continued, "investigating and that."

Jimmy put down his fork. "No. Not at all. You?"

"Nah," said Phil. "I mean – surveillance. That's just sitting around getting a sore arse watching people."

"Having to pee in a bottle."

"Yeah," said Phil. "Hours of staring at a door that might never open."

"And investigating," said Jimmy, "is just seeing people at their worst. I mean, if you enjoy puzzles, you can just do puzzles."

"Exactly," agreed Phil. "How many jigsaws have you done now?"

"One hundred and twenty-seven."

"Wow," said Phil. "That's a lot."

"It is," agreed Jimmy. "Remember how I said it always felt a shame to break them up when they were done? Well, I've got myself this clear varnish stuff now, so I can keep them together and put them up on the wall."

"Like a picture."

"Yes."

"That's brilliant."

"And your cake business is going fantastically."

"Oh, yeah," said Phil.

"I mean, instead of seeing people at their worst, you're delivering joy."

Phil smiled. "I'm like Santa."

"Absolutely."

"And you love doing jigsaws."

"I do," said Jimmy. "I love it. I absolutely love it."

"Great."

"I've never been happier."

"Right. Me either."

Jimmy noticed Phil was looking at him funny. "Is everything OK?"

"Ehm." He pointed awkwardly at Jimmy's face. "Your face is sort of leaking."

"Oh." Jimmy snatched up a tissue and started dabbing at his eyes. "Sorry. It's a side effect of the new medication. I start blubbing for no reason."

"Sure."

Jimmy looked at Phil. "You're doing it too now."

"I know," said Phil, grabbing a tissue out of the box. "It's ... I don't know where it came from, but over the last couple of years, anything and everything sets me off – TV programmes, sad music, seeing other people crying ..."

"I'm not crying," clarified Jimmy.

"I know. But whatever thing makes me do it doesn't know that."

"Not that there's anything wrong with men crying."

"Course not."

"But we aren't."

"Dead right."

"And—

The ringtone from Jimmy's mobile interrupted them. They both looked down at the phone's screen.

"Does Brigit ring you a lot?" asked Phil.

"No."

They looked each other in the eye then Jimmy pointed at Phil. "Don't say anything about crying."

Phil nodded.

Jimmy answered the phone and put it on speaker. "Howerya, Brigit."

"Hi, Jimmy. How are things?"

"Great. Great. Absolutely great."

"Super," said Brigit.

"In fact, Phil is here with me now. We're having a catch-up."

"How are ye, Brigit?"

"Hey, Phil. That actually works out well. I was going to ring you next."

"Right," said Jimmy, as he and Phil shared a pointed look.

"Jimmy, I know you're enjoying taking it easy in your retirement, and Phil, you're mad busy with the cake business, but I was wondering, is there any chance—"

"We'll do it," interjected Jimmy.

"Oh," said Brigit, sounding taken aback. "That's great, but—"

"Doesn't matter," said Phil.

"Right. I need to tell you, though – I won't be able to pay you—"

"That's fine," said Jimmy.

"Immediately," continued Brigit, "as we're financially stretched right now. Are you two OK?"

"We're great," said Jimmy. "We're in. Text us the details. Bye!"

"But—"

Jimmy hit the "end call" button.

The hug somehow took them both by surprise.

"We're back!"

"We're back," agreed Phil.

When the hug was over, they suddenly felt awkward and started looking around the kitchen. Eventually, Jimmy cleared his throat.

"Right, we should probably finish this cake, then."

6

ARE YOU SITTING COMFORTABLY?

Brigit stood and waited impatiently for Phil Nellis to park. It was like watching continental drift, if a tectonic plate had indicators. It said something for the ice water that ran through Jimmy Stewart's veins that he could sit in the passenger seat and say absolutely nothing while Phil struggled to manoeuvre his van into a space that could comfortably accommodate a building. Miracle of miracles, at the point when Brigit was contemplating whether she had died on the way home and this was, in fact, hell, Phil finally completed the task to his satisfaction.

They exchanged greetings and Jimmy looked up at the building appreciatively. "So, this is the new home of MCM Investigations, is it? Very impressive."

Brigit sighed. "Thanks for saying so, but you've not seen inside yet. Sure, the sign looks great, but the rest of it is a glorified building site."

Jimmy turned and gave her an assessing stare. "Are you OK?"

She'd noticed the testy edge in her own voice. Jimmy Stewart didn't miss much either. "I'm fine. It's just been a bit of a week."

"It's Monday."

"Don't remind me," she said. "I wanted to catch you before we go in. As you know, Paul is an invalid at the moment."

"He is?" asked Jimmy, obviously surprised.

Brigit looked between Phil and him. "I thought the two of you saw each other every week?"

"We do."

She turned to Phil. "And you never told him about Paul?"

Phil, being a man whose form was seemingly ninety percent limbs, gave the kind of expansive shrug that only he could. "It never came up."

Brigit shook her head. "Men."

"She broke his leg," said Phil.

"I did not."

"Didn't you?"

Brigit glowered at Phil. "I was holding the ladder when he fell."

"Were you?"

"Alright, technically I wasn't holding the ladder when he fell. The office phone was ringing so I went to answer it."

"Oh," said Jimmy.

"It might have been a potential client and we need the work," she said, then bit her lip while she decided what to say next. "Speaking of which, I have to be honest, the company is in a little bit of financial trouble."

"How much is a little?"

"A lot," admitted Brigit. "I'm telling you this because, as I said on the phone, I might not be able to pay you both right away ..."

Before she could finish, both men waved her away.

"I need to get out of the house in the worst way," said Jimmy. "I should be paying you."

"And I am bleedin' sick to my back teeth of cake."

She smiled at them both. "Was Da Xin all right with you taking a break from the business, Phil?"

"She started crying ..."

"Oh God!"

"No, not like that. Happy tears. Turns out she might be a tiny bit sick of me moping about the place."

"Ah, I see. Speaking of moping about the place, Paul is in a full-leg cast, which means he can't really leave the apartment – it being on the fourth floor – so he's going a little …"

"Doolally," finished Phil.

"Stir crazy. I was going to say stir crazy."

"You told me not to say he was going crazy."

"Stir crazy," repeated Brigit. "That's not the same as …" She stopped herself. It had been a little while since she'd had an extended conversation with Phil Nellis, and her skills at avoiding getting bogged down in a conversational quagmire with him were not as sharp as they had once been. "Never mind. The point is, he's in a fragile place right now—"

"He's started making his own dance music," interjected Phil. "It's like listening to a washing machine having a heart attack."

Out of loyalty, Brigit tried to find some way to disagree with that statement, but she couldn't summon the words. Phil hadn't even been subjected to the extended mixes. Two nights ago, Paul had got upset with her when she hadn't noticed that in the latest version of one of his tracks, he'd added in a glockenspiel.

"As I was saying," she managed, "he's having a rough time of it, and also, he's not fully aware of the company's financial situation." She caught the merest hint of a reaction on Jimmy Stewart's face. "I know, I know, I know – but what else was I supposed to do?"

"You were supposed to hang on to the ladder," said Phil Nellis, genuinely thinking he was being helpful.

Brigit closed her eyes and took a deep breath before speaking again. "Yes. Good point, Phil. Right, come on, then – let's get this meeting going."

She let them in and they began trudging up the stairs to the top floor.

"Has he started *Rear Window*ing yet?" asked Phil as they climbed.

"Will you stop with that," said Brigit. "He's not going to start *Rear Window*ing."

"He definitely is." Phil turned back to Jimmy. "*Rear Window* is an old film where this bloke is trapped in his apartment in a wheelchair, the same as Paul, and he spies on all the neighbours."

"Really?" said Jimmy. "Sounds interesting. Who's in that?"

"That famous actor – Jimmy Stewart." Phil stopped in his tracks. "Here, you've got the same name as him."

Brigit and Jimmy exchanged a glance before Jimmy said, "Do I? Do you know, literally nobody has ever mentioned that before?"

"Really?" said Phil. "Well, I guess lots of people aren't film buffs like me."

THEY ENTERED the apartment to find Cynthia Marsh, their new office manager, politely sitting through what Brigit recognised as "Afro Junk Slam Jam Fourteen". It was the track she heard in her dreams, right before she woke up screaming. Ideally, given that the flat was a bit of a mess, she would have preferred not to have visitors, but beggars couldn't be choosers and they were pressed for time.

Cynthia, sitting on one of their mismatched kitchen chairs in her immaculate business suit, seemed to make the whole place look a lot more dishevelled. She was smiling and nodding while Paul pulled excited faces and pointed out various moments in the track that he had no doubt also explained beforehand. Brigit cringed. If there was one thing worse than listening to an amateur DJ's dance music, it was having him explain it beforehand.

She raised her voice to be heard over the din. "Right, come on in, lads. Forgive the state of the place. Pull up a chair."

She gave Paul a look and, reluctantly, he leaned across and hit a button on his laptop that stopped the music from coming out of the Bluetooth speakers. The speakers had been expensive, but seeing as she had elected to keep her boyfriend in the dark about their financial situation, she couldn't blame him for spending money they didn't have. The bloody things packed a punch too. The big problem with living in a detached building that you own is that there are no neighbours to complain about the noise. What she wouldn't give for a moaning neighbour.

"I was just showing Cynthia a few examples of my work," said Paul.

"He's very good, isn't he?" said Cynthia, with an alarming degree of sincerity.

Brigit and Phil both flapped around in search of a suitable response before Jimmy stepped in with, "I wouldn't have any idea. I'm an old fogey." He extended a hand. "Jimmy Stewart, nice to meet you."

Brigit completed the introductions.

"So," said Phil, "you're the new Deccie?"

"She most certainly is not," said Brigit. "For a start, she's clearly highly competent. Cynthia is going to be a fantastic addition to the team."

"Yes," agreed Paul. "It'll be nice to have a woman around the place."

"Excuse me?"

"Um, I meant another woman, obviously," he said with an awkward smile. "Can't have too many women. Big fan of women."

Brigit patted Paul on the shoulder. "Maybe stop talking, sweetheart."

"Where were you thirty seconds ago?"

"Here, unfortunately."

"Before I forget, I rang Maggie's fat camp and ..."

Brigit braced herself. She had known this was coming, but she'd been hoping it would last a couple more days. Fingers crossed the damage bill wasn't too great.

"... they said she's doing great."

A pregnant pause hung in the air.

Eventually, Brigit broke the silence. "Really?"

Paul nodded.

"There isn't a 'but' or an 'and' or an extensive list of things she's destroyed that you're forgetting to mention?"

"No," said Paul, sounding as shocked as Brigit felt. "I even double-checked that they definitely knew which dog was Maggie. She's having a great time. Settling in really well."

Brigit stood there with her mouth hanging open, trying to get her brain around this description and her mental image of Maggie.

"OK," she managed at last. "Well, that's welcome, if slightly unbelievable, news. Moving on ... As luck would have it, while Cynthia certainly isn't the new Deccie, our new client is, bizarrely, the old Deccie."

Brigit had deliberately avoided mentioning this detail before now. It made no odds to Jimmy, but Phil and Deccie had a long-running feud. She'd thought it best to get Phil in the room before revealing who their client was, so he didn't have time to come up with any objections.

"He's received a death threat," she announced.

Phil snorted. "I'd imagine he gets one of them a day."

"True. But this one was written on his living-room wall."

"Oh," said Phil.

"Do we have pictures of it?" asked Paul. Brigit had rung him when she left Dandridge's office to bring him up to speed.

"Not yet," admitted Brigit. "Dandridge, his agent, said he'd contact Deccie's PA and arrange for us to go in and examine the scene."

"Deccie has a PA?" asked Phil, sounding outraged by the very concept.

"Apparently. Although, seeing as we need to provide him with twenty-four-hour protection and they don't want it to be conspicuous, she's going on holiday and I'll be taking over and pretending to be his PA."

"You're going to be taking orders from Deccie?" asked Paul.

"*Pretending* to take orders. Big difference. Speaking of his protection" – Brigit turned to Phil – "isn't it time that the two of you buried the hatchet?"

Phil folded his arms. "Absolutely no way. Never. Not in a million years. He knows what he did."

The feud had been going on for so long now that neither Brigit nor Paul was entirely sure of its origin, but the duo had been remarkably consistent in keeping it going. Before Deccie had given up his role on the St Jude's Under-12s hurling management team – because his new job meant that he was unavailable for training sessions – they had coached together while never speaking directly to one another. Brigit had seen them in action once. It had looked a lot like two grown men shouting largely contradictory advice at a group of children while Paul and Johnny Canning, the other member of the management team, stood in the middle looking like they were fast losing the will to live.

"Alright," conceded Brigit. "Seeing as Paul isn't able to get around, Phil is a non-starter due to the stupid bloody feud and we need Jimmy out investigating the source of these threats, I'm going to have to move into Deccie's spare room. That way one of us can be with him twenty-four hours a day."

Paul gave her a concerned look. "Are you sure that's a good idea?"

"No, but it's unfortunately the only one we've got. Unless anybody has any other suggestions?"

"I could move in," offered Paul.

"Yeah," Phil chirped, "you'd be great protection. You could wheel your chair around fast enough to whack somebody with your cast." Even Phil noticed when the room fell silent. "Is this one of them times where I've been overly honest again?"

His deduction was acknowledged by a sea of nods.

"Right. I thought so."

"I presume this is all something to do with Deccie's radio show?" asked Jimmy, attempting to move things along.

"I guess so," said Brigit. "While it's not the only way he winds people up, it's the way he can annoy the most people in the shortest amount of time possible."

"Sorry," said Cynthia, who had been taking meeting minutes on her notepad until this point. "This might be a silly question, but are we talking about that Deccie Fadden guy from the radio?"

"Yes," confirmed Paul.

"The guy people ring up and he argues with them?"

"That's the one."

"And he used to answer your phones? What was that like?"

"Pretty much exactly the same shtick," said Brigit. "He's been doing his current job his entire life; someone's just started paying him for it. And now, somebody's claiming they're going to kill him, which, again, is not an entirely recent phenomenon."

"What are the Gardaí saying?" asked Jimmy.

"Nothing," said Brigit. "And Oliver Dandridge, Deccie's agent, told me they're in the middle of contract negotiations so they don't want this getting out." She clocked Jimmy's disapproving face. "I know. But look at it this way – somebody had access to his apartment during the night when he was asleep in his room. If they really wanted to kill him, wouldn't they have done it by now?"

"You're assuming whoever's doing this is acting logically, which is a big mistake. Does scrawling messages on somebody's wall strike you as the actions of a sound mind?"

Brigit paused. "I take your point. In that case, we'd better find out who's behind this, and sharpish. Jimmy, you and Phil can be on the outside searching for the threat, I'll be on the inside keeping my eyes peeled for anything—"

"What about me?" asked Paul.

"You're going to be here running things, love. You're our big-picture guy."

Brigit tried not to wince. It had sounded better in her head. Paul's disappointed facial expression told the story.

"Look," she continued, "I know it's not great, but it's only for a few more weeks."

He nodded disconsolately.

Phil raised his hand. "I can install those surveillance cameras we still have from the other thing. You can watch Brigit attempting to not kill Deccie before somebody else tries to."

Paul scratched at a week's worth of patchy beard growth on his face. "Do you reckon Deccie might play one of my songs on the radio?"

Brigit smiled. "I will definitely ask."

7

HOW TO WIN FRIENDS AND INFURIATE PEOPLE

Brigit and Jimmy sat at the round table in the nondescript meeting room at Caint FM. Its only decoration was a picture of Sinead O'Connor on one wall and, on the other, a portrait of the pope. Brigit guessed that was somebody's idea of a joke.

Jimmy drummed his fingers on the tabletop.

"Alright, then," said Brigit. "Out with it."

"What?"

She raised her eyebrows and gave him a quizzical stare.

"OK. This makes me uncomfortable."

"The picture of Sinead, or the one of the pope?"

"Both, but, more importantly, all of this. If some nutter is after Deccie, then the police should know about it. I appreciate I'm a little bit biased towards the Gardaí, given that I was one for forty years, but if this goes sideways, I don't want to feel as if we should have done more."

"I get it, but ultimately, it's not our decision to make. It's Deccie's choice whether he wants to go to the guards, and I've been told he doesn't."

Jimmy shifted in his seat.

"If it makes you feel any better, I'll make the case directly to

Deccie?"

"Fair enough. Even if he says no, I might have an unofficial chat with a couple of old colleagues of mine. I won't mention him by name, I'll just check in to make sure this isn't part of some bigger trend. Maybe some nutter's making threats against every radio presenter in Ireland. Weirder things have been known to happen."

Brigit shrugged. "Seems like a good idea. I've got no problem with it." She lowered her voice and leaned in. "So, it would seem that I've drawn the short straw. Any advice for my protection detail?"

"Yeah. If anything happens, don't fight – run. Get you and him out of there as fast as possible. Nothing else matters."

"Right."

It was sensible advice, but part of Brigit wished she hadn't asked. Jimmy's solemn expression made all of this seem very real.

Before they could say anything else, there was a brief knock on the door. It was opened immediately by a short bespectacled woman carrying several large folders. Even in serious heels, she barely reached five feet and her blonde hair was pulled back in a bun so tight it looked painful.

"Hello," she said as she entered. "I am Shauna Walsh, Declan's personal assistant. He is in his weekly editorial meeting with his co-host, Rhona Phillips; his producer, Mike; and the station controller, Ms Murphy, at the moment. I have been asked to bring you up to speed on certain matters."

She could only have been in her late twenties, yet her voice had a regimented stiffness to it that was almost robotic.

"Great," said Brigit. "I'm Brigit Conroy and this is my associate Jimmy Stewart."

Shauna gave them a nod as she sat down. "Apologies for the wait. I had to print off rather a lot of material." She patted the folders. "As a matter of policy, we monitor the social media accounts of all of our presenters."

"Fantastic," said Brigit. "We can sift through all that and see if we can find any aggressive responses."

"Sorry, you misunderstood. This is the aggressive material."

Brigit gawped at the two folders Shauna placed in front of her, which reached about a foot in height. "You're shitting me!"

Jimmy cleared his throat discreetly and Brigit remembered herself.

"Apologies," she said with an awkward smile, "but that is an awful lot of death threats."

"They're not all death threats," Shauna assured her. "A lot of them are only threats of physical harm."

"Phew. You had me worried there for a minute." Brigit opened the top file and scanned the first page. "Let's see. Well, that's disturbing. As is that one ... and that one. Technically, that one is more of a suggestion. Although it is one hundred percent physically impossible to do without considerable help and it would prove fatal ... This one actually contains the word 'please', which is surprising given the rest of the message." Brigit slammed the folder closed. "Well, that's comfortably one of the most depressing things I've ever read."

"Declan receives an enormous number of positive mentions as well. The subject matter discussed on the show gets people very riled up." Shauna held up two smaller files, one in each hand. "These contain the alarming correspondence sent directly to the station and to Deccie's apartment."

"People know his home address?" asked Jimmy, horrified.

"Yes. Mr Dandridge negotiated that Declan could have his apartment in Lansdowne Towers rent-free for six months if he undertakes some promotional activities for that property and another one being built nearby."

Brigit noted Jimmy's clenched jaw.

"That is less than ideal," he muttered.

She turned back to Shauna. "Has there been anything that got people particularly excited recently?"

"Well, last week the main topics were Irish neutrality and profanity in rap music. There was also: Would the world be a better place if nobody over thirty was allowed to vote? The use of signal-controlled roundabouts. Who was the best member of the Beatles? Can polygamy work? There were a few more suggestions for the hardest people in Ireland – for what people are unofficially calling 'Deccie's army' – but by far and away, the most contentious issue was which way round toilet rolls should go on the holder."

"OK," said Brigit. "And have there been any incidents where particular groups have become upset with Deccie over something he's said?"

It was impressive how blank Shauna kept her expression. "You could say that." She flipped open the final folder, which contained several sheets of A4 paper, and began reading from the first one. "Vegetarians. Meat-eaters. Vegans. Episcopalians. The lactose intolerant. The French. Volvo drivers. People who give out about the lactose intolerant. People who walk too slowly. Babies. Small dogs. People who walk too quickly. Buddhists. The entire population of Papua New Guinea. People who chew with their mouth open. All branches of Christianity. The Dutch. People who play their music out loud on buses. Atheists. People from every county in Ireland, except Longford. Singers. Enormous dogs. Contestants on dancing shows on TV. People from Longford who claim Deccie has never mentioned them because he knows nothing about Longford. Anyone who keeps snakes as pets. The Norwegians ..."

Brigit held up her hand. "I'm getting the impression the answer to my original question was an emphatic yes."

Shauna gave a curt nod. "I'm still on page one of eleven."

Jimmy ran his hand over his brow. "Maybe we should find someone who doesn't want to kill him."

"Oh, again, don't get the wrong impression – Declan is extremely popular. He's actually up for an Irish radio award. The ceremony is on Friday."

"Fantastic," said Brigit, mentally adding *fingers crossed he lives that long*. "So, are there any particular groups or individuals who you think could be responsible for the threat that was made against Deccie last night?"

Shauna pursed her lips. "Nothing springs to mind immediately."

"Well" – Brigit took out her business card and slid it across the desk – "I know you're going to be on holiday, but if you think of anything, give me a ring."

Shauna gaped at Brigit, stunned. "I'm ... I'm sorry?"

"Oh. My bad. Did nobody tell you?"

Shauna shook her head.

"Right. Sorry. Deccie and Mr Dandridge have decided they want his protection to be as low-key as possible, so I'm going to be replacing you for the next couple of weeks to fulfil that demand." The other woman looked positively horrified and Brigit quickly sought to qualify her words. "I mean, not replacing you – pretending to fill your role while you are off on holidays. Paid holidays. You are being given paid leave, and then, when all this blows over, you'll be back as normal. I've no desire to be Deccie's PA, I assure you." She followed this with a laugh, which Shauna did not share.

"I ..." Shauna adjusted her glasses. "Forgive me, this is a surprise. I have been working for Declan for nine months now, without a break."

"Sounds like you definitely have one coming," observed Jimmy.

"I mean," Shauna continued with a faraway look in her eyes, "technically I have weekends off, but he still rings me."

Brigit and Jimmy exchanged a glance.

"I guess you just get used to it." Shauna now wore a very peculiar expression on her face. "If this had happened a couple of weeks ago, I could have gone to Auntie Florence's funeral." She turned her attention back to Brigit. "Are you sure Declan will cope OK?"

Brigit shrugged. "He's a grown man. He'll be fine."

"Someone will need to pick up his underwear from the dry cleaners."

"That's not a prob—" Brigit began. "Wait, hang on. He sends his *underwear* to the dry cleaners?"

"Mr Dandridge negotiated a deal where—"

"Free dry-cleaning. Got ye. I'm noticing a trend here."

Shauna looked down at the table and then at the floor around it, as if she had just woken up from a dream. "If there is any problem, day or night, ring me."

"I will not be doing that," said Brigit firmly. "You have yourself a proper holiday. You're definitely overdue."

"You can get some excellent last-minute deals on the internet, so I hear," Jimmy chipped in. "My daughters are always telling me about them."

Shauna studied them both earnestly. "So, I'm ... free."

Brigit and Jimmy nodded.

Without another word, the liberated PA got to her feet and left.

After a couple of seconds, Brigit turned to Jimmy. "Well, that was weird."

"Which bit?" Jimmy stood up. "You'd better have a serious chat with your protectee when he gets out of his 'who will we be pissing off this week' meeting. Phil and I are off to check out the apartment, and then I've got to figure out how to interview babies, people who walk too quickly and the Dutch."

Brigit sighed. "Welcome to showbiz. And look on the bright side – at least people who walk slowly will be easy to catch up with."

8

FRATERNISING IN THE WORKPLACE

It must be somebody's birthday.

Jimmy had headed over to Deccie's apartment and Brigit had been moved from the meeting room into what had been described to her as the green room. Certainly, it was a lot nicer, with a large floor-to-ceiling window that offered an impressive view of the Liffey lazily meandering in the late-afternoon sun. Pictures of what she guessed were Caint FM presenters shaking hands with various celebrities adorned the walls, a sofa sat on one side of the room opposite a large display of fresh flowers, which was already setting off her hay fever. The biggest and most prominent picture was of Deccie, on his own, grinning like the cat that had just got the cream.

The room also had tea- and coffee-making facilities and an array of cakes and baked goods was spread out on one table. To this point, Brigit's day had been far too busy to feature any eating beyond a hastily grabbed banana on her way out of the flat, so she was doing her best to ignore the sugary temptations.

Disconcertingly, one of the cakes featured an image of Deccie's face on it. She briefly considered the idea that today could be his birthday. Nobody had mentioned it, but then the death threats scrawled on the wall of his apartment had rather consumed everybody's attention. Besides, Brigit was ninety percent sure his birthday was in December. The only reason she had any degree of certainty about the date was because when he'd been employed by MCM Investigations, he'd asked for the day off on two separate occasions, claiming each time that it was his birthday. Brigit had been moved to check that neither date was correct. What made it even more annoying was that she had explained to him repeatedly that it being his birthday did not mean he got a day off. It wasn't something adults were automatically entitled to – or children, come to that.

Caint FM billed itself as "all talk all the time". It was undeniably the perfect home for Deccie Fadden. He had personified that tagline long before he had ever worked at the station. His show, which he co-presented with a lady called Rhona and who Brigit couldn't help but notice did not seem to get equal billing, aired between 4 and 7pm. The prized drive-time slot. It had its own podcast and, incredibly, was also repeated after midnight.

Brigit had read about this on her phone while she sat and waited patiently for Deccie to finish his meeting. It was now 3:35pm and she was growing concerned that the only way she'd end up being able to talk to him would be by ringing in live on-air. She figured he was probably, understandably, freaking out. Someone had broken into his apartment and scrawled a death threat on the wall. She might not be the man's biggest fan, but no one deserves that kind of stress in their life.

As she checked her watch for the umpteenth time, the door to the green room flew open and in strode Deccie, wearing a Caint FM baseball cap and an expensive-looking leather jacket that was a good size too small for him.

He threw out his arms. "Brigit, great to see you. How've you been?"

"I'm fine, Deccie," she said, getting to her feet. "More importantly, how are you?"

"Tip-top, thanks for asking. Not a care in the world."

"That's great. I mean, I'm glad you're doing OK, given the circumstances."

"Circumstances?"

Brigit took a step forward and lowered her voice. "You know – the death threat."

Deccie scoffed and waved her away. "Ah, that – don't be worrying about that. That was nothing."

"Nothing? Somebody broke into your apartment and threatened to kill you."

He perched on the arm of the sofa. "Yeah, but they didn't, did they? If you think about it, logically speaking – if someone has the means and opportunity to kill you and doesn't, then they are the people in life you have to be the least worried about."

Brigit re-ran that last sentence through her mind just to confirm it was as stupid as she had thought it had been the first time round. It definitely was. "Deccie, we could be dealing with a very sick person here. We need to take this seriously."

"It's just banter."

"Banter?" Brigit couldn't believe what she was hearing.

"Yeah," continued Deccie. "You know how when you were in school and one of the bigger boys would run up and punch you in the back of the head? Or when the lads in your class would gob down the back of your coat? Or when they'd set your shoes on fire? Banter."

"None of what you just described qualifies as banter, Deccie. It's bullying. And quite possibly arson. You have to take this kind of thing seriously. Shauna just gave me the files with all the nasty stuff people have said about you."

Deccie shrugged. "You can't make an omelette without breaking some eggs. Loads of people like me as well." He gestured in the direction of the cake-and-pastry-laden table. "That's all the stuff people have sent in. Fans. My fans. Some woman sends me a cake with my face on it every week. I'm a celebrity. The occasional bit of static is just the price you pay for that. Do you know what your problem is, Brigit? You have no appreciation of the fundamentals of the fame game."

Brigit felt like screaming. What was happening here was obvious – Deccie's inner macho idiot had kicked in. Being scared was, apparently, not manly. Presumably being dead was.

"That's as maybe," she managed diplomatically, "but I've been discussing this with Jimmy Stewart and the team, and we strongly advise telling the Garda Síochána about what happened."

Deccie shook his head firmly. "Nope. Don't trust the peelers. There was only one man in uniform I ever trusted. That was Bunny McGarry, God rest his soul, and he's gone now." He blessed himself. "It would be a dishonour to his memory if I was to go talking to another guard."

"That's not how that works, Deccie. Bunny would want you to be safe."

"Exactly," said Deccie. "Which is why I told Oliver to hire MCM Investigations. One of the Ms stands for McGarry. Who else am I going to trust? Besides, you and Paulie are two of my closest friends."

"We are?" Brigit realised how bad that sounded as soon the words left her mouth. "I mean, obviously, we are – which is why we want to make sure you're safe."

"Perfect," said Deccie. "So that's settled."

"Wait. Hang on ..."

He pointed at the clock on the wall. "I've got to be on air in a few minutes, so just to let you know, I'm going to this thing tonight. I guess that means you're going to this thing tonight too. My driver, Wheels, will pick us up from here straight after the show. You'll see him outside. He drives this old-school gold BMW. Pretty sweet."

"Where exactly are we going?" asked Brigit. "I need to protect you twenty-four hours a day until this is over, so you're going to have to get used to me being around you a lot."

Deccie nodded. "This brings me to the thing I think we need to talk about. Look, let's be honest, you and I have always had this sorta will-they-won't-they vibe going on."

"Sorry?" said Brigit, taken aback.

"There's no need to apologise. You're only human. Thing is,

though – you're Paulie's bird and I take the vows of matrimony seriously."

"OK, first off – Paul and I are not actually married."

"Don't try to talk me into it."

Brigit's voice came out at such a pitch that every dog within a mile must've perked up. "I am not!" She now remembered just how incredibly annoying Deccie could be. "By which I mean there is not, never has been and never will be any will-they-won't-they vibe between you and me."

Deccie made a terrible attempt at a wink that made it look as if he was having a minor stroke. "If you say so."

"I do, and if we keep talking about this, Deccie, trust me – we will no longer have to worry about trying to figure out who wants to kill you, because it will be me."

Deccie gave a sigh. "It's OK. I know that's just the hurt talking."

"I ... I ..." Brigit desperately wanted to do something incredibly unprofessional, and not in the way Deccie expected. She took a deep breath and tried to calm herself. "OK. We'll leave it at us both agreeing that spending a lot of time together will not be a problem."

"I'm glad to hear you think you can control yourself. By the way, I meant to say, bar anything else, this company has a very strict no-fraternisation policy. I take that policy seriously."

"I guarantee you it's not as strict as my no-fraternisation policy."

"Good. As long as we stick to the policy, we should be OK."

"Yeah," she managed, trying to regain her composure. "Let's just say I am extremely confident that will not be a problem. Now, let's stop talking about this ad nausea."

"I think you mean ad nauseam."

"I know what I said. Now, for the love of God, moving on – have you noticed anything strange recently? People hanging around? Have you received any threats? I mean, more than what you consider to be normal."

"No," said Deccie, shaking his head. "Things have been great."

"Other than the threat scrawled on the wall of your apartment in the middle of the night."

"Yeah, other than that."

"Super." Brigit felt her phone vibrate and looked down to see Jimmy Stewart's name appear on the screen. "It's Jimmy. He's over at your apartment right now, checking it out. I'm just going to take this quickly to see if there's any news."

"Fire away," said Deccie, and pointed towards the table of cakes, snacks and baked goods. "I'm going to treat myself."

Brigit took a few steps away and answered the phone. "Jimmy, what's the story?"

"Well," said the gravelly voice at the other end, "first things first, you'll be pleased to hear that the building manager took the decision to repaint the wall this morning, so that's the evidence gone."

She resisted the instinct to swear. "You're kidding?" Brigit turned her back on Deccie to avoid having to watch him getting stuck into a packet of crisps. She had blanked from her memory the fact that the man could chew unbelievably loudly.

"Yeah. Deccie's living in their show apartment, and I think they're extremely keen to keep this whole thing very quiet. Apparently, they spoke to that Dandridge fella first."

"I'm going to have to have a word with him."

"Best of luck," said Jimmy. "I haven't told you the best bit yet. I was particularly concerned with how someone could have gained access to the building, seeing as this place has a twenty-four-hour concierge and security cameras on every entrance. Get this – I've just interviewed the bloke who was working last night and he says somebody left a cupcake on his desk, he ate it and then conked out for five hours."

"You're kidding?"

"That's what he says, and, incredibly, the camera feeds from last night have been wiped. I thought it was nonsense, but the manager says that a couple of other residents complained that this concierge was asleep on the job. He says it's very unusual and until this point the guy has a long history of being an outstanding employee."

"Until he ate a spiked cupcake?"

"That's what they say. I just …"

The end of Jimmy's sentence was lost as Brigit yelped, spun around and in three strides was across the room. She smacked the slice of cake out of Deccie's hand.

"What the—"

"We're putting you on a diet."

9

LIFESTYLES OF THE RICH AND SHAMELESS

Phil Nellis gave the apartment a quick once-over. All right, he had to admit it was nice. Very nice. It was over on the Southside near the city centre. One of those executive apartments. Lots of cream carpets and mirrors knocking about the place. He could even see the Aviva Stadium out the window. In the front room was some kind of chandelier made from a bunch of golden tubes set at random angles with a lightbulb coming out of each one. You had to pay a lot of money for something that weird-looking. It was probably designer. People who just made stuff didn't make stuff like that. Still, the view of the stadium was pretty impressive.

Standing in one corner of the room was a gorilla wearing a pair of sunglasses. Not a real gorilla. A life-sized model. Phil had already checked. If it had been a proper one that had been stuffed, Phil would have refused to work there on principle. His daughter Lynn's favourite animal was the gorilla. He wondered how Deccie, who probably didn't even like gorillas and who certainly hadn't made up a song with his daddy attesting to his love for them, had got hold of one. Jammy bastard.

Not that Phil was jealous of Deccie's place – God, no. For a start, Lynn was still a toddler. All those cream furnishings would be an absolute disaster. Everything would be covered in Nutella within a week, and that wasn't even factoring in Maggie. As far as dogs went, she was pretty clean and she didn't chew the furniture, but she shed a lot and had a tendency to drool whenever she saw something tasty-looking on the TV. Besides, Deccie didn't own this apartment. They were just letting him stay here. It was basically charity. Phil nodded to himself – none of this meant Deccie was better than him.

As it happened, Da Xin was very keen for them to move now that her business was going so well. At the weekend she'd convinced Phil to view a fancy house out in Skerries that she wanted to buy. It had been very nice. Phil had experienced a very odd sense of déjà vu the entire time they were there. When they got back into the car to go home, he realised what had happened. He *had* been there before, back when he was a teenager. He hadn't been inside, though – he'd waited outside in the van while his uncle Paddy had robbed the gaffe. Phil knew he wasn't great at the whole tact thing, but even he knew he shouldn't say anything about that to Da Xin. She and Phil's auntie Lynn got on great, but there had never been any mention of what Uncle Paddy had done for a living, God rest his soul. As far as Da Xin knew, Uncle Paddy had worked in home security, which was more or less true.

Paddy had also taught Phil a lot about that field, which was why it was Phil's job to figure out exactly where to place the surveillance cameras Brigit had decided they would install in Deccie's apartment. The building manager had kicked off about that until Jimmy had got stuck into him about the fact that his building's security had allowed an intruder to sneak inside in the middle of the night and paint a death threat on a wall. Jimmy was typically a cool customer, but something about that bloke was really winding him up. Added to that, Jimmy wasn't wild about them not telling the cops about this. That bit didn't bother Phil in the least. He had grown up with the cardinal rule of not telling the police anything about anything.

Phil had come upstairs and left Jimmy and the building manager to it. They could argue it out between themselves. Worst-case scenario, Deccie would lose his damage deposit – Phil was fine with that. If they'd not asked Deccie for a damage deposit then these people deserved everything they had coming to them.

Phil really knew what he was doing with this stuff, which is why he'd carried out a complete survey of the apartment before he'd got started – scanning the whole place with his special doodah, checking the electrics, and so on. Once he'd done that, he'd tried to ring Jimmy, but there had been no response. Technically, Jimmy didn't outrank him or anything, and as long as everyone understood that, Phil had no problem taking orders from him. Jimmy was a smart man with a wealth of experience and Phil was someone who respected intelligence. If you couldn't do that, you'd end up like one of those idiots who went around thinking they knew everything, and before you knew it, you'd be Deccie Fadden.

Deccie's radio show primarily consisted of him winding people up by saying the first thing that came into his head – something he'd been doing ever since he first learned how to talk. It wound Phil up, too, but he also never missed the show. He'd have to listen to the podcast episode of today's broadcast.

He took out his drill and gave it a whirr, just to make sure it was fully charged. That done, he wandered into the kitchen, put on the kettle and opened the fridge to find there was no milk. Absolutely typical. Disgraceful.

Phil heard the front door of the apartment open then slam closed again, followed by the sound of Jimmy Stewart striding into the room.

"That man is unbelievable. This is why I miss being a guard. Nobody would dare be that uncooperative with a guard. The way he was talking, I think he'd be delighted if I promised that if somebody killed Deccie in his bed, we'd move the body so that his precious building wouldn't look bad. People like that drive me insane."

"Yeah," said Phil, "I'll tell you what's worse than that – Deccie's got no milk in his fridge. How are we supposed to have a cuppa with no milk? It's just basic hospitality."

"Don't worry about me," said Jimmy. "Sorry – you were trying to ring me when I was dealing with that idiot. What did you want?"

Phil was now opening cupboards at random. "Maybe he's got

some of that long-life milk. I'm not a fan personally. It looks too similar to paint. I don't trust it, but beggars can't be choosers."

"Phil?"

He looked over his shoulder. "What?"

"What were you ringing me for?"

"Oh, yeah – sorry. I just wanted to check about the cameras."

"What about them?" asked Jimmy, pulling out one of the kitchen chairs and taking a seat.

"If I'm putting these new cameras in, should I take out the other ones?"

"That wine fridge over there." Jimmy pointed across the kitchen. "Is there something in it? Might be a thing of milk or ..." His brain finally caught up with his mouth. "Hang on a second, there are other cameras?"

10

RECREATIONAL DARTS

Now that Deccie was on air, and safely locked in a studio, Brigit was able to catch up with other things. Shauna had helpfully left her a list of the tasks Brigit was expected to carry out as Deccie's PA, but there was no way she was doing everything on it. Her job was to keep him alive; he could sort himself out with clean underwear. Brigit had been shocked when she thought the list of responsibilities filled an entire sheet of A4 paper – then she'd realised that it was in fact the first page of six. She quickly scanned the rest of the document. There were people in a coma who appeared to be doing more for themselves than Deccie Fadden did.

On her way through the Caint FM reception, Brigit looked through the large window into the studio and confirmed that Deccie was sitting up and breathing unassisted. They appeared to be two of the very small number of jobs he was handling himself. That number was set to grow exponentially with Brigit in the role of PA. She had things to do, starting with meeting Jimmy and Phil at the apartment/crime scene.

She had got as far as calling the lift when the receptionist looked up from texting and leaped to her feet as if she'd just been electrocuted.

"Miss Conroy, the station manager would like a quick word." The woman behind the desk followed up her message with a nervous smile. Being the evening receptionist was probably a dull job with very little to do, and she wore the alarmed look of someone who'd almost screwed up the only task she'd been given.

Brigit turned around. The station was picking up the bill, after all. "Sure, no problem."

BRIGIT REALISED that she knew Karen Murphy as soon as she saw her face. Not "knew" knew – she had never met the woman before – but Brigit knew her type from the time she'd spent working in the Irish Health Service, where there was never enough of anything to go around. It made you an expert in identifying stress levels in others. Karen Murphy was mid-forties and had the look Brigit instantly associated with "two nurses are off sick, the junior doctor is floundering like a dinghy in a tsunami, and I've got an old man in bed eight who keeps wandering off with no trousers on."

As Brigit sat down, Karen angrily ripped up the letter she had been holding and tossed it into the bin.

"Sorry," Karen apologised. "A certain TD from Kerry is threatening to sue us for accurately repeating something he said." She pointed at the bin. "He called it a gross violation of his civil rights. Apparently, he had no idea what a microphone was."

"Only the best and the brightest," observed Brigit.

"Depressingly, he's still a lot smarter than other members of his family."

They shook hands and Karen Murphy directed Brigit to take a seat across from her. Her desk was a mess of paperwork and a half-eaten sandwich lay forgotten on the edge.

"Thanks very much for coming in. How's everything going so far?"

"Well," said Brigit, "we just got started a few hours ago, but my guys are checking out Deccie's apartment right now. I've spoken to him, and to Shauna, who's given us a lot of information about threats made against him, concerning tweets, et cetera."

Karen nodded. "Do let me know if there's anything you need."

"Thank you. I will."

"Do you have any theories yet on how serious this is, or who could potentially be behind it?"

Brigit shook her head. "We're treating it as a serious threat, seeing as somebody managed to get into his apartment, but it's too early to come up with any suspects. If it makes you feel better, I'll be taking on the role of Deccie's PA for the foreseeable future and I'll be staying in his spare room, so somebody will be with him twenty-four hours a day. For the record, we suggested going to the Gardaí about this, but neither Deccie nor Oliver Dandridge want to do that."

Brigit noticed Karen's face tighten at the mention of Dandridge.

"Well, that's Oliver for you," Karen muttered. "Never the most cooperative of men." She glanced over Brigit's left shoulder towards the door and her face went pale.

"Is everything OK?"

"Yes, I just … Yes, of course it is. Yes." She gave Brigit a desperate smile under the panicked eyes of a trapped animal.

Unable to resist, Brigit turned to look at the back of the door.

"Don't!"

But it was already too late. She had seen what Karen was desperately hoping she wouldn't.

"Oh God," moaned Karen as she stood up and rushed around the desk. "It's not what it looks like." She ripped the offending article off the dartboard.

"Really?" asked Brigit. "Because it looks like you had a picture of my client – the man you've hired me to protect after he received a death threat – pinned to a dartboard, and you'd been throwing darts at it."

Karen's body sagged as she leaned against the door. "I appreciate it doesn't look great."

Brigit burst into laughter.

Karen furrowed her brow. "Is something funny?"

Once she'd started, Brigit found she couldn't stop. She was now laughing so hard her whole body was shaking. "Sorry, but ... that is ... hilarious."

The other woman said nothing. Instead, she crumpled up the picture, chucked it in the bin and sat back heavily into her chair. "Let me explain ..."

Brigit held up her right hand to stop her, while her left dabbed at her eyes with a tissue. "Not necessary. You and I have something in common – Deccie used to work for me. Believe me, nobody understands more what you are going through. I named my punchbag after him. Actually, two punchbags. I broke the first one."

"It's not that I dislike Deccie."

"Oh God, no ..."

"It's just ..." Karen paused to find the right words. "He can be very..."

"Frustrating," finished Brigit.

The station manager smiled with relief. "Frustrating. Yes, that's an excellent word for it."

"I can think of several more, but most of them would be unprofessional to use in a business environment."

"And to be crystal clear, I don't want to kill him."

"Congratulations," said Brigit. "If that's true, so far you are the only one."

"Most of my frustration stems from the fact I'm currently in charge of trying to negotiate his new contract. Now, I'll be the first to admit that if Oliver Dandridge turns up dead, I'll be top of that list of suspects."

"I don't know about that. I've met the man, and I'm amazed he's lived this long."

Brigit could see Karen Murphy attempting to come up with something diplomatic to say, but words failed her.

"I take it negotiations aren't going well, then?"

"Oliver Dandridge is an absolute bloody nightmare to deal with." Karen leaned back in her seat. "To be honest with you, Enterprise Media, our gracious corporate overlords, are putting a lot of pressure on me. The great irony is, I sort of discovered Deccie. I can distinctly remember bringing Rhona in, sitting her right where you're sitting now and suggesting we bring that bloke who kept ringing in to argue with her into the studio."

"What did she think of that?"

"Initially, she hated the idea but, as you can see, it worked. She was in the midnight slot getting pretty tepid ratings, and now the two of them are doing drive time. It worked better than anybody ever could have expected. If anything, it works too well. To be honest with you, at that point, the radio station was in a bit of trouble. Listening figures weren't good, and we were having zero success getting anybody under forty to listen.

"Now, ironically, my job is on the line if I don't get Deccie to re-sign with us. I'm the so-called idiot who only gave him a twelve-month contract after his trial period. Everyone's forgotten that I had to beg my boss to even let me do that." Karen stopped herself. "Sorry, would you listen to me? Rambling on. You don't need to hear all this. My point is ... Look, Deccie has been great for us and we want him to be safe and happy here. I've upped the security downstairs and we'll make sure there are two guards at the door whenever Deccie is coming and going. As always, there'll be a few people outside – autograph hunters, the occasional loon with a placard – but we've never had any trouble in the past. Mind you, we never had anything quite like this before."

"That's good to know. Thanks."

Karen Murphy sat forward again. "So, if there's nothing else, I'll let you get back to work. I have two more threats of legal action and some more mundane complaints to wade through. Let me know if there's anything you need."

Brigit started to get up then hesitated. "Actually, you don't happen to have another picture of Deccie and a couple of darts, do you?"

11

BABY NAMES

Brigit came hurtling through the door of Deccie's flat so fast that she nearly tripped over her own feet. Jimmy's phone call a few minutes ago had upgraded her dropping over into an urgent visit.

"We're in here."

She followed the sound of Jimmy Stewart's voice down the hallway to an open-plan kitchen diner and lounge area, where he and Phil were enjoying a cup of tea and some biscuits. Phil had his laptop out and was playing a game of solitaire.

"I got here as soon as ..." Brigit stopped and looked around. "Damn! This place is nice."

Phil sniffed. "S'alright, I suppose. There was no milk in the fridge, though. Had to go out and buy some. The man is a savage."

"Maybe, but he's living well."

"Yes," agreed Jimmy, "although the place is somewhat lacking in terms of privacy." He indicated the three smoke alarm units laid out on the table before him.

"So, this is them?"

He nodded.

"How did you even find them?"

Jimmy looked across at Phil, who didn't even glance up from his game.

"I was putting in our cameras," Phil replied, "as per your request, and, par for the course, I always check to make sure they're not going to interfere with anything nearby." He clicked his mouse and tutted at a card he disliked. "I noticed that there were two types of smoke alarms and one of them wasn't connected to the mains, which they do as standard in these fancy-pants modern buildings nowadays. So, I ran the doodah over it and, sure enough, hidden cameras."

"Jesus," said Brigit. "This thing just keeps getting better and better."

"There was one in here," said Jimmy, pointing up at the ceiling, "one in the bedroom and one in the en-suite bathroom."

"Yuck."

"Yeah," said Jimmy. "We've been debating which one of those last two is worse."

"I'd definitely rather have a camera in the bedroom than in the bog. I'd prefer somebody watch me sleeping than somebody watch me taking a dump."

"Yes, but as I keep saying, other things happen in the bedroom beside sleep."

Phil looked up and shrugged. "I suppose I also read in bed a lot."

Jimmy shook his head and laughed. "How do you have a kid?"

"Two," corrected Phil as he returned his attention to the game of solitaire. "If you count the one on the way."

Brigit scratched her forehead with a finger and looked around the room. "OK, do we know if we found all the ..." She paused. "Hang on – Da Xin is pregnant?"

"She is."

"Why didn't you say something before now?" asked Jimmy.

"Didn't come up."

Jimmy reached across and closed Phil's laptop. "It didn't come up? You just spent a good twenty minutes telling me about the table-tennis matches on TV last night."

Phil looked at Brigit. "You should see them, Brig. The speed some of them lads can fire the ball back and forth – unbelievable."

"*You're* unbelievable," said Brigit, clipping Phil lightly behind the ear. "I don't know what's worse – not telling us until now, or telling us now in the middle of, you know, creepy voyeuristic horrible thing."

Phil shrugged. "It's not that big a deal. It's not you who is pregnant."

As Brigit looked at Phil's innocent expression, she was weighed down by that all-too-familiar feeling of having no idea what to say next. She sat down between the two men and studied the three smoke alarms. "How did we even get from these to your joyful news?"

"I've told you about the baby, so that's over now. We can get back to this."

"Alright," said Jimmy, shaking his head, "but we are coming back to the baby thing, ye big spanner. Congratulations, by the way."

"I didn't do that much," said Phil, "except, y'know ..." His eyes widened. "Ahhhh, I just got what you meant by other things you do in the bedroom."

"And the penny drops," said Jimmy.

"Although, to be fair, we are pretty sure this happened on the sofa while we were watching Netflix. Da Xin really loves *The Crown*. I think it's all the costumes."

Jimmy looked down at the table and ran his tongue over his lips. "Remember that discussion we had about things your wife probably doesn't want you to share with other people?"

"Is this one of them?"

"It definitely is."

Jimmy nodded. "Understood. Although, I tell you what – I don't care what she says, we are not naming the baby after one of the Royal Family. A man must draw a line."

A moment of silence passed before Brigit turned to Jimmy. "Anyway, back to the cameras."

"Yes. Like I said, three of them. The Father of Dragons over there tells me that they were recording audio and video."

"Do we know if they were fitted last night, at the same time as" – Brigit looked at the freshly painted wall – "that happened?"

Jimmy shook his head. "We can't be a hundred percent certain, but it's pretty unlikely, given that the smoke alarm was installed directly over Deccie's bed. Not unless he's an incredibly heavy sleeper. By the way, before you ask – yes, that means whoever put them there had a good view of the bed."

"Lovely," said Brigit, a shiver passing down her spine. "So do we have any idea how long they've been there?"

"Not really," said Phil. "I had a quick google, and these things typically have a battery life of about thirty days. You can buy them from lots of places online and there's a couple of shops in Dublin that sell them. They come with memory cards as standard, but they've been removed so we can't see what they've seen. They're connected to the wifi and are storing the recordings on a server in some place called Azerbaijan."

"I don't suppose you could hack into that server?" asked Brigit.

"You've seen too many films."

Brigit puffed her cheeks out. "Great. In summary, we know these things have been here for less than a month, but we don't know who installed them, when, or what they might have seen."

"I reckon that's about the size of it, alright," said Jimmy.

"So, not only is somebody threatening to kill Deccie, but they've also been watching him."

Jimmy shifted awkwardly in his seat. "Not necessarily."

"What do you mean?" asked Brigit.

"Look, don't shoot the messenger here, but a few years ago I was involved in a case where a drug dealer was caught red-handed talking about shipments on video. The twist was, it was his own camera that he'd installed in the bedroom because he wanted to record himself and whoever else ... Well, you get the idea."

Brigit's hand flew to her mouth. "Good God! I'm not even sure why that idea is worse, but it definitely is."

"Maybe," said Jimmy, "but it would make our lives a lot simpler. You need to sit our client down and talk to him about this. If he knows about the cameras, which is unlikely but possible, then that's one thing. If they aren't his, then that's a whole other thing."

"Fantastic," said Brigit. "That is going to be one horribly awkward conversation." She paused and gave an exaggerated wince. "Maybe, given its sensitive nature, you could do it? I don't want to compromise my relationship with the subject?"

Jimmy tilted his head and raised an eyebrow.

"Alright," she conceded, "I'd rather chew my leg off than have that chat. Could we at least do it together?"

"Fine, but you owe me."

Brigit smiled and patted his hand in thanks. "I'll stick in a bonus as soon as I figure out how I'm going to pay you." She looked at her watch. "I've to be back over at the station in an hour, and then he has to go straight from there to do this appearance thing this evening."

"Might be best to talk to him about all of this in the morning, then," suggested Jimmy. "It's not like we can do anything before then. Assuming his answer is option B – as in they weren't his cameras – we'll need to gather a list of everyone who's had access to this apartment in the last month. I'd hope the nightwatchman with the sweet tooth hasn't fallen for the same trick twice, but I'll double-check to be sure. Somebody had to install these things." He turned to Phil. "Would that take long?"

"Nah. The wifi password is up on the wall for everyone to see. You could nip into the loo, connect them to the network and then pop them up. They're designed to be installed quickly – you'd just need a minute or two unobserved."

"Ahh, the joys of modern technology," said Jimmy. "Still, we can start going through the security tapes downstairs that haven't been erased and see if we can find somebody who wasn't supposed to be here."

"Are we confident that we've found all the cameras and any other devices?" asked Brigit.

Phil nodded. "I took the doodah around three times."

She stood up and swung her bag over her shoulder. "OK, then. Good work. I'm going to head back over to the station. I'll ring Paul on the way and bring him up to speed. Jimmy, you OK to meet here at nine o'clock tomorrow morning for the awkward conversation?"

"Can't wait."

"And I'll tell you something else," Phil chipped in, "I am not calling the baby Deccie either."

12

NO

It wasn't as if Brigit hadn't seen a dead body before. She'd worked in a hospice, which meant that, unfortunately, it was part of the job. This was different, though. Context was everything.

This was a little old man sitting in the front seat of a car, his head tilted back, his mouth open, and he wasn't responding to her tapping on the window, followed by her talking quietly, followed by her talking loudly, followed by her banging on the glass. Unless there was a spate of old men parked up in classic, gold-coloured BMWs around Dublin, then this poor man was the person Deccie had referred to as Wheels. On top of everything else, when Deccie finished his show in a few minutes, Brigit was going to have to inform him that his driver had passed away. She had been working for him for less than six hours now and was already building up an alarming stockpile of tough conversations to have with the man.

She was considering dialling 999 when the corpse smacked his lips together, yawned, tilted his head forward and smiled at her. Brigit was relieved – that she hadn't made the phone call and that there hadn't been a brick lying nearby with which to smash the windscreen.

The not-dead man lowered the window. "Sorry about that," he

apologised. "I take out my hearing aids when I'm resting my eyes. Are you one of those autograph hunters?"

"No, I'm" – Brigit steadied herself to utter the words again – "Deccie's new assistant."

"What? Hang on, I'm going to have to put in the bleeding hearing aids again."

Wonderful, thought Brigit, *I get to say it again.*

"Now," said Wheels, after he'd duly reinserted his hearing aids, "what was that, love?"

"I said I'm Deccie's new assistant."

Wheels raised his eyebrows, which resulted in his twinkling blue eyes appearing from underneath the heavy brows where they'd been hiding. He was eighty if he was a day – a small man with thinning white hair atop a crinkly raisin of a head. "What happened to Shauna? I liked her. Nervous little thing, but she always brought down a couple of biscuits whenever I was picking up his Lordship."

"She's just taking a couple of weeks off."

"Alright," said Wheels, "there's no need to shout, love. I'm not deaf."

Brigit tilted her head up to the sky. The day had been sunny, but portentous dark clouds had rolled in over the course of the early evening. It felt as if the weather was getting all metaphorical and she hadn't brought either a metaphorical or an actual raincoat with her.

The car was parked on Prince's Street South, about twenty yards from the main doors of the building that Caint FM shared with a cable sports channel and a games studio. True to Karen Murphy's word, a couple of security guards were standing at the doors. Surrounding them was an odd collection of people. There were two middle-aged women wearing macs – one in red, who looked as excited as a child at Christmas, and one in brown, who looked as if she was being held there against her will. Then there were a few teenagers, and a man in his twenties holding a folder, a handful of laminated photographs of Deccie and a Sharpie. A couple of Japanese tourists were also gathered round, but were clearly wondering what was about to happen and seemed to be standing there only because other people were.

Positioned a few feet back from the main group was a man with long unkempt hair and a scraggly beard. His heavy anorak, even allowing for the inevitable rain, looked far too substantial for June. His coat wasn't the most notable thing about him, though – that would be the large sign he was holding over his head, which featured the single word "NO" scrawled on it in thick red capital letters.

Brigit took in the rag-tag group and then turned back to Wheels. "I just wanted to let you know that Deccie will be out in a few minutes. I'm Brigit, by the way."

He took her extended hand. "Martin. Pleased to meet you. Everybody calls me Wheels, though."

Brigit threw him a smile then sidled over to the more senior-looking of the two security guards – the one with the moustache and the belly. The other one was sporting similar facial hair, but was a few inches taller, ten years younger and a belly lighter. She attempted to appear casual as she leaned in to speak to the first guard. "Are we sure that's not going to be a problem?"

"What?" asked the security guard, making no concessions to subtlety as he spun his head left and right, in search of what Brigit was referring to.

"The bloke with the sign," she said through gritted teeth.

"Who? Fudgy? Don't be worrying about Fudgy. The man is a Dublin institution."

Brigit took another surreptitious glance at the intense-looking man holding up the placard. "As in, he's been institutionalised?"

"No. He's been protesting stuff since he was a young lad. They had him on the *Six One* news when he was, like, nine – he was objecting to a bypass near where he lived. He became a national celebrity for a bit there. I think it affected the poor lad. He's been protesting anything and everything ever since. Like he's trying to reclaim his former glory.

"This will be his last stop of the day. He protests outside the Office of Public Works in the morning, then he does either a couple of hours outside the make-up shop on Grafton Street about testing on animals, or the Chinese Embassy for human-rights stuff. Next it's a spot of lunch, then over to Dáil Éireann for a bit of general protesting before he swings by a Garda station to protest about protesting, and then Deccie is one of his evening gigs. He's usually here once or twice a week – depends what else is going on that needs protesting."

"But what is he actually protesting? The sign just says 'no'."

"Yeah, the sign. I met him a couple years ago on one of his rare conversational days. He normally doesn't speak, but I got him when he was in a good mood, or his medication was hitting just right. He told me he was getting a bad back from carrying a load of different signs around, so he decided he'd boil the whole thing down to just the one, on the advice of his chiropractor. The no thing covers most things when you think about it."

"But what has Deccie said to wind him up?"

The security guard shrugged. "Who knows? That Deccie fella's gas. He's always winding people up. The MMA fighter, whatshisname – Martin Regan. The guy threatened to knock him out. Be great if he turned up. I've always wanted to see him hit somebody. I hear it's spectacular up close. They say the noise of it is incredible."

"You do realise," Brigit began, "in that situation it would be your job to stop him from doing that?"

He nodded at the other security guard who was standing there stony-faced. "I think you'll find that's the young fella's job. It's my job to take a photograph to make sure we get a nice payday. Fifty-fifty split."

"But he's the one getting hit?"

He smiled at her. "Seniority has its privileges."

Brigit left the less-than-reassuring security team to it and made her way inside the building and up to Caint FM.

As she stepped out of the lift on the fourth floor, she walked towards the big glass partition, which gave a view directly into the studio. At this time of night, most of the station staff had gone home, but a thin blond man in a suit was sitting on the sofa in the reception area watching the studio with the kind of rapt attention Brigit would normally associate with a live sporting event. Meanwhile, on the other side of the glass, Deccie and Rhona Phillips were having a spirited debate. Brigit hadn't seen Rhona before except as a small face in the corner of the enormous promotional images featuring Deccie. She was attractive, with a head of short, red curly hair and a melodious Tipperary accent. She was jabbing a finger in Deccie's direction.

"You are unbelievable."

"What?" said Deccie, holding out his hands. "We all had to start washing our hands because of the Covid thing. Fine – I get that. All I said was, when it's all finally over, I'm looking forward to not having to do that any more."

"You always had to do that."

"A few germs never hurt anybody."

"We've got the Black Plague on line one, it'd like a word. Are you telling me you don't wash your hands when you come out of the bathroom?"

"No, I wash them on my way in. I'm about to touch the important merchandise – I don't want germs getting on that."

"So, if you were about to go into surgery and you saw the surgeon walking out of the bathroom, having not washed his hands, you'd be fine with it?"

"But I'm not doing surgery, am I? Besides, as far as I'm concerned, hand-washing is the main part of a surgeon's job. People make such a big deal out of surgery but it's just the same basic stuff inside all of us. You open somebody up, cut out whichever bit needs cutting, stitch 'em back together again – job done. I've no idea why someone needs to go to university for seven years to learn that. Just give me a big knife and a map that shows where all the different bits should be – I'm confident I can handle it. Being a butcher is a harder job. They have to deal with loads of types of animals. Surgeons only have to deal with the one."

Rhona shook her head. "Right – well, we are out of time. I'm amazed I have to say this, but in spite of what Deccie may have said, do not try to perform surgery on yourself or anyone else if you are not qualified to do so. We'll talk to you all tomorrow. Be good."

As the music played out, Rhona and Deccie removed their headsets and walked out of the studio.

"Well," said Rhona, as she pushed through the door into the main reception area, "I don't know why we bother having these editorial meetings every Monday. I'm telling you now, tomorrow we're going to be dealing with angry surgeons and underpaid butchers."

"Great show, guys," said the blond man.

"Yeah, David," said Rhona without taking her eyes off Deccie. "Go get the car, please." She turned towards Deccie and spread out her arms. "You're going to have to give me a hug, because I'm never shaking your hand again, you dirty animal." She and Deccie embraced then; when they broke apart, Rhona noticed Brigit and favoured her with a broad smile. "Is this the new Shauna?"

"Temporarily," confirmed Brigit.

"Yeah, that poor little thing needed a break from this monster in the worst way. I hope he told you about the station's strict no-fraternisation policy?"

"It was the first part of my briefing," said Deccie.

"Well, her loss is the gain of the rest of the women of Dublin. Are you off out partying again tonight?"

"I've got to go do a thing."

"I bet you do. Be good, and if you can't be good, be careful." She spun around to head towards the doors that led back to the station's offices and almost ran into the blond suited man standing behind her. "Jesus, David – it's like having a clumsy shadow."

"Sorry, Rhona. I'll go get the car. It was a nightmare to park as they've closed off—"

"We should get moving," she said, before heading through the double doors.

The man hurried off, eschewing the lift in favour of hot-footing it down the stairs.

"Right," said Deccie, addressing Brigit. "Let's get going – my public awaits."

Brigit waited for the lift doors to close before pulling Shauna's six-page document out of her bag and handing it to Deccie. "While we've got a second, here's the extensive list your PA gave me of the things she does for you. I've taken the liberty of going through it – the items highlighted in green are the ones I'll be doing, the ones in blue are things that Shauna shouldn't be doing, and those in red you should just stop doing entirely. I'm afraid to ask, but is 'folding toilet paper' a euphemism I'm unfamiliar with?"

Deccie looked up from scanning the list. "What? No. The toilet roll in my loo in the apartment is always in swan-like shapes. I guess Shauna must have been doing that."

"Your loo roll keeps being transformed into renderings of aquatic birds, and you never thought to ask?"

"I'm a very busy man. Speaking of which ..." Deccie rifled through the sheets of paper. "I can't see anything here highlighted in green."

"Well spotted," confirmed Brigit. "I'm only pretending to be your PA. It is my job to keep you upright and breathing. I can't do that if I'm ironing your undies and checking nothing you eat contains horseradish. For however long we'll be working together, you're going to have to dress yourself like a big boy and start reading menus again."

Before Deccie could respond, the lift doors opened into the building's reception. Following such glorious timing, Brigit stepped into the lobby and walked in front of Deccie as they headed towards the main doors and onto the street.

In what little spare time Brigit had had earlier that day, she'd found an article online that detailed the basics of close-protection work. It was written by a guy named Clint, who had been a bodyguard at one time for Prince, Michael Hutchence and Davy Jones from the Monkees. Now that she thought about it, she realised all his clients were dead. Still, Clint couldn't be blamed for that, and he had a trustworthy face.

Clint Rule Five: Stay in front of the subject when possible.

As soon as Deccie emerged onto the street, the woman in the red mac rushed at him while trying to pull something out of her pocket.

Brigit braced herself for a tackle to the ground, but the woman stopped just in front of Deccie, barged one of the kids out of the way and produced a Sharpie.

"Would you mind signing my boob, please, Deccie?"

She thrust her chest forward, just in case he didn't know where the aforementioned boob could be found. Behind her, Brigit noted the friend shaking her head and rolling her eyes.

Deccie took the Sharpie. "Sure, no problem."

The woman pulled open her blouse to reveal her cleavage and shoved her left breast forward.

Deccie paused. "It's already got Joe Duffy's name on it."

"Oh, sorry," said the woman. She readjusted herself and presented her right breast. "This one is all for you. You can put your middle name as well, if you'd like," she encouraged as Deccie started signing. "And your phone number." She giggled. "There's plenty of room."

"That would leave me open to identity theft," replied Deccie without a hint of humour.

Clint Rule Three: Always be aware of your environment.

Brigit disciplined herself to keep scanning their surroundings. The task afforded her the added advantage of not having to watch the unedifying sight of Deccie trying to autograph a body part of a woman old enough to know better. That was when she caught sight of the moped on the far side of the street. Its driver pulled over and his visored helmet turned in their direction. As he gave them a long look, Brigit felt her heart rate jump.

After a few seconds he turned away and drove off. She sighed with relief. She was going to have to get better at dealing with the tension of this. She could be doing this for days – weeks, even. Inwardly, she groaned.

As she looked to her left she was horrified to see the guy on the moped had done a U-turn and was heading straight for them.

Brigit froze like a rabbit in headlights and time seemed to slow to a crawl. She turned towards Deccie; the Sharpie had failed halfway through his signature, and he and the woman were trying various tricks to coax some further life out of it. The security guards were entirely focused on the partially signed boob. There wasn't time to do anything more than tackle Deccie to the ground and that would not provide him with any protection from an assailant working at close range.

She turned back.

The bike was twelve feet away now. The rider had one hand on the handlebars and the other inside his jacket, trying to pull something out.

Ten feet ...

Eight ...

Clint Rule Six: When in doubt, be proactive, not reactive.

Brigit ran.

13

NOBODY READS ANY MORE

As the car pulled up outside The Finn nightclub on Harcourt Street, Brigit got out and limped around to Deccie's door. She scanned their surroundings and noted two women standing at the top of the stairs that led to the nightclub, one of whom was wielding a clipboard, and both of whom were wielding alarmingly broad, expectant smiles. They did not appear to be an immediate threat.

The same could not be said for the man who stood between them and the car. Oliver Dandridge clearly wanted to give the impression of being irate, but his face's limited range of expression and varnished complexion made it a difficult task.

He stepped forward and hissed at Brigit, "What time do you call this? Where have you been? Why are you so late?"

"Do you want to pick one of those questions for me to answer, or shall I just tell you where you can shove all of them?"

Dandridge paused for breath and actually looked at Brigit. She watched as he clocked the rip in her trousers and the oil stains on her jacket. "What the hell happened?"

"There was an incident."

"Is Deccie OK?"

"Deccie is fine. As am I, thanks for asking. Step back." With a final glance up and down the pavement, Brigit opened Deccie's car door and the man himself got out.

Dandridge rushed forward and hugged his client. "Thank God you're OK."

"I'm fine."

Dandridge spun Deccie around, just to check he wasn't bleeding from any gaping wounds he hadn't noticed.

"Get off me," grumbled Deccie.

"OK. Sorry. It's my job to care."

Brigit rolled her eyes at this.

"You know how you're always saying if something happens, you need to know about it as soon as possible?"

"Yes," confirmed Dandridge, shooting an evil look in Brigit's direction.

"Well, you might hear some stuff about my PA tackling a pizza delivery guy off his moped while yelling 'gun'."

Dandridge focused the full force of his disdain at Brigit. "Really?"

"Yeah. Also, a woman is claiming I damaged her nipple with a Sharpie."

He whipped his head back around. "What?"

"Them two things happened at the same time."

"Super."

"It was a simple misunderstanding," attempted Brigit. "The delivery guy was trying to answer his phone while on a moped, which, incidentally, is illegal."

"Were you making a citizen's arrest?" snapped Dandridge.

"He's fine." At least, he was after she'd given him the one hundred euros she had on her.

"Still," said Dandridge, "how would you say your first day is going so far?"

"Deccie's alive, isn't he?"

He shook his head in disbelief. "We'll discuss this later. Right now we have important business to take care of."

Dandridge threw an arm around Deccie's shoulders and shifted seamlessly into gush mode as he guided him up the steps towards the entrance to The Finn.

"Deccie, baby – you look incredible. Have you lost more weight? Are you using those new moisturisers I sent you? Whatever it is, it's working."

Brigit hesitated, then quickly poked her head into the car. "Wheels, are you OK to pick us up later?"

"Twenty-four-seven service, Rambo," he chirped happily. "Deccie has my number."

"Brilliant." She slammed the door and quickly limped to catch up with the other two. It felt like a lightly sprained ankle and some bruising on her right knee. The body would recover quickly, but the pride might take a while longer. As she neared the top of the stairs, she realised belatedly that she had left her handbag in the back of the car. She turned to see the gold BMW merging back into traffic and disappearing towards St Stephen's Green. Perfect.

The woman with the clipboard turned her smile up to an intensity that Brigit considered appropriate only for greeting someone who had been released from captivity after at least five years.

"Well, this man certainly needs no introduction," the woman trilled as her assistant picked up a gift bag from the nearby table and handed it to Deccie. "We are so delighted to have you with us this evening, Mr Fadden."

"Please," said Deccie, "call me Deccie."

"Such a man of the people," gushed Dandridge. "I love this guy."

"Don't we all," said Clipboard. "Head straight in. I'm sure you know the way to the VIP area."

As the two men moved off, the smiles were dialled down about a thousand lumens and redirected towards Brigit. The assistant handed her a goodie bag as Clipboard said, "And you are?"

"I am Deccie's assistant."

"Lovely," said Clipboard, taking the goodie bag back off her with one hand and directing her to follow the duo with the other.

As soon as Brigit entered The Finn nightclub, she felt incredibly underdressed, even taking into account the rip and the oil stain. The room contained about a hundred or so of the young and beautiful, with about a dozen of the filthy rich and older mixed in. In her defence, armed gunmen would be able to carry out one of the highest-grossing robberies in the history of the state simply by charging in and demanding everyone remove their designer gear. There were handbags in the room worth more than MCM Investigations in its entirety. Admittedly, given the company's current financial plight, that wasn't saying much.

Brigit watched as Dandridge guided Deccie round the room and introduced him to various presumably important people. She considered following in their wake, but decided that would look rather pathetic. Besides, the most likely threat to his wellbeing appeared to be an ill-placed stiletto heel coming into contact with his foot.

Instead, she retreated to a tall stool beside the wall and promptly disappeared. Never mind the guests, much to her frustration, the black-clad waiting staff, circulating with trays of Champagne and no doubt gourmet finger foods, seemed entirely unaware of her existence. Her only chance at a vol-au-vent would involve tackling someone to the ground, and she'd already done quite enough of that for one evening.

The event was for the launch of a new magazine called *Essences*. She'd deduced that much as there were piles of the publication arranged on every available flat surface and its logo was emblazoned across the rear wall of the venue. The word was written in silver, except for the Es in it, which were all in gold. Brigit picked up a copy and flicked through it. It seemed to be full of rich people not talking about being rich. In one article a man she recognised as the disgraced former head of a hedge fund was discussing how painting had enabled him to find inner peace after challenging times. The reason Brigit recognised him was the challenging times in question had involved him fending off legal challenges stemming from a pension fund losing a lot of money in questionable circumstances.

In another article, a former model was discussing her love of

Pilates and how it allowed her to break away from the superficiality of the world. Said model was, in fact, standing across the room at that very moment, and although Brigit was a little disappointed in herself, she couldn't resist the urge to compare the published photographs to the real thing, and was able to verify that they had indeed been heavily airbrushed. There was also a large spread on the ten most inspiring places in the world to travel to in order to reconnect with nature. Several of them also enjoyed tax-haven status.

After a few minutes, the clipboard lady, minus her clipboard, took a wireless mic and introduced the editor/publisher of *Essences*. The man in his early twenties thanked them all for coming and assured them not to worry, he would not be giving a speech. Over the course of the next twenty-five minutes, while recapping a trip to Thailand that had led to his spiritual awakening, he reassured them three further times that he definitely was not making a speech. *If you have to do that*, Brigit thought, *you are giving a speech, just not a good one.* As people started to shuffle their feet, he came in for a landing then introduced the guest of honour, Deccie Fadden, who he invited to say a few words.

Deccie took the mic and nodded at the crowd. "How's it going? Very nice to be here. If you get a chance, grab one of those little pastry things with the whatchamacallit on top – they are smashing. To be honest with you, I'm surprised magazines still exist. I do all my reading on my phone while I'm on the bog. Still, best of luck with this. Dentists' offices must get them from somewhere, I suppose."

A sucking moment of silence descended before Oliver Dandridge started to laugh uproariously, and others joined in. Soon, everyone in the room was falling about the place, bar Deccie, who looked confused about what he had said that was so funny. Nevertheless, he handed back the mic and took all the back slaps and congratulations that flowed his way.

For the next fifteen minutes, Brigit watched on as those in attendance hammered the free bar for cocktails while the staff transformed the room with ruthless efficiency and a DJ took up position on the stage. The main floor was once again a dance floor with various enclaves shooting off it, and she could see what appeared to be three VIP areas.

The whole thing had a complicated hierarchical structure that reminded her of a David Attenborough documentary about baboons that she'd seen the week before. Granted, there was less poo-throwing going on here, but the night was still young. Dandridge and Deccie, the baboons with the brightest of arses, were seated in a private booth at the far side of the room. It was raised, so the privacy it afforded its occupants was more of a concept than a reality.

Brigit made her way over and sat down. "Excellent speech, Deccie. Nice and brief. The other fella could learn a lot from you."

"Thanks. I only do longer speeches if they pay for it. They just went for one of our more basic packages – the show-up plus."

Brigit smiled then realised that it hadn't been a joke. In fact, Oliver Dandridge was positively glaring at her.

"Is there a security issue?" he asked pointedly.

"No," said Brigit, "although I was tempted to wrestle one of those servers to the ground just to get a vol-au-vent."

"Only, we're expecting someone ..."

"Right," said Brigit, leaving a gap for Deccie to say something but he did not fill it. "In which case, I'll bugger off and stand somewhere I can be seen and not heard."

"Excellent."

Duly humiliated, Brigit stomped back across the room to the tall stool she had previously occupied, which now had an equally tall table beside it. After a couple of minutes, when the DJ upped the tempo of the music, presumably on some unseen signal, three women jokingly made their way onto the floor and started the dancing. Brigit guessed it didn't matter where you were in the world, from a country disco to the hippest nightclub in Las Vegas, there was an unwritten rule that the dancing was always started by three women.

Brigit looked at her watch. It was only 9:30pm, and here she was with no phone until whenever the hell Deccie decided to leave. Both he and she were probably too old to be in a place like this, but she guessed Deccie didn't know that. Her mood was turning dark. The idea of going to the bar to get herself a drink was tempting, but the odious Dandridge was still in her eyeline and she wouldn't put it past him to make something out of that too. She reminded herself that she was here because MCM Investigations was being paid a lot of money, which it badly needed, so she needed to suck it up and get on with it. It didn't mean she had to like it, though. As a mental exercise, she started to decide how she would take down each person in the room if it turned out they were the one who was trying to kill Deccie. Several of the plans included the happy possibility of Oliver Dandridge being collateral damage.

By ten o'clock the dance floor was full, but she could still just about keep Deccie in view, thanks to the elevated position of his booth. Oliver Dandridge disappeared and the next time she saw him, he was making his way back towards the booth, chatting to a man in a linen suit with a neatly trimmed widow's peak over a face dominated by a hawkish nose. Something about the man looked familiar, but Brigit couldn't place him. She watched as he was introduced to Deccie, then the three men took their seats again and started a rather intense-looking conversation. She was so focused on their table that she didn't see the man approaching hers.

"Brigit Conroy," said Johnny Canning in a cheerful voice, "this is an unexpected honour."

"Johnny! I'd forgotten you ran this place." And she had. He bent forward and kissed her on the cheek.

She knew Johnny Canning through the unlikely route of Bunny McGarry. For reasons that had never been fully explained, he was an old friend of Bunny's, although the two individuals could not be more diametrically opposed. More often than not, Bunny had looked like he had slept in his clothes, whereas Johnny, with his matinee-idol looks, looked as if he'd stepped out of somebody's dream. Despite the potential this offered to be otherwise, Brigit had found him only ever to be self-deprecating and charming. While Paul, Deccie and Phil had recently taken over the running of the St Jude's Under-12s hurling team after Bunny's passing, Johnny had been their unlikely assistant manager since long before then.

"Oh, I don't run this place any more," said Johnny with a sheepish grin as he sat down. "I own it now."

"Congratulations," said Brigit as she patted him on the arm.

"Yeah. I bought a nightclub just before the pandemic."

They both winced. "If it's any consolation," offered Brigit, "I bought an expensive building for a private investigation firm around the same time. It's fun being an entrepreneur, isn't it?"

Johnny laughed. "I'll drink to that." He looked down at the table in front of her. "Speaking of which, why do you not have a drink?"

"I've been trying to flag down a member of staff but—"

Before she could say anything else, Johnny seemed barely to raise a finger and one of the waiting staff who Brigit had assumed must be legally blind, rushed over to them, narrowly beating a colleague.

"Debbie, this is my very dear friend Brigit Conroy. She will have a ..."

"Just a soda and lime, please. I'm working."

"And I will have the same."

Debbie zipped off and Johnny glanced round the room before leaning in to shout more quietly over the music. "You're working?"

"Yes," said Brigit as the sinking feeling in her stomach grew. "I'm Deccie's new assistant."

Johnny stretched out his face for comic effect then laughed. "No offence, but the feck you are." He looked over at Deccie, then back at Brigit, and his face became serious again. "Has he been threatened or something?"

Brigit was shocked. "Who have you been talking to?"

"Nobody. At the risk of teaching my granny how to suck eggs, I applied a bit of deductive reasoning. Namely, the only reason you would pretend to be his assistant would be because it allowed you to follow him around, and the only reason you'd do that is if you absolutely had to, ergo ..."

Brigit nodded. "Let me know if you ever want a job."

"No offence, but if it involves following Deccie, I'll pass."

"Good point. You got any jobs going?"

"I'm afraid you're too old."

Brigit punched him on the shoulder and laughed.

"So, should I be worried?" asked Johnny. "Deccie hasn't mentioned anything about there being a problem in the WhatsApp group."

"You have a WhatsApp group?"

"Oh, yes – for the St Jude's management. Myself, Paul, Phil and Deccie. If you've never been in a WhatsApp group that contains four people, two of whom aren't on speaking terms, I'd highly recommend it. It's depressing and hilarious in equal measure. It's all, 'Tell Deccie I said this', 'Tell Phil I said that' – like both of them aren't reading the same messages you are. They've had entire conversations with just the two of them telling Paul and me to tell the other one what they've just typed. It's its very own little Marx Brothers movie."

"Sounds like fun. Am I crazy, or has Deccie become a lot more annoying since he became famous?"

They were briefly interrupted by Debbie's return with their drinks. Johnny thanked her then looked over in Deccie's direction before turning back to Brigit.

"I had a very odd neighbour a few years ago," he began. "An old lady. Had a dog she never let out of the house. A little toy poodle. I think she taught him to do his business in a litter tray, like a cat."

"OK," she said, confused by the non sequitur.

"When she died, in the absence of any other options, my then boyfriend and I took the dog on, as it was that or the dogs' home, and we didn't think it would last very long in there. The first time I brought little Rufus out for a walk, he lost his mind. Running around the place, barking, yelping, attempting to hump everything in sight. Total overload. I thought he was going to have a heart attack."

"I'm not sure I understand."

"The rather tenuous point I'm making," continued Johnny, "is that Deccie has gone from being the butt of the joke to the belle of the ball in a remarkably short space of time. Doing what I do for a living, I've been around celebrity types for longer than I'd care to remember.

Given where he was and where he now finds himself, I'll say this for him – he's much less of an arsehole than I would have expected him to be."

Brigit shrugged. "I guess I hadn't thought of it that way. Is your point that I should get him neutered?"

Johnny's eyes lit up. "Obviously, yes. If only so I can see him wearing one of those cones of shame. Still, Deccie's not turned into a letch, and unless my radar is completely on the fritz, he's been smart enough to stay away from the drugs. I mean – given that cocaine gives the ordinary person unwarranted confidence and an abundance of opinions, one shudders to think what kind of monumental arsehole it would turn poor Declan into."

Brigit laughed. "Thank God for small mercies."

Johnny leaned in further. "Don't get me wrong, I've nothing against arseholes in general. Look around you. They're my best chance at saving the business." He got to his feet. "Speaking of which, I need to get back to cooking the books." They hugged, and when they'd broken apart, Debbie was once again standing at Johnny's elbow. "Debbie – Miss Conroy here is my personal guest."

Debbie beamed at Brigit. The girl had lovely eyes when she wasn't using them to pointedly not see you.

Johnny tilted his head in Deccie's direction and spoke to Brigit again. "Let me know if I can be of any help with our boy."

Brigit bobbed her head in thanks and, as Johnny made his way into the crowd, she clocked Deccie get up and move quickly away from Dandridge and the other man in their booth. He seemed to be making a beeline for the gents. Brigit manoeuvred herself around the dance floor to intercept him. She wasn't going into the toilets, but she was damn well going to stand outside while he did. She didn't care if neither he nor Dandridge was taking her job seriously. She was.

Deccie had been slowed down en route by agreeing to shake some hands and take a couple of selfies, so she reached the corner of the dance floor before he did. As soon as he saw her, he had the decency to look embarrassed.

"Sorry about before," he apologised. "Oliver can be a bit ..."

"Yes, he certainly can, can't he?" She looked over his shoulder to where Dandridge was accompanying the other man across the room. Judging by their body language, their chat had not gone the way the mystery man had wanted and Dandridge looked as if he was trying to placate him. "Everything OK?"

Deccie shrugged. "Yeah, just Oliver being Oliver. Look, I'm fine. You can head back to the apartment, if you want. Get an early night."

Brigit shook her head. "I go everywhere you go."

Deccie pointed towards the gents. "I'm going in there."

She smiled. "I go *almost* everywhere you go."

As Deccie stepped inside, Brigit moved to one side and waited.

After a couple of minutes, a beaming face appeared before her. It took her a second to register who it belonged to, seeing as this was not the environment in which they normally met.

Dr Megan Wright, dressed to kill, threw out her arms to embrace Brigit. "Brigit, darling – wonderful to see you."

"It is?"

Dr Wright held Brigit at arm's length and grinned at her as if she were a dear friend she hadn't seen in years, as opposed to someone she'd tried to throw out of her office just that morning. "I'm always saying you and I need to hang out more."

"I've never heard you say that."

"I don't say it to you, silly. But still, I saw you in the background of a picture on the club's Instagram feed and I thought, no better time than the present."

It had been a long day, which was why it took a few seconds for Brigit's brain to tie everything together. Just as she did, Deccie re-emerged from the bathroom.

"Deccie, hi! Megan Wright – old friend of Brigit's, big fan of yours. She was just saying you and I need to meet." Before Brigit could set the record straight, Dr Wright had linked arms with Deccie and was guiding him away. "What say you and I get a drink and really get this party started?"

Brigit sighed. Despite her best efforts, a vicious predator had got a hold of her client.

14

CONGRATULATIONS IF YOU GET THE REFERENCE

Paul turned off the TV in disgust. Somehow, despite having access to every streaming service imaginable – the sum total of everything that had been committed to celluloid in human history – he could find nothing to watch. His timing was utterly crummy. Just as lockdown finished, he'd had his accident and ended up stuck inside for a whole different bunch of reasons. He'd completed Netflix, he was certain of it. He'd seen every last thing on there. He'd watched it in all languages, too. For a couple of days the week before, he'd become convinced he could actually speak Korean.

The PlayStation had also lost its appeal. Initially, online gaming had sounded like a fantastic idea until he'd realised it was just an excellent way to discover he could now get his ass kicked by a twelve-year-old from Belgium.

He needed a hobby. Writing music on his PC had fulfilled that role for a while, but then he'd become so good at it that he'd had to start thinking about it as a serious job. He'd even sent out some demos. It wasn't as if he wanted to give up working for the business entirely, but he figured he could be a private investigator during the day and write his music in the evenings. Still, his unquenchable thirst for perfection meant that he no longer found the music relaxing. Rewarding, undoubtedly, but not relaxing.

He slapped at the full-length cast that encased his right leg. The itch. The damned itch. The urge to try to reach it was strong, but the thing was permanently and infuriatingly just out of reach. He'd already lost a couple of pens, a straw and the bottom half of a takeaway menu from the Oriental Palace while attempting to scratch it. The best thing he could do was ignore it. Easier said than done.

Now he was on his own, too, seeing as Brigit was off working the Deccie case. While he missed her, part of him was also glad. He knew she blamed herself for his accident, despite the fact that he had told her several times that it was as much his fault as it was hers. If he'd just stayed still when she'd run in to answer the phone, nothing would have happened. Instead, he'd decided he was fine and had gone back to trying to clear a drainpipe.

Brigit was now stressed out all the time, while trying to hide that fact from him. He needed to do something for her, something real. Something she would really appreciate. He'd compose a chillout track just for her. Give her the gift of his genius.

He considered trying to ring her again, but he'd already tried her six times and it wasn't as if she wouldn't see the missed calls. She was busy, possibly surrounded by Deccie's new celebrity mates, chatting up a storm. He tried to keep his paranoia in check. It might not be all that – she might have got cornered by the bloke from the Corrs who'd gone loopy, telling her about the giant lizards that were running the earth. Like there was anything about human history that gave even the first hint that there was a higher intelligence at play.

He wheeled himself towards the balcony. Watching the city roll by below always relaxed him. Admittedly, that was a rather grand way of thinking about it. While he was four storeys up, the view mainly comprised the two apartment buildings to the left, the back of the Last Drop pub to the right, and a section of the road out front. It didn't sound like much, but the road did feature the rather ostentatiously named Feast of the Gods chip shop. To have a view of a chipper was to see all of life, particularly on a Friday or Saturday night. It wasn't quite births and deaths, but there was the occasional serious punch-up, and some conceptions had definitely taken place in the alleyway around the back.

Paul's attention was attracted to movement on the roof of the Last Drop. Mr Thorwald, the landlord, was up there again. It was impressive; he'd transformed an open space on the top of the building into a garden. Paul thought it was a wonderful idea. When he and Brigit finally got round to sorting their place out, which was going to take quite a while, he loved the idea of doing something similar with their roof.

It was almost midnight now, but Mr Thorwald was out there with a shovel, digging a hole. He seemed to enjoy working on the garden late at night, after closing time. It made sense. Doing something like that to unwind. Mr Thorwald seemed to be dealing with quite a lot of stress. Paul had heard him and Mrs Thorwald arguing a lot recently, about money and other things. Lockdown had put a lot of pressure on a lot of relationships. He hoped they came through it OK.

Mr Thorwald noticed Paul with a start, and Paul gave him a cheery wave. It was nice to feel part of the community.

15

CLUBBED TO DEATH

The problem with the human brain, thought Brigit, *is that you couldn't stop the bloody thing from thinking.* In particular, you couldn't stop it thinking certain thoughts even if you really, really didn't want to be a person who thought those thoughts.

She was still in her thirties. All right, late thirties. Admittedly, pretty late now, but she was in them nonetheless. She kept trying to think the thought that she would be fine in this nightclub at midnight, surrounded by drunken people who were younger than her or, frankly, depressing to look at, if she wasn't stone cold sober and working.

She was young at heart. At least, that was what she wanted to think. What she was actually thinking was: *If that DJ doesn't turn down the music soon, I'm going to feed him his own baseball cap. If the couple to my left, who are eating the faces off each other, bang into me one more time, I'm taking them both outside and telling them a few of the stories from my week working in the STD clinic – that will seriously kill the mood. And if the lecherous, misogynistic, drunken sop who has tried to chat me up twice already, seemingly not remembering that our first exchange ended with him informing me I was a "dyke", comes back for round three, he's going to be stopped by knockout.*

In short, Brigit was tired, irritable and feeling every second of her age, and quite possibly a few extra seconds that other people weren't using. It didn't help that she had a bird's-eye view of Dr Megan Wright ensnaring Deccie in her web. She kept reminding herself that it was none of her business and Deccie was an adult, at least as far as the law was concerned. The pair had been sitting in their not-so-private booth for a couple of hours now. Oliver Dandridge had left early, possibly to hang upside down in a cave, or maybe he was working the night shift as the child-catcher.

Brigit wondered if Dr Wright's training in the inner workings of the mind gave her an unfair advantage in these situations. Then again, she considered the woman to be a terrible therapist, so any advantage would be minimal at best. It probably had a lot more to do with the fact that she was hot. It had always amazed Brigit how incredibly attractive people could get away with so much. She considered what Pol Pot might have done if, as well as being a psychotic monster, he'd also been a stone-cold fox. There was comfort to be drawn from the fact that incredibly attractive people didn't seem to enter politics any more. TikTok might have a lot to answer for, but at least it thinned out the herd of egomaniacs who would normally go seeking validation at the ballot box.

Brigit was scanning the room for a sighting of Debbie, her reluctant non-alcoholic drink-dispenser, which is why she initially didn't see the small peppy blonde woman who had appeared in front of her. It was only when the woman shouted Brigit's name loud enough to be heard over the music that Brigit stopped looking over her head and actually looked down at her. Yet again, her addled brain couldn't quite pair the face with the name. God, she was feeling old.

Clearly she was doing an awful job of hiding her confusion as the girl grinned and announced loudly, "It's me – Shauna Walsh."

Even with the additional information, Brigit had a bit of a hard time putting it together. In her defence, the woman who had introduced herself several hours earlier as Deccie's PA looked nothing like the person standing in front of her now. Her blonde hair was down, she was dressed to the nines and the bubbliness had been turned up from a two to a ten.

"Shauna," repeated Brigit. "I didn't recognise you. You look like a different person."

"I'm on holidays," she roared, raising her arms in the air.

Brigit gave a broad smile. "Looks like you're getting into the spirit of it, too."

A hunky slab of attractive manhood appeared behind Shauna and handed her a drink.

"Thanks, babe," shouted Shauna. Then, for Brigit's benefit, she added, "This is Sebastian."

Brigit nodded a hello, which was cheerily returned.

"So, how's everything going?" asked Shauna.

"Oh, y'know." It was as much detail as Brigit felt capable of giving, out of fear that anything else might cause the dam to burst.

Shauna pointed across the room at the private booth. "Who's that with the boss?"

"The devil," replied Brigit.

"What?"

"Just a friend," she said more loudly.

"Cool. Catch you later."

Before Brigit could say anything else, Shauna turned around, grabbed the taut white vest that was clinging to Sebastian's impressive pectoral muscles for dear life, and dragged him into the centre of the dance floor. There, they began gyrating against one another with the kind of wild abandon and rampant sexuality that had resulted in dancing being banned in that town from *Footloose*.

Yeah, thought Brigit, *that would be me if I was ten years younger and I'd not crippled my fiancé by dropping him off the side of the building that we can't afford to own.*

She looked across at Deccie's booth, where Dr Megan Wright was yet again laughing so hard at something he'd said that she looked as if she might need medical assistance. "Screw it, I'm going to the loo."

This process took about ten minutes, thanks to one of the two available cubicles being taken up by the inevitable girl crying her eyes out about a bad relationship while two friends comforted her. When Brigit re-emerged, both Deccie and Megan Wright had disappeared from the booth. *Great.* Brigit started hobbling around the dance floor. They had to be here somewhere. He wouldn't have left without her. She spent two minutes scanning the room before deciding that that was exactly what had happened. Either that, or Deccie had been kidnapped. Right there and then, she couldn't decide which of the two outcomes she was hoping for.

She exited the club into the gloriously cool night air just in time to see the gold BMW on the street below, one of its rear doors about to close on Deccie and Megan Wright in the back seat.

"Wheels! Wait!"

Brigit raced down the steps as fast as she could on her still-tender ankle as the car pulled away. Luckily, Wheels drove slowly, so she was able to jog behind it, waving her arms to get their attention.

"Wait! You've got my bag!"

Unluckily, Wheels didn't seem to use his rear-view mirror at all. Brigit kept pace with the vehicle until the end of Harcourt Street, but then the BMW took a right turn and was gone. She was left standing in the middle of the road, her hands on her knees, panting for breath. Behind her, a taxi honked loudly. She turned around and screamed a wordless scream at the driver before limping back onto the pavement in defeat.

She'd been ditched. What's more, she had no phone, no money and a dodgy ankle she had just made a lot dodgier by setting off on an ill-judged hot pursuit. Her evening could not get any worse. She considered going back to The Finn and asking either Shauna or Johnny Canning for money for a taxi, but she rejected the idea. She couldn't face looking any more pathetic, and besides, Deccie's apartment was only a fifteen-minute or so walk away.

She started trudging on. Then, because God doesn't close a door without also pissing out a window, she noticed one fat drop of rain plop onto the pavement in front of her. Just a few seconds later, with exquisitely sadistic timing, the heavens opened.

TWENTY MINUTES LATER, battered, bruised and soaked through, Brigit finally reached Lansdowne Towers. Even though her bag had been left at reception – *thank you, Wheels* – the nightwatchman still had to be convinced to let her into the building. He was now taking his job very seriously – probably because he was shocked to still have it.

All the way there, she had been deciding exactly what she was going to say to Deccie, and as she squelched through the front door of the apartment, she had a bucketload of invectives ready to go. He was going to get a piece of her mind. However, from the noises reaching her ears, it was immediately apparent that Deccie was already getting a piece of something else.

The unmistakable sounds of sexy times were emanating from behind Deccie's bedroom door. She considered charging in there anyway, but she couldn't bring herself to do it. Instead, she peeled off her soaking-wet jacket and tossed it on the sofa. Then, she went into her room, got undressed and lay down on the bed.

Within a minute, exhausted as she was, she could feel sleep's warm embrace taking her. She could sleep for days.

Then it started.

"Oh, Deccie. Oh, Deccie. Deccie! Deccie! DECCIE!"

She picked up a pillow, shoved her face into it and screamed.

16

OH, DECCIE, OH, DECCIE, OH, DECCIE!

Brigit cracked the egg and enjoyed the satisfying sizzle it made as it hit the surface of the frying pan. She had rashers and sausages going under the grill, along with a nice bit of white pudding, and some baked beans warming on the hob. A full fried breakfast was a rare treat, but she felt she deserved it. Yesterday had been a long and arduous day, and she'd eaten next to nothing. This time around, she would make sure to get a good feed in first thing in the morning, so she'd be prepared for whatever the day had to throw at her.

The meal consisted of most of the contents of Deccie's fridge. Judging by the packaging, it all seemed to have come from a goodie bag given out at a restaurant launch. Not only did she not care about this, she had also decided it was a good thing. After the way he'd treated her yesterday, making him sit there and watch her eat a full breakfast while he got nothing seemed like the very least he deserved. She was no longer as furious as she had been last night – it was impossible to sustain that level of anger – but her ire had formed into a cold, hard resentment. Deccie Fadden was going to get a sizeable piece of her mind, just as soon as she'd finished eating his sausages.

Brigit jumped as Dr Megan Wright appeared beside her out of nowhere.

"My God – breakfast. You are a lifesaver."

"Ha," said Brigit bitterly. "Boy, have you misread the room. None of this is for you." She wielded her spatula menacingly to emphasise her point.

"What's up with you?"

"What is up with me? What is up with me?" she repeated. "Gosh, let's have a think about that, Doc, and see if we can figure out that mystery. Do you think it might have anything to do with the fact that the two of you ditched me last night and left me to walk home in a bloody storm?"

Megan Wright's face was a picture of innocence. "We thought you'd left. I couldn't find you anywhere."

"Bullshit. For the first time in several hours, I nipped to the loo, and you saw your opportunity."

"Where is all this aggression coming from, Brigit?"

"Don't you dare try to roll out your psychological mumbo-jumbo. I am not buying that snake oil any more."

"It's not like you were with us. For some reason, you were sitting on the far side of the room all night."

"You know damn well why I was there."

"No, I don't."

Brigit paused. Now that she thought about it, it was indeed very possible that Megan Wright did not know what she'd been doing there. "More importantly," she said, rallying, "we both know why *you* were there. Bad enough that you show up and shamelessly use me to get to Deccie" – she looked pointedly toward Deccie's bedroom door – "but then you use sex to get what you want."

"How dare you."

"Oh, please, spare me the righteous indignation act. Don't forget how we met. I was hired by your ex-husband – who, let's not forget, you are apparently screwing again – to find out who you were screwing behind his back. If infidelity was an Olympic sport, you'd be disqualified for screwing the judges."

"First off," said Dr Megan Wright, "what you know about me is covered by doctor-patient confidentiality."

"No, it is not. I'm the patient. Or I was. And the only reason I was the patient is because I got twenty sessions to cover your ex's bill after the most recent of your divorces."

"Well, detective-client confidentiality, then."

"You were not our client. You were our case."

Megan flapped her hand as if to dismiss Brigit's point. "Deccie and I had an instant, powerful connection."

"Yes, I heard." Brigit clutched at her chest. "Oh, Deccie, oh, Deccie, yes, Deccie, yes, Deccie, more, Deccie – you're amazing, Deccie," she mimicked in a panting warble before making a retching face. "Talk about laying it on thick. At least try to make it believable."

Brigit was surprised when Megan grabbed her elbow and pulled her closer. "I'll be honest, I'm as shocked about this as you are, but that man is ... a ... god! Words fail me. I can't describe it."

Brigit pulled her elbow away. "Please stop trying. It's mean to make fun of him like that."

"Make fun of him? I have never been more serious in my life. All right, he might not look like Jason Momoa, but my God, if more men performed like him in bed, I'd have no clients. It was like my body was a violin and he was ..." She looked flummoxed. "Somebody who is really good at playing the violin. Stravinsky?"

"I think he was a composer."

"Nureyev?"

"Ballet."

"Fine. It was like he was Jimi Hendrix and I was his guitar."

"Right," said Brigit. "Did he set you on fire then play you with his teeth?"

Megan Wright's eyes lit up. "Actually— "

Brigit held up her hands. "Whoa, whoa – I have absolutely no interest in hearing any more about this."

"You are such a prude. We really need to discuss your sexual repression at our next session."

"We are not having any more sessions. Yesterday was the last one, remember?"

Megan smiled at her. "I'll give you five more as a way of saying thank you for setting me up with Deccie."

"I did not set you up with Deccie and I have no desire to have any more sessions with you because, and please take this in the spirit in which it is intended, you are one of the very worst people I have ever met."

Megan glanced at her watch. "Look at the time! I can't stand around doing any more of this girly chit-chat. I've got an appointment." She rushed over to the pad and pen stuck to the refrigerator, and spoke as she wrote. "I'm leaving Deccie my mobile number … Actually, I'll leave my office number too, as my mobile is nearly out of charge … And my email. Screw it, I'll leave my Instagram too. And my Twitter. And my home address, just in case."

"Good idea. Maybe leave an article of clothing in case none of those work and he needs to use a bloodhound to find you."

"Oh," she said with a wolfish grin, "I've already left him one as a memento."

"OK," said Brigit, belatedly returning her attention to breakfast, most of which was now burned. "I'm just going to add that to the pile of things I did not want to know."

Finally, Dr Megan Wright left, whistling as she closed the door to the apartment.

Sixty seconds later, Brigit was seated at the breakfast bar, determined to enjoy her meal and completely blank from her mind the revelation that Deccie Fadden was apparently the world's greatest lover. Just as she picked up her fork, there was a knock on the door.

"Good God," roared Brigit as she slammed down her cutlery and headed down the hall. "Could you not at least try to play hard to get? It's like you're in heat, and I don't mean the magazine. Honestly, it's …"

She opened the door to find Jimmy Stewart standing there, looking bemused.

"Sorry, I thought you were somebody else."

Jimmy raised his eyebrows. "I'd certainly hope so."

BRIGIT USHERED Jimmy into the kitchen and sat back down to her breakfast.

"That smells incredible," he said appreciatively.

"Would you like some?"

"God, no. Man of my age – I've already had my high-fibre cereal, thank you very much. How did last night go?"

"I'd rather not talk about it."

"That well," mused Jimmy.

"You have no idea." Brigit got stuck into her white pudding as she spoke.

"Did you tell him about the …" He looked up at the ceiling.

"No. I thought I'd leave that to you. Finders keepers and all that."

"Technically, I didn't actually find them. That was Phil."

"I'm not sure that him telling Deccie is the best idea."

"I don't think we've to worry about that. He refused to come up. He's sitting downstairs in the van. What's the root of this feud the two of them have going on?"

"I'm not sure even they know any more," said Brigit around a mouthful of white pudding.

Deccie emerged from his bedroom, wearing a dressing gown and towelling his wet hair. "Morning. Has Megan gone?"

Jimmy gave Brigit a surprised look.

"Yes," Brigit replied. "She left all of her details up on the pad on the fridge, and the number for an STD clinic."

Brigit had been all set to rip into Deccie about his behaviour the night before and how he'd ditched her, but she hadn't factored in Jimmy's presence while she did so. She felt embarrassed to do it in front of him. Speaking of which … "Deccie, you might want to sit down. Jimmy has something he needs to tell you."

Brigit was then able to finish her breakfast while watching Deccie's face as Jimmy told him about the cameras they'd discovered. Deccie looked mortified, but then, who wouldn't? It was an appalling invasion of privacy. She'd been assured by Phil that there were no cameras in the spare room, but she'd still found herself looking around it awkwardly when she'd woken up this morning.

Deccie listened in silence, which Brigit had never witnessed before, and when Jimmy had finished, he licked his lips and scanned the room nervously. "Are all the cameras gone now?"

"Yes," confirmed Jimmy. "Except for the ones we've now installed that cover the front door and this living room area. Those are ours – don't worry, one hundred percent secure. I presume you've also seen the panic button that we fitted beside your bed?"

"Yeah, but somebody's been watching and recording me?"

Jimmy nodded his head. "I'm afraid so."

Despite Brigit's determination to stay angry, it was hard not to feel sorry for the guy.

Brigit and Jimmy shared a glance as Deccie stared down at the floor, clearly processing the revelations. Eventually, Jimmy cleared his throat. "Is there anything in particular you're concerned about?"

Before Deccie could answer, Brigit's phone rang. She looked at the screen. "It's Phil." She answered it. "Can I give you a shout back in a couple of minutes, Phil?"

"Alright," came Phil's voice. "Only Jimmy forgot to take his phone with him and he told me to keep an eye out for anything unusual, but he didn't specify exactly what he meant by unusual."

"Oh, you know," said Brigit, "the usual." Then she realised just how unhelpful a response that was. "Why? What's going on?"

"There is a fella down here going through the bins."

"Like, a homeless guy?"

"That is impossible to say, as I don't know where this guy lives."

Brigit nodded. It was a bit early for Phil Nellis logic. "It's probably nothing, Phil."

"Only, now that I think about it, he is wearing gardening gloves, and I don't think homeless people would own a pair. Like, when you think about it, one of the few advantages of being homeless is that you don't have to worry about having to do gardening."

She sat up. "We'll be right down."

17

TAKING OUT THE TRASH

Jimmy looked at the nervous expression on the face of the security guard who was sitting behind the reception desk at Lansdowne Towers. He already knew the answer to the question he was about to ask the guy, but he asked it anyway.

"Could you please show me the CCTV feed for the alley where the bins go out?"

The guard blinked a couple of times. "I'm not allowed to show people the camera feeds. You know, because of privacy."

"Yes, but your manager, Mr Tarrant, told you we were doing some security work and that you were to give us any and all cooperation."

"I'd ... I need to ask him."

"No, you don't," said Jimmy. "What you don't want to do is show me the CCTV feed, in the same way as you're not looking at it now, and that screen behind you is currently turned off for no good reason. How much does a blind eye cost these days?"

"I don't know what you're talking about," said the guard, doing his best to sound outraged.

Jimmy didn't bother to say anything else. Instead, he headed quickly out the front doors and around to the side of the building, with Brigit following in his wake. As Jimmy passed Phil, who was sitting in the van and watching with interest, he gave him a brief nod.

"What is this?" Brigit asked.

"I'm not sure, but I've got a good hunch." They turned the corner and stopped. "Yep. That's what I thought."

A tall man wearing a porkpie hat over a hoodie and jeans was standing on a crate, leaning into one of the building's bins. Engrossed in his work, he pulled out a black bag, opened it and, after a quick appraisal of its contents, dropped it and went back to rummaging around. He was also wearing gardening gloves and a nose clip. This was not his first wheelie bin.

"Who is that?" asked Brigit.

"Rake O'Reilly. I don't think you could call him 'a Dublin institution'. 'Legend' seems unjustifiably kind. Let's go with 'an unhappy fact of life' – like traffic congestion or the Liffey stinking in the summer when it gets hot."

"Is he a journalist?"

"Not exactly. I'm guessing he refers to himself as a freelance contractor. He does the crap not even the tabloids are prepared to do. If he gets something, he'll sell it to them and one of their journalists will write the story. They call him Rake because he's as skinny as one and—"

"Because he's a professional muck-raker?"

"Got it in one."

As Brigit marched over to the bins, Jimmy sensed that his suspicion that she was not in a good mood was about to be confirmed. When he was on the force, he'd been renowned for being a man who played by the book. To his own surprise, now that he had effectively joined the private sector, he was a little more flexible on these things, so he made no effort to stop her. In one fluid motion, Brigit grabbed the belt of Rake O'Reilly's trousers, tipped him forward into the bin and slammed the lid shut.

Not for the first time, Jimmy contemplated how Brigit Conroy's bad side was a terrible place for anyone to be. She held the lid closed for a few seconds as the bin bucked about, accompanied by Rake yelling and hollering something unintelligible. As she let the lid go, up he popped like an unhappy Jack-in-the-box.

"What the fuck?"

"Would you look at that, Jimmy? It's Oscar the Grouch."

Rake slapped at his head, which was now missing the hat, but there was some kind of wrapper stuck to his thinning straw-coloured hair. He eventually tugged it away then hissed at Brigit. "You shoved me in. That's assault."

"I did no such thing. I just slammed the bin closed because I heard movement inside it and assumed it must be a rat."

"Very funny," said Rake, looking round the bin, trying to locate his hat.

"Do you want to tell me what the hell you're doing rooting around in our bins?"

"There's no law against it."

"Actually," said Jimmy, "as you well know, there is."

Rake O'Reilly squinted in his direction. "Jimmy, is that you? I'd heard you'd retired."

"I have, Rake. Sorry, I must have forgotten to send out your invite to the party."

His face scrunched up. "I don't like being called that."

"And I don't enjoy having to get up for a pee in the middle of the night, but I can't see either of those two things changing, can you?"

Rake raised his hands and changed his tone to sound more pally. "Alright, you caught me. I won't do it again."

"I said I was retired from the force, Rake. I didn't say I'd forgotten their number." He looked across at Brigit. "Is it still the one with all the nines?"

She nodded.

"Come on now, Jimmy. There's no need to be like that. Cut an old friend some slack."

"I know you have friends on the force, Rake, but don't insult me by suggesting I was ever one of them. Who are you working for?"

"I'm not working for anybody."

Jimmy turned to Brigit. "Ring them."

She reached for her phone and started dialling.

"It's true," pleaded O'Reilly. "You know how it is. I find something, I take it to the papers. I work for myself and then I go to the highest bidder."

"And why would they care about a nobody like Deccie Fadden?"

"A nobody? Are you mad? He's—" Rake looked annoyed, having realised belatedly that the purpose of the question was to get him to confirm exactly why he was there. "Yeah. Very good."

"And what else have you been up to in the never-ending search for a scoop?"

"Nothing. I mean, the usual."

"Define for me," said Jimmy, "in as much detail as possible, precisely what 'the usual' consists of."

"Asking about. Following him around a bit. Checking up on his social media," Rake elaborated, before adding bitterly, "but there isn't much point in that these days. The papers have their own people doing that twenty-four-seven. You'd be amazed how many stories are just regurgitated tweets." He shook his head. "The newspaper game isn't what it used to be."

"My heart bleeds for you. And what have you got on him so far?"

"Nothing."

"I'm not finding you terribly convincing."

O'Reilly held out his hands. "Would I be dumpster-diving if I had anything?"

"Probably," said Brigit. "Rats traditionally love rummaging in the rubbish, don't they?"

"Sticks and stones, missus. I'm just doing a job here, and at least I'm not going around assaulting innocent Joe Soaps – unlike some people I could mention."

"Oh, please."

"While I'm enjoying this opening scene from an unlikely romantic comedy immensely," Jimmy began, "I'm going to knock this on the head, seeing as the stench is becoming too much. Rake – consider this your one and only warning. Those friends on the force?

I guarantee you don't have anywhere near as many of them as I do. Get out of here, right now, before I change my mind."

"I need to find my hat."

Jimmy rolled his eyes. "You've got thirty seconds."

It took Rake just over twenty, although he was far from happy to discover that his headwear had made friends with some discarded eggshells. He clambered out of the bin, shot the dirtiest of looks in Brigit's direction, and limped off down the alley.

"Jimmy ..." started Brigit, but held off as he raised his finger for quiet.

He watched Rake go then turned around and headed back towards the main doors. "In answer to your question – no, I can't see Rake O'Reilly being behind those cameras we found. He's a scumbag, but he's a scumbag who lives in that grey area. He does things that are, at best, a little illegal. Going through the bins is technically illegal, but it's not like he'd see jail time for doing it. Those cameras are way across every line and he'd know it. This little episode has told us something, though."

"What's that?"

He nodded towards the front doors of Lansdowne Towers. "The security personnel working at this fine establishment are not as immune to financial inducements as one would like."

"They might have been persuaded to let somebody in to Deccie's apartment?"

Jimmy shrugged. "Maybe. I was going to go through their security footage today anyway. Do you also want me to ask a few questions, see if there's anything to be found?"

"Absolutely. Let me know if you want me to chuck any of them into a bin."

"You enjoyed that, didn't you?"

A broad smile spread across Brigit's face. "I really did."

18

PANDAMONIUM

Deccie sat down on his bed and flipped open his laptop. He needed a distraction. He wanted to forget about the camera thing. Just the thought of it made him feel queasy. Some sicko nutjob had been spying on him. It was all too horrible to contemplate.

What he needed right now was his great weakness. The thing that no matter what was going on, had always been there for him. When his granny had died, when Tricia had broken up with him any one of the dozen or so times she had, when the St Jude's Under-12 hurling team lost their final because nobody would listen to his brilliant tactical plan. All those crushing blows had been softened considerably by one thing – YouTube panda videos.

He found them very relaxing. To be fair, almost all members of the bear family were good. Red pandas too, which, to Deccie's untrained eye, looked more like raccoons. Still, they were a good laugh. Grizzlies could be delightful as well, as long as you were careful to avoid the videos with the word "attack" in the title. Similarly, polar bears were great, but you had to make sure the video wasn't one of those the-ice-caps-are-melting-we're-all-screwed things. Not that he disagreed with what they were saying, it just definitely wasn't something that was going to relax him. And then there was the inconsiderate bastard who'd named a programming language pandas. Deccie considered the whole thing a shameless attempt at tricking people into learning some boring computer mumbo-jumbo. He'd watched that video for twenty bloody minutes, waiting for the pandas to show up.

Normally, he'd browse YouTube to see if there were any new bear videos, but right now, he was in a state of heightened anxiety. He needed to go straight for the good stuff. What this situation was crying out for was the crème de la crème of panda entertainment – pandas playing on a slide. As far as he was concerned, that single clip of one minute and twenty-seven seconds was worth ten times the sum total of everything on Netflix, Apple TV and Disney+. Nothing could ruin it. Shauna, his otherwise excellent personal assistant, had nearly done so by suggesting that the video might be exploitative. As Deccie had explained at great length, and, he had to admit, rather emotionally, how could it be exploiting pandas when they were clearly loving it? You only had to look at how they ran back around to get to the bottom of the stairs so that they could climb up to the top of the slide again. You couldn't fake that level of enthusiasm. One of them even tried to clamber back up the slide before running out of energy and clinging on halfway up. It was adorable. Pandas are many things, but one of the animal kingdom's elite athletes they are not.

He clicked on his browser icon and a window filled the screen, displaying the last page he'd had open – his private/work email. He'd had to get the new account six months ago, as the other one had been in the public domain and was regularly flooded with emails. Shauna managed it now. Or at least she had done. It was a mix of fan and hate mail, with the occasional picture or video thrown in. Some of them were entirely innocent. Lots of people thought their Jack Russell looked like Deccie. It was a surprisingly common phenomenon. He didn't see it himself, but clearly enough people did.

Then there were the people who made their own arts and crafts projects with pictures of him, or quotes of things he'd said, emblazoned across them. Some of them were good, but Dandridge told him to stop acknowledging them, as that could be seen as him endorsing them and they could start selling the items online. Every few weeks Dandridge came back to talking about how Deccie needed his own line of merchandise, but so far, talk was all it was. The man did an awful lot of talking.

Along with the home-made merch and canine impressions, other, less wholesome videos and pictures would appear in his inbox. He didn't get it himself. If he wanted to stare at naked people on his computer, there were literally mountains of professionally shot materials in that area. He didn't get why people were so determined to make that stuff themselves. It was like how, instead of going to the cinema to see the latest Marvel movie, some people got really excited about watching a pirated version of the film recorded on somebody's phone, which wobbled incessantly and was interrupted every fifteen minutes by some tubby bloke with a weak bladder blocking the view as he made his way to the bathroom. Leave it to the professionals.

Before Deccie could get to the pandas, he refreshed his email out of habit and three unread messages popped up. His heart leaped into his mouth. One of them was from Dandridge – something about the Irish radio awards that were coming up at the end of the week. Another was from the show's producer, Mike, with a suggestion for that evening's broadcast. They were not the emails that grabbed his attention, however. The final one was from an address he did not recognise; the sender's name was the Whole Truth and the subject line was "The video that will destroy your career".

In the preview pane, he read the text:

Dear Deccie,

Long-time listener, first-time emailer. I see you found my cameras. No big deal – I have more than enough of what I need. Have a watch. I will be in contact at midday today with my demands.

Your friend,
The Whole Truth

With a dry mouth and shaking hands, Deccie clicked on the video attachment. It was eleven minutes long.

It did not contain pandas.

19

DAMAGE ASSESSMENT

The group of four sat in the reception of MCM Investigations. Jimmy was doing the crossword, mainly so that he wouldn't have to talk to Oliver Dandridge. Brigit was seated in the corner – on her phone, getting annoyed at Wordle – for pretty much the same reason. Cynthia was behind the reception desk doing something that Brigit couldn't see. She took a wild stab in the dark and guessed that she probably wasn't keen to talk to Oliver Dandridge either. In fact, the only person in the room who seemed keen to talk to Oliver Dandridge was Oliver Dandridge himself.

"This is ridiculous," he muttered, almost under his breath, for about the hundredth time. "Absolutely utterly ridiculous. I need to do my job. If I can't do my job, then I can't do my job." He raised his voice to address the rest of the room. "How much longer is this going to take?"

Reluctantly, Brigit looked up from her phone. "Like I said the last four times you asked that question – it will take as long as it takes."

"It's nearly midday," he snapped. "This blackmailer person said they would email again at midday. We're wasting valuable time."

"Ultimately, it's Deccie's time, and he's the one who's decided how he wants to spend it."

"I need to know what's in that video," whined Dandridge unattractively.

"No," said Brigit, "you do not. You *want* to know what's in it, and that is not the same thing."

"It's my job to protect my client."

"And for the last time, Oliver, your client doesn't want you to see it. He also doesn't want me to see it, or for Jimmy to see it."

When she and Jimmy had returned to Lansdowne Towers, Deccie had come out of his bedroom as white as a sheet, and had explained that he'd received a video. He'd read them the contents of the email and then Brigit, trying to be as tactful as possible, had asked about the attachment. When Deccie had declined to elaborate, she'd suggested that he show it to Jimmy, reasoning that, given there'd been a camera in his bedroom, he might prefer it if a man looked at whatever it was. Deccie had rejected that idea as well. Eventually, he'd told them there was only one person he was willing to show it to. That was why they were here at MCM Investigations. At that very moment, Deccie was upstairs showing the footage to Paul.

"I think you would do well to remember who is the boss here," snapped Dandridge.

"I do remember – it's Deccie. And our bill is being picked up by Caint FM, so wind your neck in and stop trying to make threats, veiled or otherwise."

"OK, then, Miss Smarty Pants. What's your plan?"

"The plan," said Brigit, "is for Paul to give us his assessment of the threat this video poses and the damage it could do—"

"And he is qualified to do that, is he?"

"Seeing as he's the only person your client will allow to see it, he's the most qualified person in the world by default. Once we know more, we can decide whether we need to involve the Gardaí or not."

Dandridge threw up his hands. "This – exactly this kind of idiotic thinking – is why I need to be in there. You get the Gardaí involved, we might as well release the video ourselves. Every cop in this country is on the payroll of some newspaper or another."

"Excuse me?" said Jimmy, lowering his paper and narrowing his eyes into a steely glare. "Have you got anything to back up that ridiculous assertion?"

"OK," said Brigit, "everybody relax." She'd never seen Jimmy Stewart angry, and while part of her was curious, a larger part didn't want the situation getting any further out of hand. "Oliver, the only member of our staff you haven't insulted so far is Cynthia here, and seeing as it's only her second day on the job, let me be very clear – if you get the full set, I will throw you out of our offices."

"I wouldn't test her on that," advised Jimmy. "She's already thrown a member of the Fourth Estate into a wheelie bin today."

"You assaulted a journalist?" asked Dandridge, outraged.

"It was Rake O'Reilly. It would be more accurate to say she took out the rubbish."

"Oh." Dandridge's change in body language indicated he agreed with Jimmy's assessment. She guessed even Rake O'Reilly's family would have a hard time defending the man. "So wait, does that mean he's poking around Deccie?"

"It would appear so," confirmed Brigit.

"Why didn't you mention this before?"

Brigit stood up and gestured expansively. "Because all of this happened, I rang you, and then we all rushed over here." She leaned on the reception desk and smiled at Cynthia. "Were there any messages today? Other clients, et cetera?"

"Of course," said Cynthia, leaning back out of view and shaking her head with an embarrassed smile. "I've put the most important messages into this file."

"Excellent," said Brigit, taking the file Cynthia was offering her. She opened it to see it contained post – of the unhappy kind with big red letters on the front. "Super," she trilled with all the fake enthusiasm she could muster. "Perhaps, Cynthia, you could go through these and email me a summary of the cases needing our most urgent attention and I'll look at them later, when Deccie's on-air. That's assuming he's doing his show tonight."

Dandridge's head snapped round. "Of course he is. The last thing we can afford is for him to go to ground. Everything must look the same as normal. For God's sake, he's just being blackmailed. Do you have any idea how many people get blackmailed every day? I'm being blackmailed by three different people as we speak."

Brigit and Jimmy glanced at one another.

"I actually believe him," said Jimmy.

"Oh, I'm surprised it's that low a number." Brigit's phone beeped in her hand and she read the incoming message. "Right, Paul says we can go on up."

"Finally!" said Dandridge.

When they reached the fourth floor, after Oliver Dandridge had spent three flights of stairs complaining about the lack of a lift as if he'd been asked to scale K2, they walked into the flat. Paul was sitting in his wheelchair waiting for them, while Deccie was standing outside on the balcony.

"Is he ... OK?" asked Brigit.

"Yeah," said Paul. "I guess. Considering."

"He's not going to jump, is he?" fretted Dandridge. "Should I go and talk to him?"

"Are we working on the assumption that a conversation with you would make that more or less likely to happen?" asked Brigit archly.

"I love that man like a son," warbled Dandridge.

"Do you have any sons?" asked Brigit.

He straightened up. "That is currently a matter for the courts."

"Super. Just take a seat."

He reluctantly did as he was told, and Brigit and Jimmy followed suit. Dandridge took in their apartment in a way that suggested he thought he might need to burn his suit when he left. The place actually looked great. It was cleaner than it had been in months.

Paul noticed her noticing. "Cynthia insisted on doing it."

Brigit blushed. "That isn't her job."

"I said that and I tried to stop her but ..." He nodded down at his leg.

When they were all settled, Paul wheeled himself forward and lowered his voice. "OK." He looked at Dandridge. "If we can all keep the questions until the end, please, I'll explain where we're at. I've seen the video. I've agreed with Deccie not to specify what it contains." Dandridge opened his mouth to object, but Paul cut him off. "Deccie said if you weren't able to agree to that, he understands and thanks you for your service."

"As in ...?" Dandridge looked agog. "He would never say that!"

"If you like, I can ask him to come in here and say it directly to your face, but he's having a pretty shitty day and if I were you, I wouldn't push it."

Dandridge desperately wanted to say something more, but didn't.

"Right, then," said Paul. "As I was saying, I've seen the video. It contains nothing illegal or anything like that, but it is embarrassing."

"How embarrassing?" asked Brigit.

"Incredibly. If it was released" – Paul paused and scratched the back of his head, a mannerism which Brigit recognised as one he did when he was thinking – "he'd be a laughing stock. I mean, you could try to get it taken down but it'd be like trying to hold back the sea – if the sea was a sea of memes and whatever else. I'd imagine, given what he does for a living, that would make it pretty difficult for him to continue. So, yeah – I guess you could say it would probably be career-ending. Or, at the very least, crippling."

Brigit looked at Dandridge then followed the man's gaze to where it was resting on the far side of the room – Deccie's laptop. "Don't you—"

Before she could get out the word, Dandridge was out of his chair and lunging to get around Paul. Brigit threw out a leg to trip him up and sent him sprawling on the horrid rug she'd let Paul keep against her better judgement. Oliver Dandridge, splayed out on it, did nothing to improve its appearance. Before the agent could move another inch, she jumped on top of him and pinned him down.

"I need to see that video."

"Stop struggling or I'm going to hit you very hard on the back of the head," Brigit warned.

"Is it wrong," asked Paul, "that I'm incredibly turned on right now?"

Jimmy shrugged. "If this is what does it for you, you should have been there earlier on – she threw a guy into a bin."

"That's my girl."

They all looked up as the balcony doors opened and Deccie stepped inside. He looked sheepish.

"Deccie," said Dandridge from his position pinned to the floor. "You look great. Have you been working out?"

Brigit looked around, incredulous. "It's like he's got some sort of smarm Tourette's."

"Whatever this is," continued Dandridge, "I will fix it. You have my word. Money is no object. I will buy your freedom with my life!"

"Good God," said Brigit, rolling her eyes, "I'm sitting on Mother Teresa."

"I need to speak to my client in private."

Paul wheeled himself around carefully, to avoid hitting Brigit with his cast, then looked up at Deccie. "To spare Brigit from having to knock him out, can you confirm to your agent that you do not want him to watch the video?"

"I don't," said Deccie. He held up his phone, a dazed expression on his face. "The Whole Truth, whoever the hell they are, has sent me another email. It says I must pay them fifty thousand euros on Thursday and publicly announce I'm leaving Ireland at the Irish radio awards, or else everyone is going to see the tape."

20

THE TRAFFIC IS MURDER

Brigit was not feeling very chatty. It had been a hell of a day and it wasn't anywhere near over yet. She was perched in reception at Caint FM and using the time Deccie was on-air to catch up on admin. Her laptop was balanced awkwardly on her knees and she was working her way through the folder of angry correspondence from creditors that Cynthia had prepared for her. The whole thing twisted Brigit's stomach into an anxious knot, not least because she couldn't help but imagine their new office manager reading through the letters and thinking she'd made a terrible mistake by joining a sinking ship.

Brigit had come to accept that she was going to have to swallow her pride and reach out for any help she could. She'd already messaged her friend and lawyer, Nora Stokes, for an embarrassing chat about what options were available to protect the business. Increasingly, Brigit was realising that she should have just come clean with everybody earlier on rather than let her ego get in the way. She hadn't wanted to tell Paul, and as an extension of that, she'd ended up hiding the whole thing from everybody. Her last hope was that it wasn't too late to save MCM Investigations from going under. Protecting Deccie was a well-paid job they certainly needed but it was nowhere near enough to keep them afloat on its own.

All of this explained why Brigit was definitely not in a chatty mood. Unfortunately, David Phillips, the husband of Deccie's co-host, Rhona, seemed entirely oblivious to the energy she was giving off. Mind you, that wasn't a massive surprise; when they'd previously met in the same location, he'd not seemed to realise how much he annoyed his own wife either. He'd taken a seat beside Brigit on the sofa forty minutes ago and had barely drawn breath since. She had a sneaking suspicion he might be the most boring man on earth. It was like wallpaper had achieved sentience and wanted to discuss the traffic situation in Dublin city centre ad nauseam. For at least twenty minutes now, Brigit had said nothing, but despite that fact, David seemed to be labouring under the misapprehension that he was still in a conversation.

"And of course, I know what you're going to say. What about all these new cycle lanes? I'm telling you – they're only going to make things worse. Rather than improving the roads, they've taken the roads away from cars like they're the root of all evil. Cows farting causes a lot of problems, but nobody's suggesting we get rid of them. Ireland doesn't even have any ice caps. We've only got the one dry ski slope. And don't get me started on congestion charges. You see, the problem with congestion charges—"

"Right," Brigit announced, considerably more loudly than she had meant to. David Phillips gave her a startled look, like a dog who'd just realised why the vet was wearing a glove. She smiled and pointed at the clock on the wall. "Is that the time? Can't be sitting here all evening flapping my gums. I am, after all, Deccie's personal assistant. I need to be ... personally assisting him."

David nodded to the glass partition, behind which sat Rhona and Deccie in the studio, currently discussing how soccer could be improved by giving the referee a Taser. "He's busy right now."

"Yes," she said, her smile growing increasingly awkward, "but I still have lots of things to do. You know ... tasks."

"Sure. Can I ask – is Deccie OK? He doesn't seem quite himself this evening."

Brigit was taken aback. Somehow, David had the ability to

simultaneously listen to the show while talking non-stop. "He's fine," she responded quickly. "I think he mentioned having a headache earlier on, so he might be a little off, but nothing more than that."

"Sure. Happens to the best of us."

Brigit headed over to the lift and hit the button for the ground floor. The reality was Deccie was a long way from fine, and understandably so. For the last few hours he'd behaved in the most un-Deccie way imaginable. He'd been quiet. Unnervingly quiet. On the drive over, he hadn't said a single word, and had simply stared out the window at the late-afternoon traffic.

Brigit might not be his biggest fan, but she couldn't help but feel for him. He had the look of someone coming to terms with the fact that his world was about to crumble. She still had no idea what was on the tape, and she'd disciplined herself to respect Deccie's wishes and not try to squeeze it out of Paul, but it was obvious that whatever it was, it was bad. While she might be dreading coming clean with Paul about her screw-up, ultimately that was a conversation to be had with just one person. Deccie, on the other hand, was looking down the barrel of the whole world seeing his bare arse hanging out in the wind – metaphorically speaking. Nobody deserves that.

The same two moustachioed security guards that had been on duty the previous evening were again standing their post outside of the building's front doors. The older one with the pot belly grinned widely as he saw her walking across the main reception.

"Here she comes."

The face of his young apprentice lit up too, showing all the tell-tale signs of someone thrilled at the prospect of "banter".

"Are you going to tackle any mopeds tonight?" asked the older guy.

"Hard to say," responded Brigit. "I'll have to see if the mood takes me or not."

Belly pointed up the road. "A suspicious-looking fella on a push bike cycled by there about a minute ago. You might still be able to catch him."

"I'll let you do it. Looks like you need the exercise more than I do."

He looked put out by this remark. Clearly, he had anticipated that this conversation would consist of him embarrassing her, and had not considered the possibility that it would be a two-way street.

Brigit was in no mood to pussyfoot around a bruised male ego. "So," she said, looking at the small crowd gathered just down the pavement from them, "everything as normal?"

"Yeah," came the stiff response. "Just the usual."

Fudgy was back, bearing his sign with the word "NO" on it, along with a half-dozen autograph hunters, a couple of teenage boys, a gaggle of middle-aged women, and one bloke standing alone holding a large autograph book and wearing a look of alarming concentration.

"And then there's your one," said the younger security guard.

"Excuse me?" asked Brigit.

"Oh, yeah," said Belly. "Your one."

"Is there any way you could be a little bit more descriptive, fellas?"

"Your one," repeated the younger, as if Brigit was the one being slow. "She keeps casually wandering back and forth across the road there." He pointed. "Look, there she is now."

Brigit glanced up and admonished herself. She hadn't been paying attention to the far side of the street. Clint Rule Two: Always be scanning.

Despite the fact that the woman had gone all Princess Grace with the classic headscarf-and-sunglasses combo, once Brigit's attention had been drawn to "your one" she recognised her instantly. "Ah. I'll go deal with that."

"Here we go," said Belly excitedly. "Catfight." He pulled out his phone, ready to capture the encounter for posterity.

Brigit gave him her most withering glare. "Put your phone away and try to be professional, will you?"

As she made her way across the road, through the stationary traffic, she noticed the younger security guard doing a bad job of hiding his smirk. Brigit's target soon clocked her and made a bad attempt at walking away casually.

"Too late. You've been seen."

Dr Megan Wright whipped off her sunglasses and tried to style it out. "Brigit? Is that you? What a coincidence."

"Yes. An almost unbelievable one. What are you doing here, Doc?"

Dr Wright pointed up the road hesitantly. "I was just heading to the gym."

"With no bag?"

"Not to work out. I just love the smoothies there."

"Right." Brigit's tone made it quite clear how feeble an excuse she considered that to be. "So definitely not here to accidentally bump into Deccie again, then?"

"Well ..."

"Jesus. How desperate are you to get on the radio?"

Dr Wright looked taken aback by the question. "It's not like that."

Something in the woman's voice gave Brigit pause. "What exactly is it like, then?"

"Like I said, I felt like Deccie and I had this incredible connection. I've never experienced anything like it."

Brigit held up a hand. "Yes. He's Jimi Hendrix and your body was his guitar. I remember. Believe me, I've been trying not to, but unfortunately, some images, once seared onto the human brain, can't be scrubbed off, no matter how hard you try."

With everything else that had happened that day, Brigit had not had much time to think about the conversation the pair had had while she cooked breakfast, but mentally she'd decided to write off Megan's assertion that Deccie Fadden was the world's greatest lover as manipulative hype designed to achieve what she wanted. However, now that she found herself looking into the woman's big, hope-filled eyes, she looked alarmingly sincere.

"Has he mentioned me?"

"No, but then Deccie and I don't really have the kind of relationship where we discuss things like that – thank God."

"Only, I've not heard from him all day." Her tone became mildly accusatory. "You did give him my contact details like I asked, didn't you?"

"Yes, I did. He's just had a very busy day."

Now that was an understatement and a half.

"He's not seeing anyone else, is he?" Megan Wright fiddled with the sunglasses in her hand.

"Obviously I'm not at liberty to discuss my employer's private life." This earned her a look as if she'd just drop-kicked the good doctor's pet bunny rabbit into a volcano. "Oh, for crying out loud – no, he isn't. Would you like a little bit of free advice?"

Dr Wright gave a noncommittal shrug.

"Go home and relax. You're a grown woman. Stop acting like a lovesick puppy. I can't believe I have to tell you this, but maybe give playing hard to get a bit of a run. You're the psychological whizz here, but I'm sure I heard somewhere that men prefer to do the chasing." Brigit felt awkward about that statement as soon as she'd made it. "Although it is the twenty-first century, so anyone can chase anyone, obviously. Actually, maybe we should all just give up chasing entirely. It's very undignified for anyone over the age of twenty-five. Now, what was my point? Oh, yeah – go home."

"You'll double-check he's got my details?"

"OK."

"But don't tell him you saw me."

"No."

"And I'm available any time later on if he—"

"I'm not telling him that. You're a busy woman with a jam-packed social schedule."

"Right. Yes. Right."

Brigit hadn't been a fan of the old version of Dr Megan Wright, but as she watched the woman walk away, she realised she liked the new version even less. Seeing her transformed into an infatuated teenager by Deccie Fadden was like seeing a lion getting its lunchbox nicked by a tubby, highly opinionated gazelle.

Brigit looked at her watch. Deccie would be done in fifteen

minutes. Just enough time to grab a quick cup of tea and make a trip to the loo. That should kill enough minutes to avoid having to discuss traffic flow with David Phillips again. She crossed back over the street through the stationary traffic. He did have a point, though – the gridlock really was something else.

21

SMITHFIELD'S OTHER HORSE MARKET

Jimmy Stewart glanced around before he opened the door and slid into the passenger seat of the Ford Cortina. It was parked in a space in Smithfield, facing the west side of the plaza where the majority of the snazzy apartment buildings were located. Around them, the day was turning to night and, even on a Tuesday, the various bars and restaurants seemed to be doing a good business.

The owner of the car was sat behind the wheel with a cardboard box resting on his knee, and a napkin shoved into his shirt collar to protect his suit.

"Donnacha."

"Jimmy. Nice to see you."

"Apologies – I didn't mean to interrupt your dinner."

"Don't worry about it. It'll stay warm for a while."

"It smells good."

Donnacha Wilson held up the cardboard box. "Barbecue from the meat wagon place over the road there. It's incredible. I've been doing surveillance down here for a couple of weeks now – between there and the Mexican up the road, I reckon I've put on half a stone."

"I thought you were on a big health kick?"

Wilson raised an eyebrow.

"Sorry," said Jimmy. Now that he had the chance to give Donnacha Wilson a better look, he did notice that the guy was developing a bit of a spare tyre. "One of the downsides of the job, I guess. I don't miss the long hours. How long a stint have you been on?"

"Technically, I'm not here. Technically, I finished several hours ago."

"It's like that, is it?"

"I'm afraid so. You remember Sam Christie?"

"Son of John. One of two heirs apparent to the Christie crime-family empire?"

"The very same."

"Isn't he wanted for some serious questioning in relation to the fact that Stephen Godey was found floating in Dublin Bay with more than the medically recommended number of bullet holes in him?"

"Indeed he is. We were under the impression that he was off in sunny Spain, but recently there's been a bit of chatter that he's sneaked back into Dublin. Apparently, he's trying to make things up with the missus."

"Isn't love grand?"

"It would be if it meant we could find the bastard. A source of mine swore blind that he was holed up somewhere in Smithfield in an apartment owned by the Christies."

Jimmy nodded. "Which of the buildings are you keeping an eye on?"

"That's at least part of the problem. The Christies own half a dozen apartments down this way – that we know of. The likes of them have become experts in hiding stuff in case the Criminal Assets Bureau comes calling, so there's all manner of offshore companies and strawmen behind the ownership of apartments round here. You think people are angry about the housing crisis now, imagine how they'd feel if they realised drug gangs are one of the reasons they can't get a foot on the property ladder."

"Well, if you grab young Sam, it'll be a good start at fixing that problem."

Wilson huffed. "It would be, but it's been two weeks and the higher-ups are losing faith in my confidential informant. For the last three days it's just been me down here."

"You're on overtime, then?"

He gave a bitter laugh. "Never lose that sense of humour, Jimmy. So, I take it this isn't a social call?"

"No."

"You back working with the gumshoes, then?"

"I am. At my age, you've got to find a reason to get out of the house, and I can't face the idea of taking up lawn bowls."

"I'm sure you'd look very good in one of those white cardigans they wear."

"I've got one of them already. I'll pop it on next time you drop round for a cup of tea. In the meantime, I take it your lot are still the catch-all for any high-profile stuff?"

"Yeah. If it raises the Commissioner's blood pressure, we get it. Burns is her go-to for anything she really doesn't want to see screwed up."

"Would that extend to things like death threats against celebrities?"

"Yes and no. We're living in the Twitter age. Death threats aren't what they once were. One of the poor sods who presents the weather is threatened every time it rains. I ended up working a case last year after half the onscreen talent in RTÉ started receiving graphic descriptions of how someone would like to murder them, often featuring the imaginative application of farm machinery and, in one particularly memorable instance, a Dyson vacuum cleaner. We ended up tracing the threats back to a housewife in Lucan who wouldn't say boo to a goose. The DPP declined to prosecute her once she'd agreed to a spot of therapy. Waste of everybody's time."

"But there's nothing in the offing where somebody's getting threats of a more serious nature? I mean, not on Twitter."

Wilson turned in his seat. "What exactly are we talking about here?"

"I can't go into details," said Jimmy, trying to sound apologetic, "but let's just say the threat in question was delivered in a rather more dramatic fashion."

"With all due respect to you and your colleagues, if this is a serious threat, shouldn't this be an official conversation?"

Jimmy held up his hands. "I made the case for that but the client doesn't want to involve the Gardaí. I just wanted to check that this isn't part of something bigger. Like, somebody isn't off their meds and deciding they're going to kill half the celebs in Ireland?"

"Nothing springs to mind but, seeing as it's you, I'll ask around."

"Thanks. There's also a blackmail element to it."

"Hang on – does somebody want your client dead or do they just want their money?"

Jimmy slapped the dashboard lightly. "Thank you. That's exactly what I said. Doesn't make sense, does it? To be honest, that's the bit that worries me. A pro who's trying to blackmail somebody isn't going to start by making death threats. Whoever we're dealing with isn't approaching this logically."

"And, as you're always telling me, illogical people are dangerous people. That's one of the Jimmy Stewart golden rules. I keep saying you should write a book."

"That's an even less likely prospect than the bowls thing. So again, there hasn't been an epidemic of blackmail threats as far as you're aware?"

Wilson shook his head. "Although, as you well know, most things like that are dealt with without ever crossing our desks."

"True. The guards only ever find out when things go tits up."

"Does that mean I'm not gonna find out what you're working on unless that happens?"

Jimmy shrugged. "I'm not wild about it, but it looks that way."

"Still, it beats lawn bowls."

"So far, but I'll keep it in mind as an option. Anyway," said Jimmy, extending his hand, "I've taken up enough of your valuable time, and your dinner's getting cold."

Wilson shook his hand. "Take it easy, Jimmy. And remember – keep your guard up around illogical people."

FOUR MINUTES LATER, Donnacha Wilson was almost done with his barbecue spare ribs. He'd just realised that he'd forgotten to pick up enough spare napkins when there was a tap on his window. He pressed the button to wind it down.

"Jimmy, did you forget something?"

"No. As it happens, I remembered something. Or someone, to be more exact. Do you know who Martin O'Brien is?"

"John Christie's brother-in-law? That Martin O'Brien?"

"The same. Last I heard he was living out in a big pile in Malahide."

"As I recall."

Jimmy gave a broad smile. "He must've fallen on hard times, then. I just noticed him dressed as a pizza delivery guy heading into that building over there on the far left."

Wilson's eyes widened. "You're kidding?"

"Nope. I'll leave you to it." He hesitated. "Oh, and Donnacha – word to the wise, grab a salad every now and then."

22

THEY'RE NOT ALLOWED TO PRINT IT
IF IT ISN'T TRUE

Brigit sat down at the breakfast bar and placed her cup of coffee beside her open laptop. Truth be told, she wasn't a fan of coffee, but working long shifts had taught her that it was the most efficient way possible to fuel her body with caffeine, and that, she definitely needed. She'd been protecting Deccie Fadden for a hair over thirty-six hours and it was proving exhausting. The clock on the wall told her it was just past 9am. She logged into Zoom to see her face occupying one out of four of the squares on one side of the screen. The others were filled by Paul, Jimmy Stewart and Cynthia Marsh.

Her morning greeting was met with a mixture of nods and waves. "Is Phil not here yet?" she asked.

Jimmy spoke slightly too loudly and Brigit guessed he wasn't overly comfortable with the technology, despite the fact that, undoubtedly, he'd used it just like everyone else over the last couple of years. "I got a text from him saying that he would be late. He said he was, and I'm quoting" – he read off his phone – "verifying very troubling information."

"What does that mean?" asked Paul.

"It's Phil," responded Jimmy with a shrug. The others just nodded at this, except for Cynthia Marsh, who looked suitably confused.

Being new, she had yet to experience the magical mystery tour that was Phil Nellis's brain.

"By the way, Brig," said Paul, "you've not heard any more from the dog health farm people about Maggie, have you?"

"No."

"Neither have I. I mean, they said they'd only ring if there was a problem."

"Right," said Brigit. "Well, then ..."

Neither of them said what they were thinking, because once you've said it, the idea is out there in the world and you can't take it back. Maggie had been at doggie fat camp for forty-eight hours now and there hadn't been a problem. Brigit's estimate of when there would be a problem had been exceeded by forty-seven hours and fifty-six minutes.

"Alright," she said, mentally parking the thought, "let's crack on. Deccie's in the shower and I'd rather we did this without him overhearing."

"How is he?" asked Paul.

"About what you'd expect, I guess. Last night, after work, we came straight back here. He only ate half his dinner and he didn't say very much, neither of which are remotely like Deccie Fadden, are they? Then again, how would any of us feel if we knew we were about to be embarrassed in front of the whole world?"

Jimmy gesticulated unnecessarily before speaking. "Is he still intending to pay the ransom tomorrow?"

"He mentioned it briefly. I think he feels he has to, but he hasn't got the money. He gets a lot of freebies, like this place, but he's still on his Caint FM contract, which I'm guessing doesn't pay the kind of money that means he has a spare fifty grand lying around. We're supposed to be having a meeting with Oliver Dandridge later, to discuss his options. I imagine that's going to be pretty grim."

"What's his itinerary for the day?" asked Jimmy.

Brigit took them through Deccie's schedule. From here, they were going to a session with Deccie's personal trainer, followed by the meeting with Dandridge, and from there, going to talk to somebody who, quite possibly, could lend him a lot of money on very short notice. Brigit wondered if maybe she should have a chat with that person too, seeing as MCM Investigations could certainly use an injection of cash.

"Alright, then," Jimmy continued. "I had a chat with an old friend on the force last night. As far as he's aware – without me giving any specifics about what's going on, obviously – he hasn't heard anything about anything similar involving other celebrities, but he's going to discreetly ask around for me, to double-check. Odds on, this isn't part of something bigger – by which I mean some kind of concerted campaign or whatever."

"Is that good news or bad news?" asked Paul.

"No idea."

"I was thinking," said Paul. "One thing I can do from here is go through Deccie's Twitter – see if there's anybody who he's particularly wound up."

Jimmy nodded. "It can't hurt. This might shock you all, but I am not terribly au fait with the world of social media."

"Really?" said Paul with a grin. "And there was me trying to follow you on the gram."

"The what?"

"Don't worry about it. You're not missing anything. I'll let you know if I find anybody exhibiting anything more than the usual homicidal rage exhibited on Twitter."

"I don't get why anyone is on there." Jimmy blinked with bemusement. "Anyway, since this started, I've been trying to pull a suspect list together but it's proving difficult. The death-threat thing – the most likely source of that would be some unhinged person who took exception to something Deccie said on the radio. I have that list we got from his PA, Shauna, of potential groups, and I went through it with Phil, who filled me in on the details."

"Wait," said Brigit. "Phil filled you in on the details?"

"Yeah. Turns out he's listened to every single one of Deccie's shows, and he has a freakish memory for this kind of thing."

"But I thought he hates Deccie. He's pretty much his nemesis.

They haven't spoken for, like, two years. And he listens to the show every day?"

"It's Phil," repeated Jimmy – two words that could cover all manner of odd behaviour. "Best not to question it – you'll only come out of it with a headache. Anyway, my point is, this new blackmail angle changes the whole game. It's not impossible that it's some nutter who listens to the radio show from his mammy's basement, but I think it's a lot less likely – lunatics aren't usually looking for a payday. And then there's the level of sophistication with the cameras, which would again point to a highly organised person or persons being behind it. Speaking of which, I've asked Shauna to drop in for a chat this evening, to see if she can give me a list of people who might have had access to the apartment. I'm also going to finish my interviews with all the concierge staff at Lansdowne Towers today, just in case they remember somebody coming in. It's brought up nothing so far, but you never know. We've got a few weeks' worth of their CCTV footage, too. Not much good on its own, but it might help us down the line if we ever get a proper suspect."

"What about that so-called journalist scumbag from yesterday?" asked Brigit.

"The one and only Mr Rake O'Reilly. Whilst my instinct is that, even for him, this is stepping over the line, I wouldn't rule him out. He also might know if there's someone out there trying to sell footage or stories about Deccie. The problem is, if we start asking him questions, he'll start asking questions back, and the very last thing we want to do is to put him on the scent."

"Wouldn't Dandridge be able to check if someone's selling stories about his client?" asked Paul. "He'd be well in with the papers."

"I guess so," said Brigit. "I'll bring it up when we meet later."

"Speaking of later," said Jimmy, "when I started asking about people who knew Deccie in real life and who might have a grudge, Phil suggested Deccie's ex-girlfriend, one Tricia Reid."

Paul tilted his head from side to side. "I could certainly see her being responsible for the death threat. Blackmail doesn't quite feel like her style, though."

"That's more or less what Phil said. Still, he suggested Brigit should maybe go and talk to her."

"Why me?" she asked.

"He reckons she might respond better to a female."

"Plus," said Paul, "Phil is terrified of her. As is pretty much every bloke I know."

"So, I have to go because you're all big wusses?"

"Obviously I would do it," responded Paul, "but sadly, I am incapacitated."

"Yeah, yeah," said Brigit with a smile. "You can stop milking that I-dropped-you-off-a-building thing now."

"You do this and I'll consider us even."

"Christ. How scary is this woman?"

"You two will get on like a house on fire. Just don't piss her off."

Brigit pulled a face. "I can't see how I could do that. I mean, unless she takes being accused of being an unhinged blackmailer as some kind of insult."

"I'd be careful how you phrase it."

"Good tip," she said, offering a sarcastic thumbs-up.

"If you're willing to do it," said Jimmy, "Phil would be happy to drive you out to her place of work this evening, while Deccie's on-air – provided he stays in the van, of course. I can be at the station monitoring things while I have my meeting with Shauna."

"Fine. Right, if there's nothing else ..." said Brigit, preparing to wind things up.

"Actually, there is," replied Paul. "Cynthia has something."

"Oh, sorry. Fire away."

Cynthia appeared in the main window on the screen, looking rather embarrassed. "It's probably nothing."

"No, it isn't," said Paul. "Go on, Cynthia – share with the group."

"I was thinking – Caint FM, prior to Deccie becoming a hit, were having trouble getting listeners. There were articles in the paper about it. About how they might get bought out or just have to give up their licence altogether."

"OK," said Brigit, not really seeing the point yet, but trying to sound encouraging.

"And I just thought maybe there's somebody who might benefit from Deccie not signing with Caint FM again, and from him leaving the country. So I rang a couple of people I knew from a couple of jobs ago who know about this kind of thing. It turns out Callan Media are sniffing around. Deccie being gone would really suit them."

Jimmy scratched his chin. "Interesting. Very interesting. Wouldn't be out of the realm of possibility. Corporate dirty tricks happen a lot more than you think."

"Apparently, according to my friend, Callan Media has a bit of form in that area."

"Aren't they owned by that Australian guy?"

"Yeah," chipped in Paul. "Marcus Callan, self-made millionaire – if you ignore the start-up loan of a few million quid from daddy's mining company. He's in Ireland, too. At least he was. There was a piccie of him at the races last week. He's over here trying to expand his interests in the UK and Ireland."

Cynthia bobbed her head. "Apparently, his American news channel is in trouble and he's looking for fresh investments to keep his investors happy."

"Very nice work, Cynthia," said Brigit.

Cynthia tried to hide it, but Brigit could see how happy she was that her idea had been warmly received.

"I'll add him to my persons of interest list," said Jimmy. "I might need your help chasing up more detail on that angle, Cynthia."

"Absolutely. Happy to help."

"Excellent," said Brigit. "So, unless there's anything else?"

"Hang on," interjected Paul. "Here he comes. The late great Phil Nellis."

A second later Phil Nellis's face appeared on-screen.

"You've missed the whole meeting, Nellis," said Paul, with a grin. "Did you sleep in or something?"

"Don't mind him," said Brigit. "Good morning, Phil."

"Don't you good morning me, you ..." Brigit was taken aback by

Phil's harsh tone. "You ... I can't think of any words I'm willing to say as I was brought up properly to respect women – even loose women."

"Excuse me?"

"No, I will not excuse you."

"Phil," said Paul, obvious irritation showing in his voice, "exactly what do you think you have to be annoyed at Brigit about?"

"I'll tell you what." A blur of what appeared to be a newspaper filled the screen. "This!"

"Phil," said Jimmy, "none of us can see what you're holding up."

"Hang on." Phil moved the paper further away from the camera and the page came into focus.

Brigit stomach dropped. "Is that a picture of ... me?"

"Yes, it is," said Phil. "And according to this, sources believe that you are Deccie's new paramour. I looked up that word and I was very upset to find out what it meant."

"But ... that's ludicrous."

"Oh dear," said Jimmy. "Maybe pushing Rake O'Reilly into a bin wasn't the best idea after all."

"Never mind that," said Phil. "How could you do this to Paul?"

"Phil," snapped Paul. "It's obviously bullshit."

"It can't be. It's in the paper. They're not allowed to print it if it isn't true. Everybody knows that."

"No, they don't."

"You're in denial, Paulie."

"No, I am not."

"That's exactly what somebody in denial would say."

"Just ... Shut up for a minute, Phil."

While the others were arguing, Brigit pulled up the article on her laptop. The picture looked as if it had been taken outside the Caint FM offices last night when she'd been walking Deccie to the car.

"I'm described as plump. Fecking plump."

She knew that wasn't the biggest thing right now, but it still bothered her. She scanned the rest of the article. There were references to a whirlwind romance, and the implication was that she was only interested in Deccie because he was a celebrity. The text was all couched in "friends say" and "rumour has it". Friends say! As far as Brigit was aware, Deccie's two closest friends were on this call, and one of them hadn't spoken to him in two years.

"I'm ringing Nora," she muttered, flustered. "I must be able to sue these bastards."

"Never mind that," said Paul, feigning a quiver in his voice. "I can't believe you've kept this from me."

"Don't you dare find this funny."

Brigit looked up at the sound of a door opening and saw Deccie coming out of his bedroom, wrapped in a towel.

"What's funny?" Deccie asked.

Brigit muted her laptop. "Nothing. Just some bullshit in the papers." She saw his face fall and knew instantly where his mind had gone. "It's not that. Don't worry."

"What is it, then?"

She paused. "To be honest, this is something I'd much rather discuss when you are fully clothed."

23

TITLE FIGHT

Brigit looked down at the one-person bench with undisguised distaste. Who the hell came up with such a thing? A bench designed, presumably, to stop people from having a conversation. As it happened, it didn't have an impact on her – she wasn't with the person she was talking to. She sat down and shifted her phone to her other ear.

"So where are you now?" asked Paul.

"I'm outside Deccie's gym. I say gym, but the word really doesn't give you any kind of picture of the place."

"How so?"

"It's like the bridge of the starship *Enterprise* has been crossed with the inside of a Ferrero Rocher. Apparently, it's the most expensive gym in Ireland."

"And Deccie's in there?" enquired Paul. "Deccie Fadden? The little fat lad who was in charge of minding the bucket for our hurling team when we were kids because he claimed to be allergic to his own sweat?"

"Yes. He was given a membership in exchange for a promotional thing. Between that and the apartment, he's been comped one hell of a lifestyle."

"Wonders never cease. Does he stick out like a sore thumb?"

"What do you think? Mind you, so did I. I came outside because I could sense my cellulite was upsetting the staff."

"Oh, would you shut up. Don't let that crap in the newspaper bother you."

"It doesn't."

It did. And she was annoyed at herself for letting it. As she'd stepped onto the street she'd considered cracking and buying her first pack of cigarettes in a month, but she'd rung Paul instead. She tried to draw a relaxing lungful of the heady Southside air.

Everywhere she looked were buildings that seemed to be made of ninety percent glass. The entire place was a window cleaner's wet dream. There were also those trees that looked so identical to each other that the little splash of nature they provided actually made the place feel somehow less natural. As if you were a little figurine trapped in one of those scale models you sometimes see in the foyers of buildings.

Something about the area set Brigit's teeth on edge. It was all too neat. That was Ballsbridge for you, though. Everything here was too expensive to allow any chaos to enter the equation.

She turned her attention back to her conversation with Paul. "Deccie is in there being shouted at by his personal trainer, Rían, to 'work for them gains', which, I believe, is the new 'feel the burn'. You should see the place, though – it's got a bar, a snow shower, whatever the hell that is, and you can watch your personal Netflix on the screens. Apparently, the rowing machines are connected to the internet, so you can race some guy in Australia, if you'd like."

"No, thanks. Australians always grab me as being unacceptably fit. And how much does all this cost?"

"I had a google – three grand a year."

"Three grand? For that kind of money, you should be able to fall asleep and let the machines do all the work for you. Hell, for that much, you could fly to Australia and get rowed to death by Aussie Al in person."

"There are also these people called sauna masters who'll waft essential oils at you."

"I knew a bloke down Moore Street who was always doing that. I think they locked him up eventually."

"Well, anyway," said Brigit, "I figured the greatest danger to Deccie in there is Deccie himself, so I left him to it. They also have a lot of security for a gym."

"They'll need it just to stop people running in to see what the hell three grand gets you. How the other half live."

"The other half? I think you mean the one percent."

Paul lowered his voice slightly. "So, how are you doing after you know what?"

"Well, I've had calls from both of my sisters-in-law, several texts from people I used to work with, Nora absolutely ripping the piss out of me as if this is the funniest thing that has ever happened to anybody ever, and the parish priest from back home asking if I'm in need of any spiritual guidance."

"Oh God."

"Yeah. I spent so much of this morning cringing that it's quite possible my face is going to stay like this permanently."

"If it's any consolation, I always thought you had a very sexy cringe."

"Stop trying to cheer me up."

"What's the alternative?" asked Paul. "You go off seeking bloody vengeance?"

"Don't tempt me. I've not even got to the best bits yet. I mean, the phone call from Oliver Dandridge suggesting I keep it in my pants was a delight, but the call from Dad really took the biscuit."

"Ouch."

"Yeah. He was almost as hard to convince as Phil was. The good news is, despite what you think, he really does like you. He was absolutely mortified when he thought I was doing the dirty on you."

"Well, that's something, I suppose. If you like," Paul offered, sounding tentative, "we could just make our engagement public? Knock all this stupidity on the head."

Brigit sighed. "It occurred to me, but then we'd still be trampling all over Dad and Margaret's day. I don't want to announce the biggest thing in my life because some tabloid shite burger has forced us to do so."

"Marrying me is the biggest thing in your life?"

"I mean, so far, but rumour has it Gabriel Byrne is also a member of this gym, so obviously, if I see him, then that will be the biggest thing that has happened or will ever happen in my life."

"Fair enough," said Paul. "If you get the chance, invite him to the wedding."

"Screw that. If I see him, I'll be inviting him to marry me."

"He's older than your dad."

"Only in human years. Not in movie-star years." Brigit turned her head and stopped. "Something's just come up, hon. I'll talk to you later." She hung up before Paul could say anything else.

The thing in question was that a distinctive porkpie hat had caught her eye. There he was, standing outside the Starbucks across the road – the person she had to thank for the most awkward conversation she and her father had ever had. Rake O'Reilly.

Before she had time to think about it, Brigit was on her feet and walking over. A voice in the back of her brain pointed out that this was a bad idea. No good could come from it. *Relax*, said a second voice, reassuring the first one that she was just going to talk to him.

For reasons she didn't understand, Brigit had nipped out and picked up a physical copy of the newspaper this morning, and she was carrying it in her bag. *Technically*, said the first voice, *was it even assault to wallop somebody about the head with something untrue that they had written? Yes*, said the second voice, *it definitely was.*

As Brigit waited for a gap in the traffic, she noticed Rake looking over at her. He gave her a broad smile. *Oh God*, said both voices, *I really wish he hadn't done that.*

After a truck whooshed past Brigit, a gap opened up in the mid-morning flow and she was able to cross to the island in the middle of the road. She stole another glance at that smug face under that stupid hat. She was tempted to feed the stupid thing to him. He had it coming and …

It was the smile that did it. He'd done well to keep his eyes on her, not giving anything away like that, but he'd overplayed his hand. He already had one of the world's most slapable faces, he didn't need to sell it that hard. You wave the red cape around too much and even the bull starts to get suspicious about what lies behind it. Brigit looked both ways, checking the traffic, before crossing the remaining lane.

"Mr O'Reilly," she said. "Lovely to see you."

"You too, Ms Conroy. Have you seen the paper this morning?"

"I have. You should know that 'paramour' is used to refer to the lover of a married person."

He looked confused by this. "What?"

"I'm just pointing out that you're almost as horrible a writer as you are a human being."

"You came over here to give me some writing tips, did you?"

"I did also consider giving you the monumental clip around the ear that you so richly deserve, you scum-sucking parasite," she trilled, offering a wide smile of her own as she pointed down the street to where a bearded man was sitting in the front seat of a red car, poised with a camera in his hands. "But then I figured your little furry-faced friend was sitting up there in the Astra hoping to get a picture of me doing just that." There was more than one way to take that stupid grin off Rake O'Reilly's face. If anything, this way was more enjoyable. "Sorry you wasted a trip."

Rake attempted to shrug it off. "As it happens, I was here for the show, anyway."

"I've already said there isn't going to be a show."

A sly little grin played across Rake's lips, which confused Brigit. "I wouldn't say that."

With a smile, she stepped to one side to make room for two yummy mummies pushing executive baby carriages out of the Starbucks. After a beat, she spoke in a quiet voice that only Rake could hear. "When the opportunity arises, I will make sure to thank you properly for what you did today."

He leaned back against the wall. "Do you have any idea how many times I get threatened in a week?"

"Is this what you wanted to be when you were growing up, Rake? Utterly despised?"

"I wanted to play in the midfield for Leeds United, but I've got a dodgy knee."

"As villain origin stories go, that's pretty weak."

"Villain?" he echoed with a sneer. "I'm just a bloke providing a public service."

"If you're that concerned with the public, you'd make sure your flies were up."

As he reached down to check his zip, Brigit raised her voice. "Please, sir, stop fondling yourself in public!" She switched her expression to one of horror and stepped back as the heads of the two mothers snapped around in their direction.

Rake pulled his hands away quickly and attempted a disarming smile. "She's just joking."

"There is nothing funny about it," Brigit shouted. "You monster!" Without another word, she turned around and hurried back across the road, only daring to glance back once she'd crossed over.

Rake's face was like thunder. One of the mothers had taken out her phone and was snapping a picture of him. The irony of seeing just how much he clearly hated having his photograph taken was not lost on Brigit. As she gave him a cheery little wave, her own phone buzzed in her pocket. Text message from Deccie. He'd finished getting changed and was on his way down. Brigit quickly rang Wheels and told him to bring the car around to the front.

She reached the main doors just as Deccie stepped onto the pavement, his trainer Rían in tow.

"Good workout?"

"Pretty good," said Deccie. "I think I'm making actual progress. What do you reckon, Rían?"

Rían, who was about six foot three with tightly cropped auburn hair and the kind of body you got from spending every waking hour in a gym, looked down at Deccie, as if surprised to find himself in the conversation. "What?" he said distractedly. "I mean, yes – absolutely. Great gains. Big gains."

"Right," said Brigit. "Well, assuming that was your objective – congratulations. We should—"

Brigit stop talking as she noticed Deccie's face drop.

"What the hell is he doing here?" he asked.

She spun around to see a well-built man with a goatee on his bullet-shaped head striding towards them, his arm swinging in the ludicrously exaggerated swagger that Liam Gallagher had gifted a generation of males. His sharp blue eyes were alarmingly wide and his grin showed off a couple of gold teeth.

"Well, well, well, if it isn't Captain Bigmouth," said the man. "I knew I'd catch up with you eventually."

It was only when he spoke that Brigit put two and two together. In her defence, she had absolutely no interest in MMA, or whatever the hell they called it. Boxing with kicking, and a lot of rolling about on the ground hugging each other thrown into the mix. The guy was Martin Regan, some sort of champion or other, and the guy Deccie had refused to put on his list of toughest people in Ireland, much to Regan's chagrin.

Brigit took a step forward to position herself between him and Deccie. Clint's Rule One: Always make sure that you are between the subject and the danger.

"Back away please, sir."

"Back away please, sir," Regan mimicked before giving a bark of laughter. "What's going on here? Have you got women to fight your battles now, Deccie?"

"Nobody's having any battles," said Brigit as she shifted her body to make sure she stayed firmly between the two men.

Regan stretched out his arms. "Relax, love. I'm just trying to have a conversation with my buddy here. Have you got nothing to say to me?"

"I don't want to talk to you," said Deccie.

"You heard the man," said Brigit.

"Oh yeah, I heard him. Wouldn't call him a man, though. He pretends he's one when he's behind a microphone, but out on the street he's hiding under a woman's skirt. You know what you find down there."

"You shut your mouth," snapped Deccie.

"Not that it matters, but I'm not wearing a skirt," said Brigit. "Now, are you leaving or do I need to call the police?"

"Yeah. Go on, sling your hook, ye big bollix," was Deccie's contribution.

"Why don't you make me, Declan?" Regan stuck out his chin. "Go on. I'll give you your first shot for free."

"Would you cop yourself on," said Brigit. "Look at yourself, acting like an eight-year-old in the school yard. You should be ashamed of yourself."

Regan looked taken aback. "Who asked you? Mind your own business."

"Says the man bothering people on the street. You've taken one too many shots to the head – that's your problem. Come on, Deccie – let's get out of here."

As Deccie tried to walk around Regan towards the kerb where Wheels's BMW was now parked, Brigit moved herself again to preserve the barrier between the two men. Regan responded by dancing mockingly in front of them both, shadowboxing.

"Is little Deccie running away? I've not even touched you yet. Not even—"

What happened next happened fast. Regan darted out a right hand – not in a punch, just an attempt to nip past Brigit's defences and touch Deccie. Instinctively, she reached out and grabbed the arm, threw her hip into Regan's body and, in one fluid motion that her Taekwondo instructor, Keith, would have been massively proud of, dragged Regan over her body in a perfectly executed shoulder throw. Deccie leaped out of the way as the MMA middleweight champion of the world ended up on his back on the pavement in front of him.

"Oh no," said Rían.

"What the fuck?" said Regan, looking up at Brigit with genuine outrage as he reached around with a pained expression to grab his lower back. "This wasn't part of the agreement."

Brigit gawped down at him. "Agreement?"

24

KÜBLER-ROSS REMODELLED

They were standing in Oliver Dandridge's office. The man himself was sitting behind his desk wearing a pink shirt and green tie. He steepled his fingers beneath his chin and tried to give Brigit the most piercing of looks.

"I'm sensing you're upset."

"Upset?" echoed Brigit, folding her arms to resist the urge to gesticulate wildly. "Upset? No, I'm not upset – I am absolutely bloody livid. Thanks to you, Martin Regan is now threatening to sue me for millions, because apparently, this whole thing was supposed to be some sort of staged fake confrontation that neither I nor Deccie knew about."

"Yeah," agreed Deccie.

Dandridge placed his hands either side of him on the ridiculously large desk and splayed out his fingers. "OK. I will admit, there was a little bit of a communication issue. On the upside, after taking him down, I'm pretty sure you're now next in line for a title fight." He smiled up at them then quickly wiped it off his face. "I was just trying to lighten the mood."

Before she knew what she was doing, Brigit was attempting to clamber over the desk. Her heart set on throttling Oliver Dandridge once and for all. "That's it! That is ..."

Deccie grabbed her around the waist. "Don't, Brig – he's not worth it."

"No, but I'm really going to enjoy doing it."

Dandridge leaned back as far as he could, which wasn't very far. "Has anyone ever told you that you've got a serious anger-management issue?"

"Not twice."

"Brigit," warned Deccie. "We haven't got time for this."

She took a breath. He was right. Reluctantly, she put her feet back on the carpet and raised her hands. "OK. I'm calm. I am calm."

"Alright, then."

"You can take your hands off me now, Deccie."

"Probably a good idea," agreed Dandridge. "Especially given the article in the newspaper this morning."

"Really?" snapped Brigit. "You thought now was a good time to bring that up, did you?"

"Just ..." started Deccie. "Look – I still don't even understand what the hell happened."

"I'll explain," said Dandridge. "Would the two of you like to take a seat so we can discuss this in a reasonable manner?"

Brigit shook her head. "I'd rather stand. By the way, it's not what we're here for, but somebody needs to tell you, this desk is ridiculously big for this office."

"I'll have you know it was custom made."

"With this office in mind?"

"It was custom made," Dandridge repeated, looking wounded. "We had to knock down a wall to get it in."

"Someone comes in here to eat a sandwich and you'll have to knock down another one to get them out."

The agent ran a hand across the desk, as if comforting a wounded animal. "I love this desk."

One of the girls from his office took advantage of this relative lull in proceedings to poke her head around the door. Brigit and Deccie had marched in before they could make any beverage solicitations. "Can I get anybody tea?" she asked. "Coffee?"

"I asked for a cup of coffee when I was here two days ago," responded Brigit archly. "Has that turned up yet?" She saw the hurt expression on the girl's face and instantly felt like a right bitch. Taking her bad mood out on somebody who did not deserve it was not cool, regardless of the situation. "Sorry, don't mind me. I'm fine. Thank you."

Deccie said he was fine too, then awkwardly squeezed himself into one of the two guest chairs. Reluctantly, Brigit followed suit.

"OK," said Dandridge. "I got talking to Regan's manager a few weeks ago. What was supposed to happen was that you and he had a dramatic confrontation and then you'd challenge him to a fight, Deccie."

"It was dramatic, alright," said Brigit.

"Hang on," said Deccie in disbelief. "I was supposed to challenge the middleweight MMA champion of the world to a fight?"

"That's the genius of it. You were never actually going to fight him. He wouldn't be able to do it because of insurance reasons, but that would only come out after the build-up. Back and forth in the press. That kind of thing. Great profile-raising stuff. Then – we pitch it as a TV series, where you get five people who've never fought before and train them up to take on professional MMA fighters. You'd be a team captain, he'd be a team captain – it would be incredible TV. If I do say so myself, I think it's a brilliant idea."

"Right," said Deccie. "Only you forgot to tell me about this brilliant idea?"

Dandridge winced. "Yeah. Full disclosure – I was looking for the right moment and then all the stuff happened with the death threat and the blackmail, and I sort of forgot."

"How did he even know where I'd be?" asked Deccie. Dandridge went to speak, but Deccie slammed his hand down on the table, cutting him off. "Bleedin' Rían. He even said to me when we were leaving – was I ready for this?"

"Did that not strike you as strange?" Dandridge asked tentatively.

"He's a personal trainer. Most of what he says doesn't make any sense. He keeps talking about giving one hundred and twenty percent. First off, you can't give more than one hundred percent – that's just maths. Second, it used to be a hundred and ten percent – how has inflation crept into the amount of stupid extra percent we're all supposedly giving to stuff?"

"Ah, hang on," said Brigit. "It just hit me. Rake O'Reilly made some remark about being there for the show. Did you tip off that scumbag about this, too?"

Dandridge at least had the decency to look sheepish. "Well, I mean – obviously, we need to have pictures. Otherwise, it's a sort of tree-falling-in-the-forest-type deal." He turned to Deccie. "I had no idea he was looking into you when I gave him the tip-off."

Brigit held her head in her hands. "He's got a picture of me shoulder-throwing Regan to the floor." She looked up and pointed at Dandridge. "You have to stop him publishing that photograph."

"Are you crazy? That thing's going to sell all over the world. All of Rake's birthdays have come at once. You've probably helped pay off his mortgage."

"Great," said Brigit, throwing her hands in the air. "Isn't it brilliant when good things happened to truly terrible people?" She folded her arms and glared across the ridiculous desk at Dandridge. "And all it took was you making a public spectacle of me – again!"

"It's not my fault you're a psycho."

Brigit was all set to give him both barrels, but she never got the chance. Deccie stood up and jabbed a finger at Dandridge. "Don't you dare talk to Brigit that way. She is one of my closest friends. We used to run a business together."

"Well ..." began Brigit, trying to find a way to correct that assertion without undermining Deccie.

"Her, Paulie and Phil, who I haven't even spoken to in a couple of years, are the only people I trust right now. She put herself in the line of fire to help me while you ... All you ever do is come up with ridiculous schemes to make me look stupid. I'm getting death threats, I'm being blackmailed – she's here twenty-four-seven trying to help me, and all you're trying to do is help yourself. I told you I wanted to be a serious broadcaster, but all you're interested in is making me into a cheap sideshow so you can make some easy money."

Dandridge looked like a six-year-old who'd just been told Christmas was cancelled. "Deccie, baby—"

"And stop calling me baby. You sound ridiculous. And she's right – this desk is stupid, too. You don't care about me and you are no longer my agent."

And with that, after awkwardly shoving his chair aside as much as was possible in the limited available space, Deccie stormed out the room.

Brigit stood up with a triumphant grin. "That's you told."

Thanks to the aforementioned ridiculous desk, she too experienced great difficulty in extricating herself from her chair and negotiating her way around Deccie's, which is why she was afforded the questionable privilege of witnessing Oliver Dandridge pass through the five stages of grief in record time as he shouted after his ex-client.

Denial. "You can't fire me."

Anger. "I am firing you."

Bargaining. "We should talk about this."

Depression. "Why does this always happen to me?"

Acceptance. "At least I've still got the circus-skills people. Nobody can take that away from me."

It was impressive – almost as impressive as him finding a sixth stage, which involved some unexpected office gymnastics as he leaped onto the desk, slid across it and barged Brigit aside as he rushed out the door after Deccie. By the time Brigit had made it into the reception area, Dandridge was lying prostrate on the carpet, his arms wrapped around Deccie's ankles.

"Please don't leave me. I'll do anything."

Stage six – outright, undignified begging.

"Get off me," said Deccie.

"I can change. I'll be a better man. I'll be a better agent."

"I'm not interested."

"I believe in you. Give me another chance. I'll do anything."

"That's the problem."

"I mean, I'll ... I'll ... I'll pay the ransom!"

Deccie paused at this and looked down at Dandridge. "Really?"

"I'm happy to lend you the money."

The rapid self-edit was not lost on Brigit. She watched as Dandridge opened his mouth and then closed it again. She would go to her grave believing he had considered mentioning an interest rate and then thought better of it.

Deccie looked at her and then down at Dandridge again, before relaxing his body. "OK."

He started to help Dandridge up off the floor. As he did so, one of the office assistants appeared at Brigit's elbow, holding a mug and looking very pleased with herself.

"Here's the herbal tea you asked for."

"I actually—" started Brigit, before stopping herself. It was the thought that counted. "Thanks very much."

25

TRYING TIMES AND VICTIMLESS CRIMES

Jimmy Stewart was fully aware that it was his responsibility to protect Deccie Fadden, he just wasn't quite sure how to fulfil that duty in this situation. Was it possible to get mothered to death? Brigit had "delivered the package" to Jimmy at the offices of Caint FM before she headed off with Phil to have what would no doubt be a fun conversation with Deccie's ex-girlfriend. The package in question, Deccie, was sitting in an office chair, fending off a tsunami of concern and looking rather gormless.

"Are you sure you're OK, Deccie?" asked Karen Murphy. "You don't have to do the show this evening if you don't want to. You've had a very trying day."

She was Deccie's boss, so that made sense to Jimmy. She had to make sure he was actually capable of going on-air. There was a duty-of-care thing, and then there was the fact that if you were to stick someone on live radio when they really weren't up for it, it would become very obvious, very quickly, and be very embarrassing for all concerned.

"Karen's right," chimed in Rhona, his co-host. "Let's not forget – you were attacked. That's a traumatic experience. You might have PTSD."

That, on the other hand, thought Jimmy, was out and out ridiculous. First off, Martin Regan had not actually laid a hand on Deccie, thanks to Brigit's rather emphatic intervention. As he'd heard it told, Deccie had been pretty much a bystander as Brigit had taken down the MMA middleweight champion of the world and opened an entire can of worms in the process.

Rhona ran a hand up and down Deccie's upper arm in an effort to comfort him. "I cannot believe that animal tried to attack you in broad daylight."

Jimmy could. To be fair to the other people in the room, Jimmy had the advantage of having received a full update from Brigit on what had really happened, which they hadn't. According to Brigit, Oliver Dandridge, the genius behind the whole hare-brained scheme, had spent most of the afternoon convincing Martin Regan's people that it would be worse for him if he decided to sue or press charges against anyone. Thankfully, his injuries from the coming together with Brigit were a bruised backside and a severely wounded ego. That being said, from what little Jimmy knew of the man, Martin Regan was ninety-five percent ego, so that really was a serious injury. Getting taken down by a woman looked undeniably bad for him, but so did admitting that he'd been taking part in an ill-judged publicity stunt that had gone awry. It was an example of why Jimmy Stewart had always told his kids to tell the truth in life – not for strong moral reasons, per se, it was just that in the long run, the possibilities for embarrassment when getting caught out by your own lie were far worse than the truth could ever be.

"Honestly," said Deccie, "I'm completely fine. Everyone just relax."

"Can I get you anything?" asked Shauna Walsh. "Anything at all?"

Jimmy felt bad that Shauna was even here. The poor girl was supposed to be on holiday, but he'd asked her to come in.

"I'm fine. Let's just get on with the show."

"What I don't understand," continued Karen Murphy, "was how on earth he knew you'd be there? If he was just passing by, it would be a hell of a coincidence."

Yes, thought Jimmy, *it really would be.*

"I don't know," said Deccie with a shrug. "We'll probably never know."

Seeing as neither side could admit what was supposed to have happened, Jimmy reckoned that was the only truth anyone had spoken so far.

"You were coming out of your gym up in Ballsbridge when it happened, right?"

"Yeah. We were just heading back to the car."

At this point, the other person in the room, who Jimmy had forgotten was there, piped up.

"That's the problem, you see," said David Phillips, who had been sitting in the corner playing on his phone. "The parking over there is an absolute nightmare."

"Oh, do shut up, David," snapped Rhona.

"I mean," said Karen, consciously or subconsciously trying to divert attention from the domestic squabble, "you're having some week. Between this and the—" She stopped herself, realising belatedly that not everyone in the room was supposed to know about the death threat.

"What?" asked Rhona, sounding suddenly suspicious.

Karen hesitated for a moment then recovered well. "The Irish radio awards on Friday. It's an awful lot to deal with in one week."

Deccie got to his feet and dusted down his trousers. "Look, I appreciate all the concern, but I'm fine. Let's just crack on and do the best show we can."

The rest of the room agreed. Jimmy couldn't help but feel a little sorry for Deccie. He hadn't asked for any of this, and Karen wasn't wrong – he was having a terrible week and she didn't even know all of it. Not by a long chalk. The bit she didn't know about was why he'd asked Shauna to come in for a chat.

∿

Ten minutes later, with Deccie safely installed in the studio working on his pre-match prep with Rhona, Jimmy guided Shauna into the meeting room with the pictures of Sinead O'Connor and the pope on the walls. He looked across the table and was startled to realise that Shauna looked positively terrified.

He tried to give her a reassuring smile. "Thanks so much for coming. I'll try to keep this as brief as I can. I'm painfully aware that I'm messing up your holidays. Sorry about that."

"No problem at all," said Shauna, readjusting her glasses.

"It's just that I need to get together a list of anyone who would have had access to Deccie's apartment in the last month."

"Why?" She shifted in her seat. "I mean … The writing appeared on his wall on Sunday night. It definitely wasn't there before then."

"No. I know." Jimmy hesitated then took his own advice on sticking to the truth. "In the course of our investigation, we've made a bit of a disturbing discovery. It turns out that somebody installed cameras in Deccie's apartment."

"What?" Perhaps it was the glasses that made Shauna's eyes look as wide as they did when she spoke. "Cameras? There are … Somebody's been watching Deccie?"

"Yes. Please keep in mind that obviously this is confidential, but I figured, seeing as we need your help in trying to find out how they got there, you should know the truth. In fact, Deccie's currently being blackmailed. Before we get to the list of who had access, have you seen any correspondence anywhere that mentions blackmail, cameras or used the name the Whole Truth?"

Looking dazed, Shauna shook her head and bit her lip. "I mean … No. Nothing that would … No." She held her hand to her mouth. "This is so awful."

"Yes, it is," agreed Jimmy.

"I was in and out of there all the time, and I never saw … Where exactly were these cameras?"

"There was one in the front room, one in the bedroom and one in the bathroom. All disguised as smoke detectors." Jimmy noticed the discomfort on Shauna's face and guessed where her mind was heading. "Only in the en-suite bathroom," he added. "Not the main one."

She blinked a couple of times then exhaled loudly. "That's ... That's just awful."

"It is. So now you see why it would be a big help to know who had access."

"Of course. Can I ask, have you taken over Deccie's protection from Brigit?"

"God, no," said Jimmy. "I'm just filling in for a couple of hours while Brigit runs an errand. Don't you worry, she'll be sticking to Deccie like glue. I mean, she already took on an MMA fighter today. No better woman to make sure Deccie is safe."

Shauna nodded. "OK, then. Like I said, if Deccie needs anything, anything at all – please let me know."

"I'll pass it along and I'm sure he'll appreciate the offer, but honestly, the best thing you can do now is help me with this list." Jimmy flipped open his pad. "So, is there anyone you can think of who had access to the flat?"

"I should warn you – this list is going to be extensive."

Jimmy clicked his pen on. "Fire away."

26

MEAT MEET

The sun was hanging low in the sky, a driver-dazzling ball of awkwardness, as Brigit and Phil finally reached their destination. It had been a long drive in Phil's van, heading west through the Dublin rush-hour traffic and out on the N4 towards Meath. Back in the days when planning officials were a bit more "amenable", it had been a running joke that the county of Meath to Dublin's north-west was getting smaller every year. Any developer worth their salt wanted their houses to be in Dublin, as it added to their value. One of the doctors in Connolly Hospital in Blanchardstown, where Brigit had worked for a few months, had explained that the same house in the exact same spot could be twenty grand more or less expensive, depending on which county the postcode said it was in. Brigit didn't know if she really believed that, but it wasn't beyond the realm of possibility. The property market in Ireland had long ago ceased to make any kind of rational sense to anyone.

They were now definitely in the Meath part of Meath, though. They'd passed a tractor and everything. Brigit was reminded yet again that for all the convenience that city living brought with it, nothing beat the countryside when the weather was decent and there was a grand stretch in the evening. The last part of the journey, at least, should have made for a relaxing drive. In theory.

Somehow, in a way that Brigit couldn't explain, she had allowed Phil Nellis to get onto the subject of the moon landings. He had a lot of takes. So many that Brigit had occupied herself by counting down every minute as the GPS's estimate of the time to their destination slowly shrank. You were never really in a conversation with Phil Nellis, it felt more like you were there while it was happening. Like a natural disaster or someone deciding to perform music on public transport.

"And don't get me started on Mars," concluded Phil.

If there was anything Brigit was sure of in this life, it was that she didn't want to get Phil Nellis started on Mars. If there were two things she was sure of in this life, it was that on the way back, Phil was definitely somehow going to get started on Mars.

As she tried to clear the fog of confusion from her mind that had been brought about by a fifteen-minute exposition on how flags flutter in space, she looked up at the sign over the building they were now parked in front of.

"Flannery Meats. By any chance, is this an …"

"Abattoir," finished Phil. "Yes. Yes, it is."

"And Deccie's ex-girlfriend, Tricia Reid, works here?"

"She does."

"In admin or …"

"The killing," said Phil. "I believe she mainly does the killing. Like, with a bolt gun or something like that."

"Right." Brigit paused to consider this. She wasn't naive. She'd grown up on a farm, after all – she knew where all those steaks and sausages came from. Like everyone else, she'd been a vegetarian for about a fortnight when she was sixteen, but it hadn't lasted. The reality was, the human mind was very good at blocking things out when it suited it, and burgers were tasty. Still, there was knowing and there was knowing.

"How long has she worked here?"

"Couple of years. She moved out here for the job."

"I see."

A weird tension had descended in the van, and not just because thirty minutes ago Brigit had suggested that, with the level of organisation required for even half of the conspiracy theories Phil was suggesting, it would have been easier just to go to the moon. It had been a hectic few days, to put it mildly, so Brigit's brain was only belatedly catching up on something. Looking back, Paul and Phil had both been oddly evasive when the name Patricia Reid had come up before. Admittedly, odd was Phil Nellis's default position, but she had a sneaking suspicion her fiancé hadn't given her a full briefing on what to expect either.

"Phil, what are you not telling me about Tricia?"

"Nothing. I think Trish is lovely. Please tell her I said that."

"Phil?"

He started rubbing at his face with the heel of one hand, as if he was warming it up for something spectacular. "You didn't hear any of this from me."

"Really?" said Brigit. "You work for me, you drove me here, but you'd like to be treated as a confidential informant?"

"Yes."

It didn't matter how many times you experienced it up close and personal, somehow Phil Nellis's utter failure to grasp the concept of irony still came as a surprise. "Fine. Whatever. Just tell me what you're not telling me. Is this Tricia some kind of nutter?"

"I would never say that," said Phil quickly.

"So what is she, then?"

"She is ... She was ... She can be ..."

"Do you reckon you'll be doing a full sentence any time soon, Phil?"

"She grew up around our way, so we all knew each other as kids. Tricia didn't have it easy. Her mum died early and her dad was ... Well, she spent more time taking care of him then he did of her."

"OK."

"Tricia used to play football with the lads. She was like one of them ... tomboys?"

"Is that all?" asked Brigit. "Christ, Phil – so was I. Well, a bit."

"Larry Dodds – who is an absolute prick, by the way – one time, when we were kids, he tried to put my hand in a saucepan full of water when I was asleep, only—"

"Sorry, Phil. I know this story – Paul intervened."

"Right. Yeah. That Larry. Anyway, when we were maybe thirteen, he said some stuff about Tricia. She said he asked her out and she said no. He said he never did, but that they'd done some stuff. Y'know."

"I can guess."

"Right. Pauline Rogers backed him up. She said Tricia had told her all about it, but then Pauline also claimed that she was secretly a member of the Corrs, so make of that what you will. One time, Pauline said that—"

"Maybe cut to the end, Phil."

"Tricia broke Larry's arm."

Brigit sat back in her seat. "Oh. I see."

"Then Larry's big brother Dermot went looking for Tricia and she broke his arm too."

"Jesus! Did anybody around where you lived ever talk through their problems?"

"Yeah. In fact, Larry and Dermot's uncle went around to talk to Tricia after that."

"Let me guess, she broke his arm?"

"God, no," said Phil.

"That's a—"

"She did put his head through the window of his own car, though."

"I'm starting to see why nobody wanted to come and talk to her today."

"Honestly," said Phil, "Tricia is lovely – and please tell her I said that."

"Will you stop saying that?"

"She is. I mean, she wasn't very good at conflict resolution, but in her defence – Larry, Dermot and the uncle – all renowned pricks.

Anyway, after that, Tricia got sent away somewhere for a bit, and then she came back."

"And she went out with Deccie?"

"She did. Lots of times, in fact."

"What does that mean?"

"They kept breaking up. You see, Tricia has a bit of an anger-management problem, and Deccie ..."

"Is incredibly annoying," finished Brigit. "That sounds like a bad combination, alright. And you think she could be involved in all this stuff that's happening with him now?"

"No," said Phil, his eyes wide with alarm. "I never said that. Don't you tell Tricia I said that."

"So, what am I doing here?"

"Jimmy asked if there was anyone Deccie had a history of conflict with."

"I see."

"And if anyone had ever threatened to kill him."

"To be fair, I've probably threatened to kill Paul." As soon as Brigit saw Phil's face, she instantly regretted her words. "I mean, not really. Not seriously. But when you're in a relationship with somebody and they're annoying you ... Da Xin has probably threatened to kill you?"

"No," said Phil, shaking his head emphatically. "I get the impression she quite likes me."

"It's not ... Do you know what? Never mind." Brigit looked at her watch. "It's almost six thirty. You sure she's OK for a chat?"

"Oh yeah. I've been texting her. She's working the late shift, and now's when they stop for a smoke break. She said she doesn't smoke, so she's happy to spend the time talking."

"OK. How will I know which one is her?"

"She said she will be the only woman there. I think she broke the glass ceiling in the abattoir killing business. To be fair, they probably don't have a glass ceiling – because of all the blood and that."

"Right." Brigit put her hand on the door handle.

"Hang on." Phil reached into the back of the van and brought out a cake box, which he handed to Brigit. "I got Da Xin to make her a cake specially. I thought it might help with the questioning."

"Sure. Good idea."

Yeah, that'll work. Here's a cake – are you threatening or blackmailing your old boyfriend?

Brigit opened the van door.

"Hang on," said Phil again.

"Hurry up. It's nearly time and I'm very keen to get this incredibly awkward conversation over with as quickly as humanly possible."

"There's just one thing. Now, I don't want you to overreact when I say this."

"I'll try not to."

"Good. It's possible, and I'm only saying possible, that Tricia – who again, is very nice, please mention I said that if she asks – may have killed a couple of people. For money, I mean – not for no reason."

Brigit closed the van door slowly and turned to Phil. She spoke in a very slow and calm voice. "I know I'm going to regret asking this, but I'm going to anyway. Just so I know, what do you think is an appropriate reaction to that statement?"

"When I say possible, I don't believe it. I'm only mentioning it as I wouldn't like you to hear the rumour later on and feel like I should have said something and didn't."

"OK. I'll be honest, I'm a teeny-tiny bit annoyed that you're only mentioning this now, and that you spent a good ninety minutes on the way here discussing the moon landings." Brigit jabbed a finger at Phil to silence him. "Don't! I can see you're about to say something about the moon. Trust me, that will not go well for you. Now – who is Tricia supposed to have killed?"

"A couple of scumbags. There was a rumour that she was doing contract killing, which again, I never believed. I would not be surprised if Larry Dodds was behind the whole thing. He's still holding a real grudge about the arm-breaking thing. The problem is, the rumour went around, but everybody is too afraid of Tricia to ask her anything about it. By the way, when we had the baby a couple of years ago, she sent us a lovely meat basket. It's like a fruit basket only—"

"Full of meat," snapped Brigit. "It's a simple concept."

"Does that sound like something a contract killer would do?"

"Have you ever watched any gangster films, Phil?"

"No."

"Spoiler alert – it is exactly the kind of thing a contract killer would do. Have you ever heard the phrase 'sleeps with the fishes'?"

Phil wrinkled his nose. "That's disgusting!"

"It doesn't mean ... You know what, life's too short. Is there anything else you feel I should know?"

"That's absolutely it," said Phil.

"Great." Brigit opened the door again. "You have been a massive help, Phil."

"Don't mention it."

Every time. The man just did not get irony.

BY THE TIME she left the van, cake box in hand, Brigit was expecting to meet a large woman with arms like tree trunks and a face like a side of beef, wearing blood-drenched overalls with a nail gun slung over her shoulder. That was, of course, ridiculous. She admonished herself for leaving Phil Nellis – of all people, Phil Nellis – in charge of her imagination. She loved Phil the same way she loved exercise. What she enjoyed most about it was when it stopped.

Tricia Reid was, in fact, svelte, five foot three, with a mop of blonde hair over a cheerful face that featured prominent dimples. The woman didn't look like a hired killer, but Brigit didn't want to fall foul of lazy sexist thinking. Women were just as capable as men of being violent psychopaths. Even as the thought passed through her mind, she bailed on the idea. There was way too much evidence to the contrary. Some things men really were "better" at. Still, while the whole killer thing was theoretically possible, Brigit was willing to believe it was actually a ludicrous lie made up by a dipshit whose arm probably still ached in the cold weather. Tricia was also, thankfully, not wearing bloody overalls. Her outfit of choice was a pair of DM boots, jeans, and a T-shirt with a picture of Elmo on it.

After a brief hello, Tricia guided Brigit to a sloped patch of grass where they were able to sit down and enjoy the last rays of the evening sun. Near to the enormous doors of the abattoir, about a dozen men milled around, smoking and chatting in a mixture of English and Romanian.

"Phil tells me that you're Paul Mulchrone's girlfriend?"

"That's right. Yes."

"Ah, that's lovely. I always liked Paul. He was one of the good ones."

"I like to think so."

"Tell him I was asking for him."

"I will," said Brigit.

"He and Phil were thick as thieves back in the day. God – Phil Nellis as a married man with kids now. If that doesn't make you feel old, nothing will."

"Speaking of Phil." Brigit handed her the cake box. "He made this for you. Actually, he didn't. His wife did. She has this amazing cake business."

"Fantastic. I'm supposed to be being good, but then again, if I open it up on the main break later on, that shower of hungry beasts over there" – she nodded towards the big doors – "will all be begging for some, so it shouldn't derail the diet too much."

Brigit laughed. They made a few more minutes of small talk and she found herself really liking Tricia. If you blocked out the entirety of Phil's briefing and took the girl at face value, she seemed lovely. They went through how Brigit and Paul had met, which was a complicated story that led on to how they were running a private investigation business together now, and what that was like. Then they chatted about the pandemic, because everybody chats about the pandemic, and they talked for a bit about Tricia working in an otherwise all-male environment. She said it was fine. A couple of the older men quickly slapped down any of the young lads if they became inappropriate, and besides, she could handle herself.

At a natural lull in the conversation, Tricia looked at her watch. "While it's been fun having a girly chat for once, this break is nearly over. I think you'd better get to what you're here for."

Brigit rubbed her hands up and down the thighs of her jeans, feeling suddenly very awkward.

"I'm assuming this is something to do with Deccie?" prompted Tricia.

"What makes you say that?"

"Well, he and I went out for quite some time." She gave a rueful grin. "On and off. Plus, you and he were in the newspaper this morning."

Brigit cringed. "Oh God, you saw that?"

"It wasn't a good picture of you."

"I wish it had been worse," said Brigit. "Then I wouldn't have got so many phone calls. All that stuff suggesting Deccie and I are a couple. Just because I'm a woman standing in close proximity to a man. I mean ..."

Tricia shrugged. "People are always making crap up. The rule I live by is you can believe half of what you see and none of what you read. I think that's from a song or something."

"Very sensible." Brigit reflected on everything Phil had told her. Tricia knew what she was talking about. "So, yes, as you probably figured out, Paul and I – the whole agency really – are working for Deccie. You see, he's had a death threat."

Tricia raised her head and pursed her lips. Brigit caught the briefest flash of hurt in the other woman's eyes and felt awful.

"Ah, I see," Tricia said after a beat. "And you need to come and check that Terrible Trish isn't on some vendetta or other?"

"No," said Brigit quickly. "It's just ... You and he were together for a long time, so we thought maybe you might know somebody who Deccie had wound up?"

She raised an eyebrow. "I think we both know that it'd be a lot easier to find somebody he hasn't wound up over the years. To answer your question – no, I know nothing about this. Deccie and I had a tumultuous relationship, but it ended a few years ago now. To be honest with you, I think we were only with each other because neither of us fitted in. Thing is, that isn't anywhere near enough to build a relationship on. It's why we argued all the time. Deccie can be a surprisingly sweet guy, but giving you his opinion on absolutely everything is some kind of compulsion. He can't help himself and, even though you know that, you can't help but get annoyed by it. It wasn't all bad, though – the sex was great."

"Really?" Brigit winced at the tone of disbelief in her own question. "I mean ..."

Tricia laughed. "I know what you meant. It's the last thing you'd expect. And to be clear, it was terrible initially. Frankly, I gave Deccie Fadden the mother of all boot camps. In all honesty, I think I became a bit obsessive about it. It was the easiest thing to fix, if that makes sense? Every woman who's slept with him after I did should all contribute to some sort of GoFundMe page, to send me on a very nice holiday as a well-deserved thank you."

Brigit put her hand over her mouth as she giggled. "Sorry. Just ... I mean, I'll have to take your word for it."

"Probably for the best. I have a lot of issues in my past – and believe me, we have way too little time to go through them now – but I decided, come hell or high water, I was going to enjoy sex. And so, I made damn sure I did."

"Right." Brigit viewed Megan Wright's emphatic assertion that Deccie Fadden was the world's greatest lover in a whole new light now. She briefly considered passing on the doctor's glowing testimony to her new acquaintance, but it felt like way too weird of a conversation to be having.

"In the end," Tricia continued, "long after we broke up, I finally figured out why I wasn't enjoying sex as much as I hoped I would. Took me long enough to realise, but it turns out I shouldn't have been having it with men."

"Ah," said Brigit. "You're ..."

Tricia laughed. "I am. I can see what Paul sees in you. You look adorable when you're all embarrassed."

Brigit chuckled and shook her head. "Sorry. You kind of caught me off guard there. I was expecting ... Hell, I've no idea what I was expecting."

"Sure you do. You were expecting some kind of violent nut job, because that's the reputation I've got and I couldn't shake it off if I tried. I had a lot of anger issues – with the emphasis on the word "had" – and with good reason, but I'm in a much better place these days. Phil must have told you about me breaking the arms of the Dodds family, and then, I'm guessing he told you the rumours that I've been working as a contract killer?"

"No, he—"

Tricia whacked Brigit's arm playfully. "You are a terrible liar. If you want the truth – all three of the Dodds had it coming, but yes, I could and should have handled it differently. So there's that. As for the other bit – honest to God, I got a job as a contract cleaner, and people – by which I mean men – are idiots. All it took was somebody hearing something wrong."

"You're kidding?" said Brigit. "Why didn't you correct them?"

"Because it's taken me a long time to get where I am in my life, and one of the first steps was to figure out that if you want to get happy, start caring a hell of a lot less about what other people think. Besides, don't tell any of them I said this, but people being terrified of you isn't the worst thing in the world. I didn't get hassled in pubs, I'll tell you that."

"I can imagine."

Tricia looked up to see her co-workers filing back into the building through the big doors. "I really do need to get going." She got to her feet. "So, for the record – I wish Deccie nothing but the best, and we listen to the show inside every night. He's got quite the fan club here. I don't tell the boys about mine and Deccie's past because, well, it's none of their business. I moved out here for a fresh start, and I found one. I'm afraid you've wasted a trip as I'm one of the few people on the planet who has nothing but fond feelings for

Deccie. I hope all this gets sorted out and he goes on to do great things."

Brigit stood up too. "Thanks very much for your time."

"No problem." Tricia held up the cake box. "And thank Phil and the missus for the cake."

"You're very welcome."

Tricia glanced over her shoulder. "In fact, do you fancy sneaking a slice before that lot get their grubby paws on it?"

"I shouldn't, but seriously, these cakes are incredibly ..."

Brigit trailed off as Tricia opened the cake box. They both stood there for several seconds, looking down at its contents in complete silence.

Eventually, Tricia spoke first. "Am I losing my mind, or has Phil given me a cake with me shooting a cow in the head on it?"

27

ONE WAY OR THE OTHER HE'S GETTING SCREWED

Brigit waved goodbye to Phil Nellis as he pulled the MCM Investigations van out into the late-evening traffic and disappeared into the night. The drive back from Meath had been a lot more pleasant than the drive there. Phil, picking up on what he might well have considered to be subtle hints, had clearly realised that he had exhausted Brigit's limited interest in the moon and whether or not man had ever set foot on it. Instead, he spent most of the journey explaining the revolutionary things Da Xin was doing with cake. In all honesty, listening to him had made Brigit incredibly hungry, but she'd found she could happily listen to a man being unashamedly proud of his wife for hours, even if it had left her craving a Victoria sponge something rotten.

She'd headed straight back to Deccie's apartment as it was nearly 9pm, the result of stopping en route to pick up some shopping, some of which was for her and Deccie, and the rest of which Phil had agreed to drop over to Paul in the morning. She was worried about Paul being on his own so much, although he'd messaged to tell her that Cynthia had said she was coming over to cook him dinner.

Brigit chalked her instinctive dislike of the offer up to ridiculous jealousy brought about by her guilt over not being there for Paul while he was incapacitated. He knew why she couldn't be there and she knew that he knew why, and it wasn't like she didn't trust him. She had determined not to give in to her inner idiot and had sent Cynthia a heartfelt thank-you for helping out. Internally, the persistent inner idiot pointed out that by doing so she was also letting Cynthia know that she knew she was there.

Brigit pulled out her phone and speed-dialled Jimmy Stewart, who picked up on the second ring.

"How did it go?" he asked.

"Dead end."

"You sure?"

"If Tricia Reid is behind this, then we should give up now because not only is she a criminal mastermind, she's also the world's greatest actress. She doesn't have motive either."

"But Phil said—"

"I know what he said, but trust me, she's not our girl."

"Fair enough."

"Where are you now?"

"Back at Lansdowne Towers," said Jimmy. "Deccie wanted to come straight back." He lowered his voice slightly. "Between you and me, I think all of this is really starting to get to him."

"Understandable. I'm just outside – I'll be up in a minute."

"Hold on," said Jimmy, "I've rather buried the lead. When we got back here, I was informed by the two guards downstairs, who are belatedly very on the ball now, that they caught someone trying to break into the apartment."

Brigit stopped in front of the building doors, so abruptly that the six-pack of baked beans in her shopping bag walloped painfully against her shin. "Who is it? Did they call the police? Do we think this is the person behind all of this?"

"They've not called the police yet, and I told them to hold off."

"Why?"

"Because I'm pretty sure this isn't our criminal mastermind, and because the individual in question asked to speak to you."

BRIGIT MET DERVLA, the female concierge, at the door. The woman wore her hair short and spiky, and her mouth was fixed in a straight line of disapproval at everything. She showed Brigit through to the back room-cum-storage area that they were using as a temporary, unofficial holding cell. Sat among the mops and containers of floor wax and window-cleaning fluid was therapist and proud owner of distressed oak doors, Dr Megan Wright, wearing a trench coat and a face like a wet weekend.

"Thanks, Dervla," said Brigit, "I can take it from here."

Dervla eyed the prisoner suspiciously. "Are you sure? She can be violent. She walloped Alan with her handbag when we caught her."

"Oh, please," huffed Megan.

"You," snapped Brigit, "should shut up right now. You're very lucky you're talking to me and not to the police."

"On what charge?"

"Breaking and entering, to start with—"

"And GBH on Alan," Dervla chipped in.

"GBH?" echoed Brigit.

"Well," said Dervla, "definitely a bit of BH. She caught him right on the ear. That can be surprisingly sore."

"I'm sure she's very sorry about that," said Brigit while giving Megan a very pointed look.

Megan mumbled something that might have been "sorry" but could also conceivably have been almost any word in any given language.

Once Dervla had left, Brigit held up a hand for silence while she cleared some toilet rolls off the only other chair in the room and took a seat. Only then did she lower her hand. "Now, do you want to tell me what the hell is going on?"

"I could ask you the same thing!"

"What?" said Brigit. "I spoke to you last night and we agreed you were going to give Deccie a bit of space."

"Yeah." Megan leaned forward and glared at Brigit. "And then, this morning, I opened the newspaper."

Brigit threw back her head and roared at the ceiling. "For Christ's sake – you as well? How is it that normally intelligent people seem incapable of holding on to the idea that tabloids are full of crap."

"You're denying it?"

"Denying it? Not if Deccie Fadden was the last man on Earth and the survival of the human race depended on it."

"He is a bit out of your league."

"The hell he is," snarled Brigit. "Deccie Fadden? Has the world lost its mind? I could have him in a second if I wanted him, which, again, to be clear, I do not. Jeez – I even told you I'm engaged to Paul. What would I be …" Brigit stopped herself. "Sorry, I just realised who I'm talking to. Infidelity is the closest thing you've got to a hobby."

"That's a low blow."

"And what exactly was that 'out of your league' comment?"

Megan tilted her head. "Fair point."

Both women sat back, some of the tension having dissipated from the situation.

Brigit looked around the room then turned her attention back to Megan. "Alright, I have to know – are you naked under that coat?"

Her enquiry was met with a shrug. "Technically, we're all naked under what we're wearing."

"That's deep. So, talk me through the plan for this evening."

"If you must know," Megan began, readjusting her coat carefully, "originally, I considered doing the whole turning-up-at-his-door thing, but then I realised he wouldn't be home. So, I thought he could walk in, find me lying on the bed and …"

"Scream because someone had broken into his apartment?"

"No, he wouldn't."

"Trust me, given the week he's having, he would have done."

"What's that supposed to mean?"

Brigit waved away the question. "Some of it will probably be in the bloody papers tomorrow. Did you not think you might have come across as … I'm trying to find a nicer way of saying desperate?"

Megan tipped her head haughtily. "Men find this kind of stuff a big turn-on."

"Depressingly, you're probably right."

Brigit's phone pinged. It was a message from Jimmy.

Deccie has received another email.

"Oh, crap," muttered Brigit, more to herself than anyone else.

"What?"

"Never you mind." She eased herself to her feet. "Right. I'm busy and we've got far bigger things to worry about than whatever mid-life-crisis-libido-overload-mental-breakdown you're going through. Go home. I'll double-check Deccie has your contact details, but I'm telling you now, he's going to be far too busy dealing with other things for the next while to think about any woman. He's under more pressure than you could possibly imagine."

"If he's in need of stress relief ..."

Brigit made a retching face. "Good God, woman. You really need to seek professional help. Somebody like you, only, y'know, good."

"And what was that for?"

"Let's call it payback for poor Alan."

"I barely touched him."

"Yeah, but you leave a big impression."

Brigit opened the door to the room to find the two guards doing a poor job of pretending they hadn't been listening. "Folks, you can show Dr Wright out, and if she comes back, you have my permission to turn the hose on her. Cold water."

DECCIE SAT on his bed and, with a trembling hand, opened his inbox and read the email again.

Dear Declan,

I hope you're well. I also hope you've got the money, as agreed?

Fifty thousand euros. Have your assistant bring it to St Stephen's Green tomorrow evening in a blue plastic bag. At precisely 6pm, she is to place it in the stone bulrushes that sit in the drained water feature in the centre of the park, then leave immediately. If you involve the Gardaí, I'll release the tape. Any funny business, I'll release the tape.

Do that, then announce at the radio awards the following night that you're leaving Ireland, and the recording will never see the light of day.

If you don't follow any of these instructions, I'll release it at the precise moment you're receiving the award you don't deserve but everyone says you're going to win.

Best of luck. :)
The Whole Truth

EVERY TIME HE READ IT, Deccie found the knot in his stomach growing tighter and tighter. He was so screwed. Either he paid the ransom and had to hope some nutjob kept his word, or he didn't, and then the nightmare would begin.

He flopped back on the bed and hugged a pillow to himself. Screwed. Totally screwed.

28

TWENTY-FIRST-CENTURY REAR WINDOWING

Phil reached the top of the stairs and stopped to catch his breath. He liked Brigit and Paul but, frankly, thought they were insane for buying a four-storey building. He checked his pulse. He didn't know how to do it properly, but judged it by how fast it was in relation to the tempo of the film score to *National Treasure*, starring Nicolas Cage. At the bottom of the stairs it had been 'Nic Cage looks up some stuff in books in the library'; after three flights of stairs it was now 'car chase number two'. That wasn't good.

It wasn't as if Phil had ever been fit – his was not a body predisposed to athletic endeavour. His limbs rarely worked in unison, and it was one of the reasons he'd never run away from a fight. He was so bad at moving at speed that he'd end up falling over and doing himself an injury. Lads would have taken the piss then. As it was, they'd done that a lot anyway – invariably, it was how he'd ended up in the fight in the first place. You couldn't let people walk all over you.

That aside, Phil was fundamentally opposed to stairs and lifts. He felt everything should be built on one floor and then all the trees and bushes and crap like that should be put on the roofs of big, long, flat buildings. It'd be good for nature, it'd be good for wheelchair users and people who were afraid of heights, and, most importantly of all, it'd confuse aliens as they wouldn't be able to see us from space. He had written to the council about his proposal but had yet to hear back.

The sound of Paul's dance music was coming from the other side of the door – loudly. Phil didn't like dance music because it was invariably crap. He also didn't like dancing – see fighting.

He banged on the door and waited. No answer.

"Paulie?"

He banged more forcefully. Still nothing.

"Paulie? I'm coming in. I'll give you the count of five to put pants on."

He had no reason to believe that Paul didn't have pants on, but after an incident when he'd been delivering a cake to a woman out in Dalkey last month, he now had a hard and fast rule on the matter.

"... four ... five. Ready or not, here I come."

Phil pushed open the door.

Paul had pants on. He was in his wheelchair, staring at the wall upon which he had scrawled lots of bits and pieces in various colours of marker pen. Arrows pointed furiously between the numerous elements. What looked to be hundreds of sheets of paper were scattered on the floor all about him.

"Paul."

Paul screamed in surprise.

Phil screamed because people screaming scared him.

"What are you doing here?" asked Paul.

Phil held up the shopping bag in his hand. "Cynthia let me in. I've got the shopping Brig bought for you last night. What the bleedin' hell have you done to the wall? Those had better not be permanent markers."

"I'm close. I'm really close to a breakthrough."

"Have you been to sleep?"

"What day is it?"

"Thursday."

"Then, no. You have to come look at this."

Phil walked towards him.

"Careful," snapped Paul. "I've got everything organised just how I like it."

"Right." Phil pointed at the coffee machine on the table. "Is that the one from downstairs?"

"Yes. Cynthia brought it up last night. Said that seeing as nobody's coming in to the office, I might as well get some use out of it."

Phil clocked the pile of used espresso pods beside it. "Do you reckon you might have got too much use out of it?"

"Maybe a little." Paul's eyes were wide and bloodshot as he turned to look at Phil. "I've started seeing this kind of golden glow around everything. It's a bit like that old advert for Ready Brek."

"That's probably not a good thing."

"I'm fine. Better than fine. I started going through all the threats that Deccie's received on Twitter and I've noticed a pattern – lots of patterns. I think loads of these accounts are interlinked. The phraseology used. The time of posting. I'm telling you, there's something much bigger going on here. Hear me out – I think it might involve the Chinese, a specific sub-section of *Star Wars* fans and, possibly, a dude from Belgium called Angelus."

Phil took in the room and waved his arms about. "I knew it! Nobody would listen to me, but I knew it."

Paul turned around so quickly he almost fell out of his wheelchair. "You knew about Angelus?"

"Nah. All of that is nonsense. Well, apart from the Chinese thing. They're basically behind everything these days. But think about it – social media, Twitter, is your window into the world, and you've become obsessed with looking through it. You're *Rear Window*ing. It's twenty-first-century *Rear Window*ing. Just like I predicted."

"I am not. There's nothing to see out my window most of the time. Well, bar that nice Mr Thorwald, the landlord of the Last Drop, over the road. He's up at all hours working on that rooftop garden of his. So much so, between you and me, I think Mrs Thorwald has left him." Paul leaned on the arm of his wheelchair and spoke in a stage whisper. "I think he's become a little obsessive. You know the type."

"I do," said Phil. He reckoned this Mr Thorwald sounded like a bit of a visionary, embracing the gardens-on-top-of-buildings idea in that way, but now wasn't the time. "Still though, Paulie – do you think maybe you need some sleep?"

"Sleep?" Paul laughed. "I've almost got it."

"Exactly what have you got, though?"

"I'm unravelling the mystery."

"Which is?"

Paul waved at the wall. "This. All this." He was sounding increasingly less sure.

"Is any of this going to help us figure out who is messing with Deccie?"

"Of course it ..." Paul looked at the wall and at the piles of paper on the floor. "I ... It definitely started out that way."

"Did you know," said Phil, changing tack, "that when the first engineers were working on mobile phones, the only reason they had SMS messaging was to test the network? They didn't think it would have any use to the customers. Couldn't conceive of the idea that people might text when they could just phone."

"I get you," said Paul, perking up. "So, you're saying this might be useful after all?"

"No," said Phil. "This is utter bleedin' madness."

"What was your point, then?"

"I don't always have one." He moved across the room and started to wheel Paulie in the direction of the bedroom. "C'mon, let's get you cleaned up and into bed."

"But ..."

"Question," said Phil. "There was a milk bottle on the floor beside you there, containing a liquid. Would I be right in saying that it ..."

"Yes, it is. It's hard to get to the loo in this thing and I was drinking a lot of coffee."

"Right. Two things: first, it should definitely not be that colour. I'm taking that coffee machine back downstairs."

"What's the second thing?"

"Have you got some socks and a pair of shoes I can borrow as what was in the bottle has just spilled all over mine?"

"Sorry, Phil."

"S'alright, Paulie. These things happen."

29

THE VIEW IS NICE, THE FALL IS NOT

Brigit stood on the roof of Lansdowne Towers and took a drag on her cigarette. She had finally cracked and bought a pack yesterday, mentally blaming Oliver Dandridge for the slip. She promised herself that she would only smoke the ten she'd bought, and that would be it. If she had to, she'd go back on the patches.

There was a metal railing around most of the rooftop, with gates to allow window cleaners to lower down a platform. That was why she was up here – at least it was, initially. She'd noticed the platform on her way back in from the shops earlier, and had nipped up to check that the window cleaners were who they said they were. She was being paranoid, but then again, it was that kind of week. After a rather confused conversation with a Polish father-and-daughter team, she had decided they were legit. Assassins didn't bring that many kinds of sponges with them.

Still, the view from up here really was something else. Dublin didn't find itself draped in glorious morning sunshine often, but when it did, it really made the most of it. The old lady sparkled. Brigit had been up here for twenty minutes now, enjoying the view and the guilty nicotine hit.

Her phone vibrated in her free hand and she answered it on the second ring. "Jimmy. How did it go?"

After Deccie had received the latest email from the Whole Truth last night, they'd agreed that Jimmy would go down to St Stephen's Green first thing to scout out the proposed drop site.

"Not to be a cliché," said Jimmy, "but I have good news and bad news."

"I believe it's now my job to ask what's the good news?"

"A couple of things, although they're somewhat related. First off, why are we doing this at all?"

"I don't get your meaning."

"It was Phil who pointed it out. Why have we not been asked to just pay the money into an untraceable bitcoin account where it'll disappear into the ether? No, we are doing a physical money drop, which, for the recipient, carries way more risk. Doesn't make any sense when you think about it. And that brings me to the second thing – why announce the drop location nearly twenty-four hours before it's going to happen? I mean, yes, they could always change it, but not at the last minute. The only line of communication we have is through an email address that contacts Deccie, who will have been on-air for two hours before the drop is supposed to happen. None of that makes sense, unless ..."

"Unless what?"

"A nasty little thought has occurred to me. I'm not saying this is the case, but it's not something we can ignore. Pretend you are whoever is behind the Whole Truth. Why do this when Deccie is on-air? One reason might be that you will definitely know where he is. And, thanks to the drop, you will also know that we will be busy somewhere else, leaving Deccie unprotected."

Brigit ran her fingers through her hair. "This whole thing started with somebody daubing 'Deccie must die' on the wall of his apartment."

"Exactly," said Jimmy. "Maybe the whole blackmail thing from start to finish has been a ruse to misdirect us."

"So, whatever happens, we must not leave Deccie unprotected."

"Right," agreed Brigit. "I'll do the drop, you stay with him."

"Which brings me to our next problem. If we're going to run surveillance to try to find out who we're dealing with – and we should, of course – we were already going to be dangerously stretched with only me and Phil, but now it'll just be him. With the number of people milling around St Stephen's Green on a Thursday evening, assuming the weather stays good, it'll be all but impossible for one person alone to carry out covert surveillance."

Even over the phone, Brigit could sense it was taking Jimmy every ounce of his self-restraint not to make the case yet again for the Gardaí to be brought in. They had broached the subject with Deccie last night, and he had been as emphatic as ever in his rejection of the notion. In his head, the more people who knew what was happening, the worse it got.

"Do we know anybody we could bring in to help?" asked Brigit.

"Not professionals," Jimmy replied. "Unless you just want to hire another agency, but then we'd be introducing more people into the equation who we don't know or trust, which I imagine Deccie will reject as an idea for the same reason the Gardaí are a no-no."

Brigit bit her lip. "OK. I'll have a think. Leave it with me."

"You're the boss."

"Am I?" said Brigit. "It really doesn't feel like it. Between Deccie and this ... Can we come up with another name? I really hate referring to whoever this prick is as the Whole Truth."

"Phil mistakenly referred to them earlier as the Wholewheat."

Despite herself, Brigit laughed. "Perfect. The Wholewheat it is."

"So ..." Jimmy hesitated. "How is everything else?"

"As in, have I seen the newspapers?"

"It's fine if you don't want to talk about it."

Brigit smiled. "I appreciate the offer, Jimmy, but if you and I don't talk about it, I imagine we'll be the only two people in the country who aren't."

She had nipped out early that morning and bought a copy of each of the papers. The pictures of her hip-tossing the MMA middleweight champion of the world had featured prominently.

Brigit's only solace was that most of the images seemed to have been taken by passers-by on their mobile phones. Rake O'Reilly wouldn't have got as big a payday as he'd been expecting.

"If it's any consolation, it really is Regan who comes out badly. From what I saw, you were regarded as the one who dealt with the situation after he behaved appallingly. The *Indo* compared you to Wonder Woman."

"I know. There was also the 'She's a knockout' headline you may have seen on a certain front page. The same newspaper that yesterday had me as a harlot."

"Normally they build you up just to knock you down," said Jimmy. "You seem to be getting the reverse treatment."

"So far. From my extensive two-day experience of being an unwilling celebrity, I fully expect them to put the boot in again at some point really soon. I take your point, though. I've had Oliver Dandridge on to me. Enquiries have been made as to whether I'd like to be paid quite a bit of money to give an exclusive interview."

She hadn't considered the offer – not really. Admittedly, given her current financial plight, ten or twenty grand would be a very welcome gift from the gods, but Brigit was not about to sell her story, especially as her story would put her client right in the shit. The way things were heading, she might only be a professional private investigator for another few days, but be that as it may, she was going to go out being professional.

"Is Dandridge your agent now?"

A shudder passed through Brigit. "Don't. Not unless hell freezes over – which is where I'd have to be to spend any more time in the company of that man than is absolutely necessary."

"I imagine he'll have an office there, eventually. Speaking of which ..."

"Yes," said Brigit. "I checked and he's getting us the money, in cash, this afternoon. He assures me he's cleared it all with his bank and just has to go in and collect it."

"I'm still surprised he's coming through for us."

"Not for us – for Deccie. He's not happy about it, but he doesn't want to lose his golden goose. He's also paranoid about Deccie going to this other agent, Eddie Warring, which seems to be helping. I mean, he did ask me to guarantee that the money will come back to him."

"What did you say?"

"I told him to blow it out his arse."

Jimmy barked a laugh. "I'd imagine Dandridge was thrilled about that."

"To be honest with you, I just put the phone on mute and let him rant about it for fifteen minutes. Help him work out some of his issues."

"From what I've seen of the man, it'll take a lot longer than that."

Brigit looked at her watch. "I should get going. Deccie has a suit fitting for this awards show tomorrow."

"Grand," said Jimmy. "Fingers crossed he gets a chance to wear it."

30

THREE AND A HALF PEOPLE

Brigit needed to hold the MCM Investigations team meeting somewhere and, in the absence of any better options, they were sitting round a table in a pub just off Grafton Street. Normally, at 5:15 on a Thursday evening, finding a table in any pub in the area would have been a challenge but, luckily, the sun was out, which made Irish people feel compelled to stand out in the street and stare up at the burning ball of gas in case they never got the chance to see it again. Brigit had wanted everyone to meet in Bewley's Café, but had discovered that it closed at 5pm. Her not knowing that rather salient detail didn't inspire the greatest confidence in the operation the team was about to embark on. And, for better or for worse, it was a team.

After a mercifully uneventful trip to the tailor, she and Jimmy had briefed Deccie on the details of the plan. Using the cash provided by Dandridge, Brigit was going to make the drop exactly as instructed, and then leave St Stephen's Green just in case anyone was watching her. The rest of the team would then keep eyes on the drop to see who collected the money. If they could find out who the Wholewheat – aka the Whole Truth – was, then the tables, while not exactly turned, would be somewhat repositioned in their favour. Blackmail was most definitely a crime.

It would be risky if they were spotted during their surveillance, which was why their approach would be loose and any attempt to follow the Wholewheat needed to be executed carefully. The idea of using a tracker on the money had been considered and discounted as being too risky. The same scanner that Phil had used to find the cameras hidden in Deccie's flat could also detect a tracking device and was available to purchase for €150, including next-day delivery, from some of the same shops where you could buy said trackers and cameras. Welcome to the twenty-first century, where it has never been easier to keep your friends and loved ones under twenty-four-hour surveillance.

Their best chance of finding out who they were dealing with was playing along by paying the money and hoping that the surveillance would work. Phil would be in the park, keeping eyes on the drop. Brigit hadn't mentioned this part, but his ongoing feud with Deccie actually worked in their favour here, as anyone who had been watching them up to this point would never have seen the two of them together.

Once completely clear, Brigit would make sure she wasn't being followed, then change outfits and be ready to pick up the tail on Wholewheat once they exited the park. St Stephen's Green had several exits, but it was the best they could do with their limited resources. Speaking of limited resources, they knew they were going to need more eyes in the field as spotters, or else the chances of this thing working were going to be severely reduced. That left them discussing who they could trust to fill the role. And that conversation was how Brigit and Phil had ended up sitting opposite three and a half people in a pub with only forty-five minutes to turn them into a smoothly functioning surveillance machine.

The first individual in question had been Phil's suggestion and was a very good one – Johnny Canning, nightclub owner and fully signed-up member of the St Jude's Under-12s hurling squad's management team, who Deccie agreed was entirely trustworthy. The only downside of using Johnny was that he was, frankly, too attractive to blend into the background anywhere. Still, you wouldn't look at him standing around and think, that man is conducting covert surveillance. You'd look at him and think, who on earth is stupid enough to keep that man waiting?

The second person was Shauna Walsh, Deccie's PA – or at least she was when Brigit wasn't pretending to fill her role. In all honesty, Brigit hadn't wanted her to be involved, but Deccie had insisted. She'd tried to put the young woman off by suggesting that Wholewheat would probably recognise her, given how much time she spent in Deccie's company, but Shauna had assured Brigit that would not be a problem. Brigit had thought she'd maybe don a pair of sunglasses and a baseball cap, perhaps. Shauna, however, turned up to the meeting having had her flowing blonde locks shorn down to a mohawk that had been dyed pink. She also now sported a nose ring and was wearing a ripped Green Day T-shirt under an unbuttoned checked shirt, some cycling shorts, and a pair of red DM boots. Brigit hadn't recognised Shauna when she'd approached her and said hello outside of Bewley's. The transformation was both convincing and alarming – the girl needed to be nominated for a PA of the Year award or, more probably, be the guest of honour at a serious intervention.

The third person was Nora Stokes, legal eagle and Brigit's best friend. Obviously, Brigit had vouched for her – she would trust Nora with her life. Having said that, she was less confident about trusting her with this assignment. For years, Nora had been hounding Brigit to let her come along on a case. She was extremely good at her job, but she regularly held court over a bottle of wine about how deathly dull it was. Despite Brigit's best efforts, Nora had an overly glamourised impression of what PI work was really like, and Brigit's worry was that she might try to make this assignment more exciting than it needed to be. While she didn't look the type, Nora was seriously addicted to Jason Statham movies.

These three people had a strict brief to carry out an observational role only, and earlier, Brigit had spent a good thirty minutes on the phone to Nora, reiterating this and attempting to calm her friend down. She was not confident she had succeeded in this task. The woman was a loose cannon, as proven by the fact …

"Why is there a kid here?" asked Phil, with his trademark inability to politely say the thing everyone else was far too polite to say.

"This is my son, Dan," explained Nora. "You've met him before."

"I didn't say I didn't know who he was, I asked why he was here."

"I couldn't get a babysitter."

"I'm not taking care of him. The last time I did that he crayoned my face."

"For God's sake, Phil," said Brigit. "He was only two when that happened. He's grown out of doing that now, haven't you, Dan?"

On cue, Dan nodded and gave them all a winning smile. Brigit had babysat the little guy enough times not to be taken in by it. In fact, he'd only got worse with age. They should use him to advertise condoms. He might look angelic, but animals ran for the hills at the mere sight of him, and he'd been unofficially banned from most of the childcare facilities in Dublin. Nora had been relieved when he'd been old enough to go to school. As she'd put it, "Legally, they have to take the little monster." None of this was to say she didn't love him more than life itself, just that she was tiring of domestic appliances mysteriously blowing up.

"Don't worry," said Nora. "He's staying with me."

"People don't take kids on surveillance operations," insisted Phil.

"Exactly!" said Nora with an air of triumph. "But they do take them to the park. It's the perfect cover. Frankly, you should all have children with you."

Phil looked across at Brigit. "I could ring home and see if Da Xin would drop off Lynn. I think she might have a play date but—"

Brigit cut him off by patting his hand. "Don't worry about it. Nora was just making a suggestion."

"If I'd have known," said Johnny Canning, giving Brigit a sly grin, "I could have rung around. Might not have scored a baby on short notice, but I'd bet a kidney somebody must have an annoying small yappy dog in need of a walk. Some stereotypes really are bang on."

"You're all perfect as you are," said Brigit. "Although Shauna, I reckon you deserve some kind of award." She'd expected her comment to raise a smile from the PA, but instead Shauna just glowered at her intensely. Brigit had no idea why, but she had no time to worry about that now. "Right, Phil is going to give you all your earpieces and radios, and will explain how everything works."

Brigit let Phil get on with the briefing, only interjecting to explain to Nora that no, everyone did not need individual call signs, and there would be no need for coded messages. She spent the rest of the time texting Oliver Dandridge. He'd assured her that he had the money and was on his way, but she trusted him about as far as she could throw the Ha'penny Bridge. If he didn't get here soon, then all this would be for nothing and Brigit could only speculate at what kind of annoyed looks she'd then get from beneath that pink mohawk. Sacrifices had been made.

In the end, Dandridge turned up with fifteen minutes to spare, by which point the three and a half spotters had been dispatched to take up their assigned positions in various areas of the park. Before Brigit could say anything, Dandridge opened the satchel he was carrying and pulled out a blue carrier bag.

"Alright, alright, alright – don't go giving me attitude. I'm here, aren't I?"

"Thanks very much," said Brigit, taking the bag and glancing inside.

The two stacks of new-looking €100 notes was smaller than she'd expected – each about the size of a clutch. She reached into the carrier bag and handed the money straight to Phil, who ran his detector over it. With absolute predictability, it pinged. Brigit took back the wad of notes and handed it to Dandridge.

"And now, as previously discussed, we will not be attempting to use a tracker for the reason you have just seen. So, please remove whatever you went to the time and effort to buy."

Dandridge glared at her. "It's all very easy for you to say – it's not your money."

"No, but it is your client's career, so let's stick to the plan, as agreed."

Sulkily, he flipped through the notes and plucked out a device the size of a five-cent coin. Phil ran the detector over the money again, and, once it had been cleared, Brigit put it back in the bag.

She studied it again with interest. "Doesn't look like much, does it?"

In hindsight, even Brigit had to admit that was probably not the best thing to say in the circumstances. Luckily, she and Phil had somewhere they needed to be, so she popped the blue bag into her handbag and they left Oliver Dandridge ranting at a double whiskey as they headed out into the sunshine. Phil, baseball cap and sunglasses on, proceeded up Dawson Street to enter the park from that direction, while Brigit headed towards Grafton Street, disciplining herself to walk at a casual pace. There was no point in rushing and getting there early. If this thing was going to work, then the timing, along with so much else, needed to be perfect.

She gripped her bag tightly. It had already been an incredibly tough week and she'd be damned if she was going to end up the victim of the world's luckiest bag snatcher.

This really needed to go well.

31

INEVITABLE GORILLAS

At the sight of the Grafton Street gate across the road, Brigit got a sickly feeling in her stomach. It wasn't like she hadn't been in highly stressful situations before, but something about this felt all wrong. As Jimmy Stewart had pointed out, the entire set-up made little sense. Why do it like this? There were only two possibilities: they were dealing with either a properly crazy person or someone who was supremely confident that they were several steps ahead. Neither of those options filled Brigit with joy. She felt like Wile E. Coyote, just before he noticed that he'd run out of cliff.

While she crossed the road, Brigit admonished herself. *Get it together.* Whatever this was, they were in it now, and the best she could do for Deccie was to keep her wits about her and stick to the plan.

As expected, given the glorious sunshine, the park was absolutely rammed. As she passed through the gate, Brigit had to bob and weave to circumnavigate the gaggle of teenagers who had stopped to excitedly discuss something or possibly nothing. The grassed areas of the green were thronged with young couples, old couples, families of tourists, yet more teenagers, office workers just finished for the day and keen to catch up on what they'd been missing, a toddler with an

ice-cream-smeared face bawling her eyes out. Ireland didn't get much
sun, but you could never accuse the natives of letting the little they
did get go to waste. The air was rich with the smells of summer – the
heavy, hay-fever-inducing scents of burgeoning flower beds mixed
with a hint of somebody somewhere enjoying a sneaky joint.

Brigit kept her eyes forward, aware that she could be being
watched. It was an unnerving feeling. Within seconds, she had her
feeling confirmed.

"Alright," came Phil's voice, loud in the earpiece concealed
beneath Brigit's hair, "Brigit has entered the park. Everyone fully
alert. Comms check."

"What is a comms check?" asked Johnny Canning.

"It's checking that your radio works," explained Nora. "Dan – do
not touch that. That's dirty."

"Oh," said Johnny. "Well, obviously it's working."

"Shauna?" asked Phil.

"Confirmed. Over."

"I was told we weren't supposed to say over," said Nora, before
adding, "over."

"You don't have to," said Phil. "But you can if you want to."

"It feels like all of us should say it or none of us should say it,"
continued Nora. "I promise I will get you an ice-cream in a minute.
Sorry, that last bit wasn't meant for you lot. You lot can get your own.
I'm not made of ice-creams."

As they talked, Brigit made her way along the path that ran
beside the lake where a few swans were gliding regally across the
surface, looking positively put out by the number of people who had
dared to enter their domain. Brigit had spent a couple of hours
staring at a map of St Stephen's Green, discussing with the others
where the spotters should be placed.

At the heart of the park was a circular lawned area surrounded
and crisscrossed by paths, which split it into four symmetrical
sections, each of which featured circular flower beds at their heart.
Other patches of lawn lay to the east and west of the central circle,
and featured more horticultural displays. The perimeter of the

central area was lined with trees, but beyond that, the feeling of symmetry broke down. Paths curved away in six different directions – the lake to the north of Brigit's approach; a large grassy area to the south, which featured a bandstand that always seemed to be undergoing renovations; a playground to the east beside another large lawned area; and the space to the west, which was dominated mostly by trees. The central area also featured a number of gazebos and a plethora of benches, plus two fountains that, for some reason, were currently bone dry. The location Brigit had been given for the money drop was in one of said fountains. Thanks to the layout of the park, it could be seen only from inside the central area or from across the lake.

As well as a view of the drop, Phil's station across the lake also gave him a quick route back to the MCM Investigations van to help pick up a tail. Johnny was to position himself over on the west side of the park, Nora and Dan on the east, with Shauna to the south. Technically, all four of them would be able to see who came to pick up the money, and they hopefully had enough sets of eyes to track the direction that person headed off in.

Brigit crossed over the bridge into the central area and resisted the urge to look around, to confirm everyone was in position.

"She's in the main area," said Phil. "Everybody shut up and keep your eyes open."

Brigit jumped and grabbed at her bag as a kid on one of those new-fangled electric scooters zoomed past her. "Jesus!"

"You're not wrong, love," said an old lady with a strong Dublin accent, who was sitting alone on the bench to her left. She was wearing a thick overcoat unsuited to the weather and clutching a handbag big enough to transport a small hatchback car. "Those things are a menace. They should be banned."

Embarrassed, Brigit tried to smile. "We never had electric scooters when I was a kid."

"I meant children," said the woman without a hint of irony. "If I wanted to be surrounded by annoying ankle-biters, I'd have not spent seventy-four years keeping my legs together."

Brigit nodded and kept walking. Some statements really didn't call for a response.

She was coming up to the fountain with the stone bulrushes at its centre now. When she'd been imagining this part of the plan, she hadn't factored in the number of people who would be sitting all around the edge of the waterless water feature. Seating was at a premium in the whole central area – all the benches were occupied and, for reasons past Brigit's understanding, prominent signs instructing all and sundry to keep off the grass were everywhere. This grass was apparently more delicate than the grass not more than a couple of dozen yards away.

When Brigit reached the fountain, she edged around the two-foot stone wall until she found a gap in the crowd and stepped over it. She now needed to place the bag containing the money in the fountain without drawing anyone's attention, which seemed damn near impossible. Brigit pulled out her phone as if she was trying to take photographs of the bulrushes. If she did it for long enough, people would just go back to ignoring her. Before that, though …

"Here, Rowena," came a young female voice, "check out your one. Taking pictures of the Mickey Bush."

"Here, Mrs," came a second young female voice, "are you a big fan of the Mickey Bush?"

Brigit turned to see two sour-faced teenage girls perched on the wall, puffing away on cigarettes and favouring her with sneers. Brigit forced a laugh. Like they were the first people to notice the bulrushes looked like penises. Everyone thought that – even other plants, probably.

"I know," she said with a smile. "It looks funny, doesn't it? They're actually bulrushes."

"Check out David Attenborough over here," said the first girl, wafting her cigarette around. Her voice dropped into a lower register. "The Mickey Bush, with its distinctive dick crop, is extremely popular with old ones who aren't getting any."

Her friend cackled in appreciation before adding, "There's an

Ann Summers shop up the road there, love. You can get yourself something better than a picture of the old Mickey Bush."

"What's happening?" asked Phil over the radio.

"Brigit is being bullied by a couple of teenage bitches," came Nora's response. "Let me know if you want me to tag in, Brig. I can tear down those two in a heartbeat. I could do five minutes on the size of the one on the left's calves alone. I was the quiet girl in school and I've got a lot of unexpressed rage to work through."

Brigit blushed and gave an awkward nod at the two girls in a pathetic effort to pretend like she was part of the joke and not the butt of it, before she started to move around and take pictures of the centrepiece from different angles, while simultaneously edging away from the Dublin reboot of *Mean Girls*. No one was more surprised than she was when it worked.

The first girl tossed her cigarette butt, which bounced off the bulrushes, then got to her feet. "Come on, Rowena – all this talk of mickeys is after making me hungry. Let's go to KFC."

As they headed off, Brigit glanced around to confirm she wasn't being watched then opened her handbag.

"Here, now," came a male voice. "You can't be in that fountain."

With a sinking heart Brigit turned to see that the mean girls had been replaced by a park warden, who was giving her a stern look, his arms folded across his hi-vis jacket.

She smiled at him. "I'm just taking a few pictures."

"You can't be in that fountain," he repeated.

"Why not?" asked Brigit, holding out her arms in exasperation. "I'm just taking pictures. What harm is there in that?"

"We do not allow people in the fountains, and we never have."

"Thing is, seeing as there's no water in it, is it even still a fountain?"

"Look, love – I'm not here to debate philosophical questions about what constitutes a fountain. It's my job – one of my many jobs – to keep people out of the fountains, and that is what I'm going to do. Now, are you getting out of there, or do I have to ring the guards?"

Before Brigit could answer, the park warden was grabbed by a concerned mother with her bemused child in tow.

"Oh, thank God," said Nora, "a park warden. The sixth emergency service. I need your help immediately."

"I'll be with you in—"

Nora started to shake the man. "But officer, my poor son has been attacked by a squirrel!"

"They don't normally do that," said the warden.

"Yes, I know," cried Nora. "But then, do they normally foam at the mouth?"

"Jesus!" exclaimed the warden, now giving Nora his full attention. "I told them this would happen, but nobody listened to me. Where's this squirrel? Show me."

Nora gave Brigit a quick, furtive wink before heading off, followed by the park warden, her son, and the attention of everyone within earshot. After a quick glance around to confirm she was free to act, Brigit darted her hand into her handbag, pulled out the money and bent down to place it among the bulrushes. With a last look around to make sure that everyone around her was still distracted, Brigit stepped out of the fountain and started walking back the way she had come in.

As she headed towards the bridge, she rubbed her hand under her nose to cover her lips then spoke. "A lot bloody harder than it needed to be, but the package is now in place. Has anyone noticed anything unusual?"

"Unusual?" came Phil's tremulous voice. "There are rabid squirrels running around this park. It's the start of *28 Days Later.*"

Brigit rolled her eyes. Thankfully, Johnny Canning stepped in before she had to. "There isn't, Phil. That was a lie Nora made up to create a distraction for Brigit."

"Are you sure?"

"I guarantee it."

"Sorry to interrupt," said Shauna, "but you know when you asked about anything unusual? Well, I've just seen a gorilla."

"What?" said Brigit.

"Holy shit," said Johnny. "I've just seen one – no, three of them."

"Four of them just ran by me," yelled Phil. "Forget *28 Days Later* – it's *Planet of the Apes*."

Brigit had just reached the bridge over the lake when she had to step aside to avoid being run over by a gaggle of people in gorilla suits who had just come sprinting around the corner. She turned to see the incredible sight of countless more gorillas pouring into the central area of the park from all sides. A crowd of onlookers was spilling in too, as the people of Dublin were always up for a free show, and whatever this was, it looked like it might get interesting.

In the middle of the central lawn, one gorilla held up a massive boombox. He pressed a button and a loud fanfare of bellowing brass blasted out the speakers. After about fifteen seconds, Brigit estimated there were now between thirty and forty people in gorilla suits more or less evenly spaced around the outer perimeter of the space. The fanfare came to an end and was replaced by a thumping dance track. All the gorillas raised their hands above their heads and started clapping in time with the music, encouraging the still-growing crowd to join in – most of whom did. Then, four gorillas ran halfway down each of the paths that bisected the circle, stopped and launched into a synchronised breakdancing routine, much to the delight of their audience, who whooped their approval.

"Keep an eye on the package," shouted Brigit, trying to be heard over the din.

The park warden from earlier reappeared and rushed towards the gorilla holding the boombox. "No music. No music allowed. And get off the grass. There is a sign. There is a sign!"

The crowd booed him while the boombox-wielding gorilla took off across the lawn. Their boos turned to cheers and the park warden gave chase. Despite the cumbersome costume and heavy stereo, this particular gorilla had been chosen for his task clearly because he was fleet of foot, as he easily evaded the red-faced and flailing warden.

After about a minute, the song ended abruptly and was replaced by what Brigit recognised as the Martha and the Vandellas classic 'Dancing In The Streets'.

Phil said something over the radio that Brigit didn't catch amid the hullabaloo. She placed her hand to her ear. "Say again?"

"Aren't you supposed to leave the park, Brigit?"

"Screw that. Can anyone see the package?"

The gorillas were now running around pulling people off the park benches and encouraging the crowd to dance. To her left, she clocked the old woman she had spoken to earlier. One of the gorillas had grossly over-estimated her desire to join in, and she was walloping him with her gargantuan handbag, sending him sprawling. Elsewhere, though, people were getting into the party spirit. A couple of conga lines were already starting up and several of the gorillas were kicking one off around the fountain, blocking it from view.

Johnny Canning's voice came over the radio. "I think ... I think one of the gorillas might have taken it now."

Brigit swore under her breath. "Has anyone got eyes on it?"

Everyone spoke at once, but nobody seemed to know anything. Brigit started to head back towards the fountain, then stopped herself. Phil was right. She was supposed to be getting out of there. The instructions had been very clear on that point. When a gorilla grabbed her arm, she almost screamed. She turned, her fist already clenched, and was greeted by the sight of a gorilla doing the twist.

She stepped around him. "Has anyone got eyes on the package?" she repeated, but received no intelligible response.

Once again, the music stopped abruptly and was replaced by 'Teenage Kicks' by The Undertones. Everywhere Brigit looked gorillas were now pogoing about, while more and more people flooded into the centre of the park, either to watch or, increasingly, to join in. The poor park warden was there in the middle of it all, his hands on his knees, gasping for air as his world collapsed around him.

After just a verse and chorus, that song ended too, and, following a brief three-second reprise of the fanfare, the gorillas all offered a clenched-fist salute before running off through the crowds in every direction, high-fiving people as they went – one of them €50,000 better off.

Brigit turned and took a seat on a nearby bench, and held her head in the hands. "We have been completely outplayed."

"What the fuck was that?" came Nora's voice.

Before she could answer, Brigit heard panting over the radio, followed by a loud grunt and the sounds of a struggle.

"I've got one," shouted Shauna excitedly.

"Oh God. What do you mean?"

"She's beside the bandstand," said Johnny. "Brigit, you'd better get over here quickly."

32

IT'S THE QUIET ONES YOU HAVE TO WATCH

It's always the quiet ones you have to watch.

Brigit reached the bandstand to see Johnny standing in its shadow and attempting to convince Shauna to release her prisoner. She was ignoring him entirely, while sitting astride the face-down gorilla, pinning its arms behind its back and screaming 'Who has the tapes?' over and over again. This spectacle hadn't drawn its own crowd yet but only because the throng was still excitedly discussing what had just happened. That wouldn't last long.

Brigit shook Shauna by the shoulder. "OK, up you get. Everyone else, just calm down."

"I got one of the bastards," yelled Shauna.

"Yes, but he probably has nothing to do with why we're here and doesn't know why you're so incredibly angry at him." *To be honest*, thought Brigit, *even I don't quite understand the second part.*

Shauna shook off Brigit's hand and glared up at her with so much hatred that she felt compelled to take a step back.

"Get her off me," shouted the gorilla in an alarmed male voice.

Johnny Canning got down on his haunches and placed himself in Shauna's eyeline. Brigit knew that he had worked on counselling hotlines in the past, and she could really see his experience coming through. He gave Shauna a calm smile and spoke in a soft, infinitely reasonable tone of voice.

"OK, Shauna, I know you're upset. This has been a mad old day, hasn't it? What do you say you get off this guy, and I'm sure he'll answer all of our questions if we ask nicely? Right?"

The gorilla only realised the last bit was aimed at him when Johnny tapped him on the back of the head.

"What?" he asked, initially bemused before catching on. "Yeah, sure. Just let me go. My arm is hurting me."

"See, Shauna," said Johnny. "You're hurting him. I know you don't want to do that."

Shauna paused then, in one swift movement, got to her feet and released her prisoner.

"Great," said Johnny.

The gorilla, for his part, was a lot less complimentary. He spun around, pulled off the head of his costume, and looked around in disbelief. "What the fuck? Crazy bitch clotheslined me."

"Language," warned Nora, who had just turned up with Dan by her side. "There are children present, ye dipshit."

Phil was jogging awkwardly up behind them now too, in the kind of uncoordinated stumbling motion that only Phil could pull off.

The guy in the gorilla suit couldn't have been much more than twenty, with a head of floppy brown hair and a face that was red from exertion, anger, embarrassment or, most likely, a combo of all three.

"I have been assaulted." He jabbed a finger at Shauna. "I'm going to sue you."

Nora swiftly produced a business card. "Nora Stokes, Miss ... ehm, Shauna's legal representative. You, a large man wearing a disguise, ran towards my diminutive client and she, a woman on her own, enjoying a quiet evening stroll, defended herself from a masked and potentially aggressive attacker. Exactly who do you think will be suing who here?"

"What?" asked the gorilla, clearly feeling like he'd lost his grip on the conversation.

"Or," interjected Brigit, "you could just answer a few questions and we'll chalk it all up to a bit of harmless confusion."

The gorilla said nothing, just rubbed his shoulder and gave a curt nod.

"Super. Who are you and what were you doing here?"

The man raised his chin with defiant pride. "We are the Devil Dance Collective – an anarchist anti-capitalist dance troupe committed to disrupting the status quo through performance art. We got a very good write-up in *Hot Press* last month."

"Congrats," said Brigit. "How do you organise something like this?"

"Various methods."

"Name one," said Brigit, a hint of steel in her voice.

"There are Facebook groups, subreddits, a discord, friends of friends."

"Is there a membership list for this group?" asked Nora.

The gorilla sneered. "What part of 'anarchist' don't you understand?"

She nodded. "Shauna, I think he's attacking you again."

"Alright." Gorilla Boy held up a hand as Shauna took a step forward. "No, there isn't. We organise everything online. I don't even know the names of any of the other members of the group."

"How do people join?" asked Brigit.

"They just join – we're not a secret. They put the links in the *Hot Press* article. It's why we got so many new members."

"Is there anyone in these Facebook groups with the nickname the Whole Truth?" Phil chipped in.

"No."

Brigit nodded. "And I'm guessing this thing has been planned for weeks?"

"Yeah. We even organised a group discount on gorilla suits. They're cheaper to buy than to rent. The costume-rental business is an absolute capitalist clusterfuck, designed to deny the proletariat ownership of—"

"OK, OK," interrupted Brigit. "Keep it in your pants, Comrade

King Kong." She looked at her team. "I'm guessing Wholewheat just knew about this and piggybacked onto it?"

A wave of nods bobbed around, except for Shauna, who was glaring at the ground like she was about to kick the crap out of it.

"Great," said Brigit. "So we've got precisely nothing."

"Brig," said Johnny, nodding pointedly to her left. She looked and saw the park warden, accompanied by two reluctant-looking uniformed gardaí, heading towards them.

"Christ. Alright, Monkey Boy – off you pop."

He regained the use of his feet, being noticeably careful to stay well away from Shauna as he did so. "Just so you know, gorillas are not monkeys."

"Sure. And you're just somebody in a silly costume with too much time on his hands."

"Fascist!"

Brigit pointed over her shoulder. "You think I'm bad? Wait until you meet the bloke who normally spends his day stopping Yogi Bear from getting picnic baskets."

She saw the precise moment he clocked the incoming trio before turning and sprinting away. A couple of seconds later, the park warden, trailed by the two gardaí, ran past.

"Why'd you let him go?" the warden called, exasperated.

"He swore he was an endangered species," shouted Nora, before turning to the team. "Well, that was apeshit crazy. Am I the only one who fancies a banana daiquiri now?"

33

ENDANGERED SPECIES

Brigit looked across the table in the meeting room at Caint FM as Jimmy Stewart sat there, listening to her with a contemplative expression on his face.

"So," she finished, having completed her account of the frankly embarrassing events that had taken place almost two hours beforehand in St Stephen's Green, "what we've got is a grand total of nothing. No idea who is behind this and no leads. Actually, less than nothing, if you take into account Dandridge's missing fifty grand."

"How has he taken that?" asked Jimmy.

"I've got about four hundred missed calls from him. I'll tell him later. After I tell Deccie."

Jimmy sighed. "Well, at least the ransom is paid, so, theoretically, this Whole Truth person might stick to their word and not release the tape."

"Only if Deccie announces he's leaving Ireland at this award show tomorrow night."

"Oh, yes," said Jimmy. "I forgot that bit."

"I doubt he has. And even after all that—" began Brigit.

"What are the odds they release it, anyway?" finished Jimmy.

Brigit slumped in her chair. "We've made a royal mess of this. I mean, I have," she corrected. "Not you."

"You've done what you could in a crappy situation, and it's not like I've been getting anywhere." He tapped the folder on the table in front of him. "I'm afraid my suspect list hasn't moved on much. Paul's been checking online stuff, but it's just an endless pit of faceless idiots spewing bile. I've gone through all the post, and so on. Most of it's crap, notable mainly for the shockingly awful standard of spelling. The interviews with the concierge staff at Lansdowne Towers have got us nowhere either. I'm going through the list Shauna provided us with of people who potentially had access, but nothing is jumping out from that, and my friend on the force has come back to confirm that there's no broader trend that they're aware of. That's not to say it isn't entirely impossible that fifty celebs are being blackmailed. It's just that nobody has told the Gardaí."

"That is both thorough and thoroughly depressing," concluded Brigit.

Jimmy flipped open the file. "There is this."

He drew out a sheet of paper and slid it across the table. It was a photocopy of an article from the *Financial Times* about how Callan Media had received an unprecedented fine in the US for misleading investors.

"Callan Media is indeed sniffing around acquisitions in Ireland," Jimmy explained, "and Cynthia's source was right – they have a rep for dodgy business practices. Still, all this doesn't seem—"

"Holy shit." Brigit cut him off.

Jimmy sat up. "What?"

Brigit spun the article round and pointed at the accompanying picture. "That guy."

"That's Marcus Callan."

"And he's the guy I saw chatting to Deccie and Dandridge in the nightclub on Monday night. I'd not seen a picture of him before."

"That is interesting," said Jimmy. "What were they discussing?"

"I don't know. I was at the far side of the room, but thinking back, it looked like Deccie didn't want what Mr Callan was selling and they didn't part particularly amicably." Brigit slapped the table as a thought struck her. "Karen, the station manager – she told me her job was on the line if she didn't get Deccie signed to a new contract."

Jimmy nodded. "He is the supposed jewel in the crown around here, alright."

Brigit held up the picture of Callan. "Maybe if Deccie won't play ball, Callan's found a way to force him out."

"Hang on, though," said Jimmy. "This is all a bit thin."

"But it is a lead," said Brigit, failing to keep the excitement from her voice.

"Yes," conceded Jimmy, "but trust me, just because you've only got one lead doesn't mean it's the right one. Don't fall into that trap. Still, I'll get checking."

"And I'll ask Deccie about it." Brigit drummed the desk excitedly. "Finally, we've got a lead!"

Jimmy's lips tensed into a tight, straight line.

"I know," said Brigit, "it might be nothing. Still" – she looked up at the clock on the wall – "Deccie finishes in ten minutes and at least now I've got something more to tell him than a gorilla nicked his pocket money."

34

THE KLF

Irony of ironies, given the week Brigit had already had, the media had helped her to explain to Deccie what had happened in St Stephen's Green earlier in the day. TV3 had footage of the goings-on, which they rather grandly labelled "an exclusive". Still, it had been a lot easier for Deccie to sit on the couch in his apartment and watch the clip on his phone than it would have been for Brigit to have tried to paint him a picture.

Him witnessing the crowds and the general level of mayhem also meant that Brigit and her team hopefully didn't look as incompetent as she felt they did for failing to get any information on who was blackmailing him. Still, she'd expected him to be mad and had a defence for what happened all mapped out in her head. Instead, Deccie was something far worse – he was understanding. He'd even thanked the team for trying their best.

Back when he'd worked for MCM Investigations, Brigid had seen Deccie criticise how Paul opened a bottle of Coke. Until that point she hadn't even realised that there was more than one way to do it. Finding fault with what other people did was Deccie's *raison d'être*. Watching him meekly accept her explanation when there were plenty of grounds for criticism was like watching Tom sit down and accept that Jerry had just as much right to live in his house as he did.

She decided to reach for the one positive they had. As Deccie put his phone away, she placed herself on the sofa opposite him. "One thing I wanted to ask you about," she began. "On Monday night, you met with a guy called Marcus Callan."

"Oh, yeah, that gobshite. That was Oliver's idea. I said no to even meeting him, but Dandridge sort of sprang him on me."

Brigit nodded. "What did he want to talk to you about?"

"He wanted to offer me a wheelbarrow full of cash to sign a contract with him. Told me I could do what I like, when I liked. Set my own agenda."

"Doesn't sound too bad."

"Doesn't sound too bad?" repeated Deccie, outraged. "He wants to put Caint FM out of business. That's my home. They gave me my break. If you've not got loyalty in this world, you've got nothing. I don't know much, but I know that."

Brigit found herself temporarily speechless. "Oh."

"Look, Dandridge is doing all this negotiating nonsense and I was letting him get on with it because he says it's how we get the best deal, but between you and me, I just want the gig I've got. I don't want to go anywhere or do anything else. I spent my whole life looking for something that felt like it fit, trying to find somewhere I belong, and now I've got it, I'm not giving it up."

He stopped and studied his hands, which were clenched together in his lap.

"At least, I didn't want to, but thanks to this Whole Truth prick, if I'm going to have any career at all, it'll be outside of Ireland. I don't want that." With a snotty sniff, he wiped a hand across his face. "Me grandad is still here, and even if he's not always on the ball with what day it is – or what year, come to that – he always knows who I am, and as long as he does, I'm going to be in there twice a week chatting to him about whatever he wants me to. Loyalty. Without loyalty, you're nothing."

Brigit nodded and fixed her attention on the table, doing her best not to notice the tears in Deccie's eyes. "I get it, I do," she said softly. "So, is that what you told Callan at this meeting?"

"Yeah, he repeated the offer Dandridge had already told me about and I told him it was still a no. Then he offered me a bonus to sign a contract with anyone that wasn't Caint FM. I'd never do anything to hurt the station and I made that clear. It got quite heated. I told him Flipper was better than Skippy, too."

"What?"

"Skippy – the kangaroo."

"Yes, Deccie, I've heard of Skippy, but ... how was that relevant?"

Deccie shrugged. "He called Caint FM a two-bit operation and I wanted to get a dig back in response, but I don't know much about Australia. To be honest, it wasn't my best work. Bar anything else, it's obviously not true. Flipper is a dolphin – when it comes to rescue/crime-fighting animals, Skippy is clearly better. He can be on land, y'know – where stuff mostly happens. He's fast, he can box the head off somebody, and he's got that pouch for collecting evidence. Flipper has none of that. Plus, dolphins are creepy buggers – they're murderers, riddled with STDs, and one of them once made a very aggressive pass at Demi Moore in Las Vegas. Google it."

Brigit opened her mouth to speak, but she discovered she had too many questions for just one to come out.

"Who I should have gone for," continued Deccie, "is Lassie or, ideally, Mr Ed. I mean, Lassie is a bona fide tracker who can bite your leg, but Mr Ed could talk, and I don't care who you are – if a talking horse corners you and starts asking questions, you're going to crack and confess."

"OK," said Brigit, realising she was probably going to spend quite a lot of tonight thinking about Deccie's assertion, whether she wanted to or not. "Just to go back to what we were discussing before – how did Callan take you telling him where to go?"

"Badly. Told me I'd live to regret it."

"Right. Thing is, though," said Brigit, "this Callan fella, he's got a bit of a rep for doing whatever it takes to get what he wants. We were wondering if maybe ... If you won't take his deal, has he found another way to get rid of you?"

Deccie's head drew back on his neck, causing his chins to pile up. "D'you mean he could be the Whole Truth?"

"Maybe," said Brigit. "I mean, not him directly. He'd have hired help. It would mean he's been planning this for a few weeks."

Deccie made a face. "I dunno, though – he seemed really surprised when I told him where to stick his deal. Like he wasn't expecting it."

"OK," said Brigit with a nod. "Well, like I said – it's just one possibility we're looking into."

"What are the others?"

Brigit tried not to wince. "We're still developing theories on other possibilities."

"Ah, right," said Deccie, trying not to look disappointed. "Yeah. That's grand." He stood up. "I'm just going to nip to the bog."

Brigit slumped back onto the sofa. "We're still developing theories on other possibilities," she muttered to herself. *Christ, that sounded weak.*

The fact that Callan had seemed shocked when Deccie turned down his deal wasn't great, but it was possible the guy was pretending. On the upside, it sounded like Deccie had properly annoyed him.

She looked up at the feature wall of the apartment where the scrawled words "Deccie must die" had kicked all of this off. That had happened the day before Deccie had met Callan. Perhaps Jimmy did have a point – maybe she was trying to force a theory that didn't really work, just because she was desperate and looking for any ray of light in a crappy week.

"Jesus!" exclaimed Deccie from the bathroom.

Brigit sat up, debating whether to ignore him, following the logic that whatever had proved exclamation worthy in the bathroom was very much Deccie's own business. Before she could decide either way, the door slammed open and he stood there in the doorway, ashen-faced, holding up his phone.

"Is everything alright?"

"No. Nothing is alright. We've had another email. I'm screwed."

Brigit managed to get Deccie to sit back down then took the phone out of his unresisting hand. As expected, another email from the Whole Truth, although the content was another story.

Declan,

Just because you're an embecile, you shouldn't have made the mistake of thinking everyone else is. Did you really think that I'd not spot counterfeit money?

Enjoy the awards tomorrow night. Know that when you're standing on stage, I'll be releasing our little video for the world to see.

The Whole Truth

A PICTURE WAS ATTACHED, which showed what looked an awful lot like the money she'd delivered earlier in the day being set on fire.

BRIGIT RE-READ THE MESSAGE. "I don't understand. I delivered the money. Dandridge gave it ..."

Deccie and Brigit looked at each other. "Dandridge!"

Deccie stood up. "I'm going to feckin' kill him!"

35

FALLEN HEROES

Brigit rested against the cool granite wall and enjoyed a few moments drinking in the mid-morning sun. It felt inappropriate. Glorious sunshine in a graveyard felt like a clown showing up at a funeral – some sort of cosmic booking error. At least the mood in the car on the drive over here had been suitably funereal. Brigit had tried to start a conversation with Deccie but had given up after his third grunted response.

She looked again at the figure of Deccie Fadden, who was standing about sixty yards away from her. She knew that, ideally, she should be closer – Clint Rule Four: Remain physically close to the subject at all times – but with all due respect to Clint and his mirrored sunglasses, she doubted he'd ever dealt with a situation quite like this one. Besides, Deccie was standing in a wide open space and she had an unfettered view if anyone tried to approach him. He needed the time alone, and while there wasn't much she could do for him, she could at least manage the space. The chances of a sniper taking pot shots at him didn't seem all that likely.

She answered her phone on the second ring.

"Hi, hon."

"So," said Paul, "how did it go?"

"Well, Oliver Dandridge is no longer Deccie's agent. The little weasel tried to explain how he'd used counterfeit money to protect Deccie."

"What? How?"

"Don't ask me. I heard the explanation direct from the horse's arse and I don't think even he understood what he was saying. He had all night to come up with something that was as least comprehensible if not believable, and that was his best effort. I expected more from the utter toerag. I don't even know where he got the forgeries from."

"Phil did some digging on the subject. Apparently, it's remarkably easy to buy them over the internet. I had to talk him out of getting some."

"Dandridge said it cost him six grand. I swear to God, I think he was angling at trying to get the money back from us – i.e., you and me. Claimed it was our fault it got lost."

"But the plan was always to pay the ransom."

"I know. Dandridge is really quite something."

"So, are you over at the home visiting Deccie Fadden Senior?"

Brigit lowered her voice slightly, for reasons she didn't understand. "No. Deccie didn't want to. I think … I'm not sure why."

She had a good idea, though. Deccie's grandad might be confused quite a bit these days, but she guessed he would still have picked up on Deccie's mood and known something was wrong. From her days working in the hospice, Brigit knew all too well that dementia patients could still be alarmingly perceptive in certain situations. Some combination of not wanting to worry his grandad and not being able to face explaining it all to him had made Deccie break from his routine.

"Where are you now, then?" asked Paul.

"Would you believe Glasnevin Cemetery?"

"As in …" Brigit could hear the wince in Paul's voice. "Oh God."

"Yeah. He wanted to come to Bunny's grave."

She could hear Paul drawing a breath through clenched teeth.

"I know but … what was I supposed to do?"

"You did the right thing," said Paul quietly.

"Feels crappy, though. Not being able to help him, and now this."

"Has he changed his mind about the awards tonight?"

"No," said Brigit. "Says come hell or high water, he's going. Apparently, he's never won a prize in his life and, in his words, even if it all comes tumbling down minutes later, he's going to pick it up if he wins. He said something about how they can't take it back once they've given it to him. I mean, that's probably the case, I assume, unless ..."

Her words hung in the air as neither she nor Paul said anything for a few seconds.

Eventually, Paul broke the silence. "It is. Look, I'd tell you what's on the recording if I thought it'd help."

"No," said Brigit, "you're right. Sorry. Don't tell me. If I don't need to know, I don't need to know. That was stupid of me."

"No, it's just ... I mean, give it a few hours and it sounds like you're going to see it anyway."

Brigit looked over at Deccie then turned her eyes away again. "Don't say that. I mean, you're right, but ..." She kicked at the dried ground beneath her feet with the toe of her shoe. "Any word from Phil and Jimmy?"

"Yes. They've successfully acquired that Marcus Callan fella and they're tailing him. Do you really think that'll lead anywhere?"

"Probably not," admitted Brigit. "If he is behind this – and that's a big if – the chances of us getting blindly lucky on a tail are not great."

"There's always a chance, though," said Paul.

"Yeah, but only in the might-get-hit-by-a-bus-while-crossing-the-street sense."

"Hey, I thought I was supposed to be the pessimist in this relationship and you were supposed to be the chipper one brimming with optimism?"

"I forgot," said Brigit. "Give me a long hot bath, a good meal and three days in bed, and I'll take another run at it. Right now, I'm feeling hopeless, listless and pretty much useless."

"Well, you're not. And neither am I," said Paul. "I've got

something. I mean, it's not much. I don't know if you could call it a lead, but ..."

"I'll take anything."

"The email from the Wholewheat wanker from last night ..."

"Yeah?"

"He or she spelled imbecile wrong."

"OK," said Brigit, not really seeing how that was relevant.

"It's quite unusual, though. Both using the word imbecile in the first place and mistakenly spelling it with an E. And when I couldn't sleep last night, I remembered seeing it recently. I checked and it appears in a few tweets from the file of threats to Deccie. I've been re-checking all morning. Four Twitter accounts all referred to Deccie as an imbecile with an E."

"Four?"

"Yeah. Odds on, it's someone using multiple burner accounts. Pretty common for trolls. All the accounts post around the same time, too. Always within minutes of each other, always between six and seven pm, when the show is on-air."

"That's great," said Brigit enthusiastically. "That's a fantastic lead."

"Hang on, love. Don't get too excited. It might be a coincidence, and even if it isn't, which is a decent shot, we don't have any way of tracing Twitter accounts back to a source. I've gone through them. They don't have any identifying information, and the history on all of them is exclusively commenting on Deccie and Rhona's show. The guy likes Rhona and, unsurprisingly, is constantly giving out about Deccie. An endless stream of pure vitriolic and untraceable hate."

Brigit kicked at a stone in frustration, sending it skittering across the path in front of her. "Brilliant. Isn't technology great. What a time to be alive."

"Yeah," agreed Paul. "Appropriately enough, I keep thinking of what Bunny would do."

Brigit gave a sad little laugh. "Slap the internet around the earhole until it gave up the information."

"If only it was that simple."

Brigit looked across at Deccie again, who was standing with his head bowed, talking quietly to a gravestone. "If only."

~

DECCIE LOOKED DOWN at the fresh flowers. All red and white, of course. The colours of Bunny's beloved Cork but, probably more relevantly, also the colours of St Jude's. It was good to see that though a few years had passed, he had certainly not been forgotten. The grave was immaculate. A small unopened bottle of whiskey sat by the headstone. Now that was respect. Not someone leaving it – although that was something in itself. The fact that it remained untouched was the truly impressive bit. Even though he was dead, no little scrote within three postcodes had the balls to swipe Bunny McGarry's drink.

Deccie spoke quietly. "Howerya, boss. You're looking well. I mean – the whole grave thing. Suits ye." He paused and shoved his hands into his pockets. "Sorry, that was a stupid thing to say. I'm not very good at this sort of thing. I should have come before now, but ... Well, I should have. I used to bring Grandad to me granny's grave on her anniversary every year, but we stopped doing that."

"He's doing alright, but his brain isn't what it was. He's OK in himself, but he asks for Granny a lot. If we just tell him she's coming in tomorrow, he's happy enough. The last time I brought him to see her, though, he got very upset. It's better if he thinks, you know, she's doing her shopping and she'll be in to see him tomorrow and she's bringing fig rolls. He's always loved them. He's doing OK, though – all things considered. Not knowing who the current taoiseach is hasn't stopped him arguing that he's the worst one ever."

Deccie paused and looked around, making sure he was alone. Brigit was standing over by the far wall, chatting on the phone. Other than that, there was an elderly woman sitting on a bench at the far end of the cemetery, with one of those little dogs sitting at her feet.

"Back in the day, you and Grandad – you were the two people I always used to come to for advice. Well, Granny too, obviously, until she passed. I'll be honest with you – I could really use a chat now." He felt a tear roll down his left cheek and wiped it away quickly. He didn't want to be crying in front of Bunny.

"Things were going great. I'm on the radio now. Sort of fell into it, but I'm good at it. To be honest, I never really felt good at anything before. I'm up for this big Irish radio award tonight, and everybody says I'm gonna win it."

He bent down and picked up one of the small shiny coloured stones that formed the bed of the grave, upon which all the flowers sat. He turned it over in his fingers as he spoke.

"You know the way you never really believe it when things are going well? You know me, I always had big ideas but, almost always, they never came off. I guess at some point, you just get used to failure. What happened with my parents, what things were like when I was younger – I guess I just got used to not expecting things to go well. It's hard to be really disappointed if you never expect things to go your way in the first place. Well, it turns out, it's a lot harder to get used to success. You always think you'll be found out. And now ..."

Deccie paused and looked up as an aeroplane sailed across the blue sky, leaving a trail of vapour in its wake.

"Actually, that's the annoying thing. What's happened is really nothing to do with the job. I didn't do anything wrong. Honest. I know I used to always say that, but this time it's really true. There's this tape, though – doesn't matter what's on it, let's just say it's embarrassing. Really embarrassing. Some monumental bollix stuck cameras in my gaff – can you believe that? Thing is, if it comes out, I'm a laughing stock. I'll be honest with you, boss, after tasting what it's like to be taken seriously, I don't know if I'm ready to go back to that. Part of me wants to run. Get on an aeroplane and never come back, but you always said to me that it's better to face up to your problems."

Deccie scratched his forehead and looked over towards Brigit. "Paulie and Brigit are helping me. You always said to trust your friends and family, and that's what I'm doing. They're pretty much all I've got left these days. They're trying their best. Speaking of which, you should have seen Brigit a couple of days ago. She kicked the crap out of that Martin Regan prick – the MMA boxer fella. I mean, I could have handled him normally, but this sneaky sod waited until I'd finished my workout and I'm all knackered out and then he comes at me. That's poor form any which way you cut it. That's the guy's problem all over, though – he's got no appreciation of the fundamentals of the game." He tossed the shiny pebble in the air and caught it. "I'm not worried about him. This other thing, though – I need a lot of help with that or else by the end of tonight, I'm over."

He took a few steps around the side of the grave then placed his hand on the headstone. "I miss you. Everybody does, boss. To be honest, this town hasn't been the same without you. The only honest copper in Dublin."

Tears suddenly filled his eyes, and Deccie turned away so they remained unseen. He ran a sleeve across his face and sniffled. "Damn allergies are killing me. Still, though, don't feel like I've ever needed you as much as I need you right now, and that's saying something, isn't it? All we've been through."

He straightened himself up. "I'd better get gone. I hope you're doing alright wherever, you know, whatever comes next." Without turning around, he held the pebble between his thumb and forefinger. "If you don't mind, I'm going to keep hold of this. For luck."

He looked back up again at the white trails the aeroplanes were painting across the sky. "Yeah, boss – sure could use you now, alright."

36

DENTED HOPES

Brigit walked over to the corner of the meeting room and turned down the speaker that was playing the live feed from Deccie and Rhona's radio show. She hoped it wasn't as obvious to everyone listening as it was to Brigit, but it felt like poor Rhona was doing everything in her power to carry the load as Deccie sleepwalked through the broadcast. His co-host had even tried to tee him up for a couple of his trademark rants on his favourite subjects, but Deccie had simply watched the chances float by without taking a swing.

It was 6:45pm. As soon as the show was finished, the plan was to head straight from the studio to Clontarf Castle for the awards ceremony. Brigit could hear the weight of the ticking clock on Deccie. He was hours away from humiliation unless …

Brigit snatched her phone off the desk as soon as it rang. "Jimmy."

"OK," he said, "now, don't get your hopes up, but … this might be something."

"Callan?"

"Callan," he confirmed. "We've been on him all day, doing a two-car follow. Mostly meetings, lunch, some shopping—"

"Jimmy?"

"But he's just pulled his Porsche into a deserted car park out on an industrial estate in Tallaght. I can't think of any earthly reason why someone like Callan would be here. But he's clearly waiting for somebody."

Brigit felt the pounding of her heart in her chest. "Oh my God, please let this be something. Have you got eyes on him?"

"Yes," said Jimmy, a hint of admonishment in his voice. "Phil's in the van and he's got the camera recording through that one-way thing he installed on the back. He parked up and walked away and I'm watching the live feed from my car."

"Right. Sorry. Not your first rodeo. I didn't mean—"

"I know. A car pulled up beside him ... A massive muscly fella just got out, mohawk, tattoos ... They're talking ..." The level of excitement in Jimmy's Stewart voice rose a little. "Callan's just handed the guy an envelope ... We've got the other car's reg and ..."

Brigit let the silence hang for several seconds before she couldn't take it any more. "What?"

"Oh," said Jimmy, sounding considerably less enthusiastic.

"For Christ's sake – what?" snapped Brigit.

"I'm afraid this isn't what we hoped."

"What do you mean? What's happening?"

"Call me an old prude, but I'd rather not describe what's going on. Let's just say it's no good to us but might be of use in his divorce proceedings."

"I don't ..." Brigit trailed off as her brain caught up with her mouth. "Ah."

"Yeah."

"Shit."

"Yeah. Sorry," said Jimmy. "And ... Jesus, I don't know how much Callan is paying for this, but it's going to cost a lot more to get that dent out of the bonnet of his Porsche."

Brigit slumped back into her chair. "So, we've got nothing?"

"I'm afraid not," confirmed Jimmy. "Not unless Mr Callan has entered into a very risky relationship with a man he is paying to blackmail Deccie."

She let out a deep sigh. "Alright. Well," she said, glancing at the clock on the wall, "I'd better go. I've got to get changed as I've got a bloody awards ceremony to get to."

37

PENGUINS TO THE SLAUGHTER

Deccie stood in the reception of Caint FM, looking for all the world like a man who was on his way to his own funeral.

"You really do look fantastic in that suit, Deccie," said Brigit.

"Thanks. They might bury me in it. Any news?"

Brigit shook her head. "Sorry."

Deccie shrugged. "Don't worry about it. You look very nice, by the way."

"Thanks." Brigit was wearing a summery peach dress she'd originally bought to wear to her dad's wedding. The nuptials had been put back so many times in the last two years, who knew if it'd suit the time of year when they finally nailed down a date. Thanks to the lockdown-generated backlog, wedding venues in Ireland were now harder to find than someone you wanted to marry.

"We should—"

Brigit was cut off by Rhona's grandiose entrance into the office area as the swinging double-doors were flung open and in she strode. She was wearing a bright red dress with a split seam and plenty of cleavage on display.

"Who's ready to party?"

"Wow," said Brigit, "you look amazing."

"I'd better," she said around a wide grin. "I've been on a bastard diet for six months and this rag cost me a decent holiday. You two look fabulous." She gave Deccie an assessing look. "Sorry, Mr Idris Elba, but I think we've found our new James Bond." She placed her hands on Deccie's shoulders. "Are you alright? The nerves aren't getting to you, are they?"

"No," said Deccie, "I'm grand."

"And so you should be. Whatever happens, you're a winner to me, you lunatic. I'm tempted to go into the story about when you first rang in, but if I do, I'm going to screw up this make-up and we're already running late." She turned around. "Speaking of which, where the hell is my date?"

"Oh," said Brigit, "I've actually not seen David."

"He can't make it," said Rhona quickly, "so I'm bringing producer Mike. He deserves to be there tonight, and besides, he's better craic."

"Right." Brigit turned to Deccie. "Wheels is downstairs so we should probably …"

"Yeah," said Deccie flatly.

"I'll see you there," said Rhona. "And you, handsome man – you'd better save me at least a couple of dances. Never forget," she said with a giggle, "I made you, and I can break you."

BRIGIT AND DECCIE got into the lift in silence. Brigit didn't speak until it started moving.

"Alright, I'm just going to say this – if you want, we can say you're ill. Nobody would be any the wiser."

He looked across at her and shook his head. "Nah. Whatever happens after tonight, if I'm going to get an award, then I'm going to bloody well get it. It might sound daft but I want the win. Everything else is out of my hands now, but I still want a silly trophy I can look at and remember how things were."

Brigit opened her mouth to say something, but nothing came. They reached the ground floor and the doors pinged open.

The crowd outside was pretty much the usual, and the moustachioed security guards stood to attention on either side of the main doors. Just up from the entrance sat Wheels's gold BMW, its engine running. A few autograph hunters were hanging around, and Deccie stopped to sign for them and pose for the requisite selfies. He looked like a man savouring his last moments.

In the background was the ever-present Fudgy, holding up his sign that simply read "NO". He was wearing his anorak, as usual, although today his sartorial choice was potentially the right one. The sun was throwing reflections off the windows of the opposite building, but despite the sunshine, there was a hint of rain in the air.

Brigit felt a drop of water hit her bare arm. "Deccie, we should probably get moving."

He posed for the last selfie then headed towards the car. As Brigit turned to follow him, she heard a wolf-whistle from behind her. Instinctively, she spun around and saw the older security guard standing there, belly pointed resolutely ahead, while his younger colleague failed to suppress a giggle. Normally, Brigit would have ripped the idiot a new one, but looking at him right then, she just couldn't be bothered. Instead, she muttered "wanker" under her breath and turned to follow Deccie.

She looked up at the sky and checked the clouds. With everything else that was going on, she'd forgotten to bring an umbrella. Hopefully, Wheels would have one in the car. Otherwise, if the heavens opened, she was going to end up looking like a soppy dish rag for the evening.

Her eyes were drawn to a flash of reflected light from up on the roof opposite. Not a window. Above a window.

She caught the briefest of outlines then an instinct she didn't even know she had kicked in. Deccie was six feet ahead of her, in contravention of several of Clint's rules.

Rule One: Always make sure that you are between the subject and the danger.

Rule Four: Remain physically close to the subject at all times.

There was still Rule Six, though: When in doubt, be proactive, not reactive.

"GUN!" She raced forwards, tackling Deccie as he was about to open the car door, slamming him into it instead. Her head hit the side of the car, sending a sickening jolt through her brain as her world became a disorientating blur.

The first shot rang out as they fell.

Brigit's head smashed into the pavement. Her mind couldn't process if there was a second shot, or if it was just the echo of the first.

She tasted a wash of blood in her mouth. She must have bitten her tongue.

Somewhere a woman screamed. "He's been shot!"

And then the world faded to black.

38

IT'S A LOT EASIER TO GET DOWN
THAN TO GET UP

First there was noise.

Low-level hushed conversations set against a backing track of hustle and bustle. It rang bells, for sure. She'd been surrounded by it more than enough to recognise the particular melody of a working hospital.

Then there was a light. A bright light. Followed by a voice she vaguely recognised.

"Brigit. Can you hear me, Brigit?"

Her eyelids flickered and the world came into focus around the smiling face of an Asian man in his mid-thirties. She smacked her lips and when her voice emerged it was hoarse.

"Dr Sinha?"

"Ah, former nurse Brigit Conroy, I am glad to see there is nothing wrong with your memory. I haven't seen you in here for a while, with an injury sustained in the line of duty. I was worried you'd chosen a quieter life."

She cleared her throat then spoke in a more definite voice. "Nah. It's just there was a pandemic on – you might have heard?"

His smile widened as he shook his head. "No, nobody mentioned it around here."

Brigit reached up and touched her head, feeling the bandages wrapped around it.

"Yes, I'm afraid you took a nasty bang or two to the head. You needed a few stitches to a wound on your scalp. We'll be keeping you in for a while, for observation, but it doesn't look too concerning. How do you feel?"

"Like I've been run over by a bus. Foggy but ..."

"That will be the meds."

Brigit heard movement nearby.

"Ah, you have some visitors." Dr Sinha nodded to the other side of the bed. "Gentlemen."

She looked over to see Phil Nellis and Jimmy Stewart standing a couple of feet apart. Her two friends then lifted Paul up out of his wheelchair, so that he was standing between them. His eyes were damp, but he wore a broad smile. "There were easier ways to get me to leave the apartment, you know."

"I ..." Brigit tried to sit up, then her brain kicked into gear. "Christ, Deccie!"

"He's fine," said Paul quickly. "Relax."

"Mr Fadden just has a sprained wrist," confirmed Dr Sinha.

"But ..." Something about Brigit's mouth felt weird but she did her best to ignore it as she tried to piece things together. "I heard somebody shout something about him being shot."

"That would have been in relation to a Mr Donal Farrell, commonly known as Fudgy, for reasons I cannot begin to understand. He suffered a flesh wound to his leg, but it is a minor wound and he will make a full recovery. In fact, he has already checked himself out and given some interviews to media outlets about his experience. I will let your friends update you on everything else as it is a Friday night and the sun has been out, which I know you know means we will have plenty of customers in A and E this evening." Dr Sinha picked up a handset attached to the bed. "I will raise your bed so Mr Mulchrone can sit back down."

As he adjusted the position of the bed, Jimmy and Phil lowered Paul back into his wheelchair.

"How did you get here?" asked Brigit.

"Phil picked me up," said Paul.

"Yeah," agreed Phil, standing back upright. "The absolute lunatic had crawled down three flights of stairs by the time I got there. Wouldn't wait."

Brigit caught Jimmy trying in vain to signal Phil to shut up.

"It was a lot easier to get down than it was to get up," said Paul.

Dr Sinha touched Brigit's arm gently. "Ignoring the circumstances, it's good to see you again, Ms Conroy."

"I think we can go with Brigit, please, Doctor," she said with a weak smile. "And thank you for everything."

"You are most welcome ... Brigit." He looked across at Paul. "Don't keep her talking long. She needs rest."

Paul nodded.

Jimmy slapped Phil on the arm. "C'mon, Phillip – you can buy me a cup of tea."

Phil looked at him. "But you just had some tea."

"Right. What I'm trying to find a subtle way of saying is, let's leave these two alone."

"So why didn't you just say that, then?"

"Because ... Ah, never mind."

After they'd left, Paul reached forward and clasped Brigit's hand. "Don't you ever do that to me again."

"Which bit?"

Paul furrowed his brow in frustration.

"Yeah, alright," she said. "I know which bit. Don't get shot at. Don't let go of ladders." She squeezed his hand. "You're so demanding these days." As foggy as her mind was, she noted a sibilant quality to her voice.

"Yeah. Get used to it. You should probably also get used to being known as the woman who saved Deccie Fadden's life."

"Oh God. I think I preferred paramour, hussy or street fighter."

"Tough. Seriously, though – well done, love. Just incredible."

"It was luck. Pure, stupid luck."

"Crap. You did it. That's what matters," said Paul.

"Did they ..." Something in Brigit's brain finally put two and two together. "Ah, hang on, have I chipped one of my teeth?" A quick exploration of the front of her mouth with her tongue confirmed her fears. "Fuck!"

"Don't worry. We'll get it fixed."

"We can't afford to."

"Course we can."

"No," said Brigit, "we can't." She looked at Paul. "I ... I should have told you a long time before now. We're broke. Flat broke. In fact, deep-in-a-hole broke and it's my fault. I'm sorry."

"But ... Why didn't you tell me?"

"Because ... I dunno. I thought you'd be mad." Brigit turned her head away. "I lost the run of myself and put us in a hole."

"There was also a pandemic," said Paul softly.

"Yeah, but – I still was the one going all gung-ho, and you were saying be cautious and I didn't listen. I keep thinking back to what you said and how I basically ignored you, and honestly, it's embarrassing to realise how much of a bull-headed know-it-all I was being. I've screwed up pretty big."

"Look at me."

She turned back to see her fiancé smiling at her, the gentlest of looks in his eyes. "You think I give a crap about that? It's only money!"

"But ..."

"But nothing, sweetheart. I spent most of my life up until now being broke. I'm a master at it. I don't mind that bit. It's the being-alone part that bothers me. You are alive and semi-coherent. That's all I'll ever need. You'll have to try an awful lot harder than that to get rid of me."

His smile was doing a better job of numbing the pain than whatever they'd given her.

"Now, normally I'd kiss you at this point," he continued, "but I can't stand up and you're not allowed out of bed."

Brigit laughed. "We're quite the pair."

"You almost killed me, but you saved Deccie. You've got some messed-up priorities, missus."

"Speaking of which, what exactly happened? It's all a bit of a blur."

"Well," said Paul, "you tackled Deccie to the ground, much to the annoyance of whoever was shooting from the top of the building over the road. They fired two shots in total. They reckon that poor Birdy guy got—"

"Fudgy," corrected Brigit.

"Right. Sorry. Fudgy. He got hit by a bullet as it ricocheted off the pavement."

"Have they caught the shooter?"

"No," said Paul, "not yet. They've recovered the gun from the rooftop, but nothing else. They're checking CCTV and all that, though. The Gardaí are all over it, so I can't see whoever it was getting away with it for long. It's our old mate, DSI Burns, in charge of the investigation, by the way. Turns out assassination attempts on major celebrities are a big no-no that warrant the special attention of her team. Deccie is talking to them right now, and Phil, Jimmy and me are due back in next. There have been a lot of questions."

"So does that mean Deccie's telling them everything?"

"Yeah. I mean, blackmail is one thing, but who the hell saw this coming? Bit of an escalation. We're dealing with one serious nutter here."

"They really didn't like that funny money from Dandridge, did they? Speaking of which ..."

Paul shook his head. "No recording released yet. As far as I know."

"I realise I've taken a serious wallop to the head, but does any of this make sense to you?"

Paul threw his hands up in the air. "Not a thing. I think let's just let the Gardaí get on with figuring out this shitshow. We were hired to protect Deccie, and you absolutely nailed that." He rubbed her hand again. "You need to get some rest, my darling girl, and I need to go and help the police with their enquiries." He looked over at the door and then back at her with an awkward grin. "Or at least I will when Phil remembers that he needs to come and pick me up."

"In the meantime—"

Without warning, the door flew open and in burst Shauna, still sporting the pink-mohawk, which her baseball cap couldn't entirely hide. "Where is he?"

"Hi, Shauna," said Brigit.

"Where's Deccie?" she asked, her eyes wild. "Is he OK? They won't tell me anything."

Paul gave Brigit a confused look. "Who is ..."

"Shauna is Deccie's PA."

"Ah, right," he said, turning back to their visitor. "Relax. He's OK. Everyone's OK, well, more or less."

Shauna physically sagged with relief. "Can I see him?"

"Well," said Paul, "I'm not sure if he's still here or if the Gardaí have whisked him away, but if you want to wheel me out, we can go check."

Shauna rushed over and grabbed the handles of Paul's wheelchair.

"Great, so— whoa!"

Shauna spun him around and rushed him out the door as if the building were on fire.

"I'll ring you late—"

The rest of Paul's sentence was lost as the door slammed shut behind them.

"Bye, then," said Brigit mildly. She tentatively touched her bandaged head again. "I'm fine, by the way. Thanks for asking."

39

THE GOLDEN BOY

DSI Susan Burns sat behind her office desk and took a sip of one of Garda HQ's rightly derided cups of coffee. It was a running joke that whoever elected to buy this awful sludge in bulk had done more damage to Garda morale than the combined efforts of every defence lawyer in Ireland. Still, she needed the caffeine.

She was tired. Beyond tired. It had been a long week, and her weekend off had started at 6:30pm but finished at 9pm with a call from the Commissioner herself. Assassination attempts in the city centre were the kind of thing that got the higher-ups all worked up. It was now 1am and she hadn't even had a chance to change. She would never wear something this strappy in the office and she was feeling self-conscious about it.

The only upside was that at least this situation had saved her from a dreadful date. The man's profile picture had been an open and shut case of tampering with evidence, and his halitosis had been a crime in and of itself. Then, of course, he'd gone for the tedious handcuffs joke within ten minutes of them meeting. Why the hell were men so intimidated by strong women?

She had been picked up from the restaurant by a squad car. The food there had looked good too. The packet of Tayto crisps she'd acquired from the vending machine downstairs had been a crappy second prize. After a quick visit to the crime scene, she'd set up camp in the incident room, from where she was coordinating the search, compiling CCTV footage, interviewing multiple witnesses and ruining a whole lot of other people's weekends as she resourced getting all the above done as quickly as possible.

There had also been the mandatory statement to the press, carefully worded to sound in control while not saying anything more than was absolutely necessary. Given that the person involved was a celebrity, the interest levels were stratospheric and rising. As Superintendent Mark Gettigan, head of the press relations office, had put it – never mind Ireland, this thing would make the global news. The world was full of people who gave opinions for a living, and they were all going to have opinions on one of their counterparts getting shot at.

The Commissioner had made it clear that the case needed to be handled sensitively, by the book and, most importantly, quickly. She'd refrained from proposing a timeline but she didn't have to. Burns knew they'd like the news cycle to be about the Gardaí making arrests within twenty-four hours. With that in mind, she wasn't exactly doing it "not by the book", but some of the decisions she'd made, given the highly unusual circumstances, might raise some eyebrows, or indeed the hackles of a tribunal. The one thing everyone in a position like hers in Ireland knew was that the politicians of this country loved nothing more than a tribunal, providing they weren't the ones being investigated, of course.

The bare facts of the case had done nothing for her blood pressure. Declan "Deccie" Fadden had received a death threat, unreported, five days ago, through the medium of it being scrawled on the wall of his apartment in red paint. A crime scene that had been painted over almost immediately. He'd then received blackmail demands relating to footage obtained from hidden cameras in the self-same apartment, which had led to a ransom of fifty thousand euros being paid – or rather not being paid, as one Oliver Dandridge,

Fadden's agent, had acquired a large quantity of forged one-hundred euro notes.

She had met Dandridge briefly, when he had demanded to speak to 'the man in charge'. Two minutes in the room with him had been enough for her to email DS Moira Clarke with the instruction to pass the forged-notes matter on to the relevant team on Monday morning. He had actually called her "sweetheart" while requesting total access to the investigation and twenty-four-hour protection for his client, who, it quickly emerged, was no longer his client as far as everyone else was concerned. She'd seen to it that Fadden was getting the protection, but not because some blowhard in a tuxedo had demanded it.

One upside in that particular tsunami of shit was that Burns had a pre-existing relationship with MCM Investigations. They weren't a conventional operation exactly, but they more or less did good work. They also had a knack for getting themselves into trouble, almost matched by their ability to find a way out of it. She had therefore agreed that, at least initially, Paul Mulchrone would show the recording that was the leverage for the blackmail to her and her alone.

She'd watched it and agreed with his assessment – it contained nothing criminal, no evidence that she could determine would assist the investigation and, not that it was her concern, but yes, it would kill Deccie Fadden's media career stone dead. The blackmail angle would be kept from the public; instead, the focus would be on the hunt for the would-be assassin.

Another positive aspect of the situation was the presence of Jimmy Stewart on the MCM Investigations team. Formerly DI Jimmy Stewart, they'd never worked together, as his retirement from the National Bureau of Criminal Investigation predated her arrival, but she knew him by more than reputation. Her contact with him since had been enough to convince her that the mandatory retirement age on the force had robbed her of a valuable resource.

Stewart had given her a briefing on everything MCM Investigations had and a precise account of how the previous week had unfolded. That was what had brought them to where they were now and the chance, just a chance, of a quick result. The National Bureau of Criminal Investigation had access to resources that MCM Investigations did not, and one important resource in particular.

There was a knock on her door, and Detective Donnacha Wilson popped his head around it. "Boss, Mick Cusack is here with the WMD."

"Right – never call him that to his face."

"It's a cool nickname, boss."

"To you, maybe. He's a little ..."

"Odd?"

"Different. I had to pull in a massive favour here. Let's not piss him off."

Wilson held up a hand. "Not a problem. I've already offered them coffee."

"Jesus, Wilson – that virtually constitutes an act of war."

She got to her feet and drew a deep breath in preparation. Inder O'Riordan, aka the WMD – Weapon of Mass Detection – was an almost mythical figure in Irish law enforcement. He was Irish-Pakistani and had a brilliant mind in the area of computer crime, one that could earn him at least ten times his salary if he were to go private, and God knows how much more if he were to go rogue. Instead, to everyone's amazement, he remained a civilian employee of An Garda Síochána.

They actually lent him out to other forces occasionally, such was his burgeoning reputation. He'd received immense offers from all corners but turned them all down flat. The reason for that, other than O'Riordan's almost insane disinterest in money, was Mick Cusack, O'Riordan's boss. It was he who had brought O'Riordan in on a six-month placement and had then been smart enough to realise what an asset the force now had. They managed to keep him by making sure he dealt with Mick and Mick alone, and he wasn't asked to fill out unnecessary reports, carry out assessments and get dragged into all the crap that wasn't the thing he was good at and enjoyed.

She'd only managed to get him in here on a Friday night because she'd pulled in a massive favour with Cusack. Last year, a certain assistant-commissioner had got an idiotic bee in his bonnet about the computer-crimes division's lack of oversight and had decided that steps would be taken, starting with moving their office and O'Riordan being asked to attend regular meetings with higher-ups to deliver reports on his work. Burns, when briefed by Cusack, had gone to bat for the status quo, and had successfully burned several bridges in the process. In another life, Burns might have been more interested in playing politics, but in the last few years she'd decided she was far more interested in being good at the job she had, rather than worrying about the next one.

She walked outside her office and met Cusack and O'Riordan in the incident room. She was taken aback by O'Riordan's appearance, but she had the sense not to say anything.

"Mick, Inder – thank you so much for doing this."

O'Riordan nodded and smiled. They'd met at least a dozen times and she'd yet to break the small-talk barrier.

Cusack nodded. "Don't thank me, but if you could explain this to my wife ..."

"We get a result here, I'll happily come round personally and do so."

"You look nice."

"Thanks," said Burns, before adding self-consciously, "I was on a date."

"Oh dear, sorry."

"Don't be. If this hadn't happened, I might have been forced to shoot my way out of there. Shall we?"

She and Wilson led the way into a meeting room, where Jimmy Stewart, Paul Mulchrone, Phil Nellis and Deccie Fadden himself were seated. Jimmy was there because he was an invaluable source of information, Mulchrone because he'd found the lead they were pursuing, Deccie Fadden because they needed him if they were to have any chance of this working, and Phil Nellis because ... There was actually no reason at all for him to be there, but he'd just come along and nobody had thrown him out.

"OK," began Burns. "Gentlemen, this is Mick Cusack and Inder O'Riordan from the computer-crimes division."

"Mick," said Jimmy with a nod.

"Jimmy. Good to see you."

"Of course," said Burns. "You two would know each other."

"Oh, yeah," said Cusack, "I'm pretty sure I was the first person to explain email to him."

"And one of these days," replied Stewart, "I'll get it."

"Do you know Inder as well?" asked Burns.

"Only by reputation. I know they refer to you as the golden boy, Mr O'Riordan, but I'd no idea the name was meant quite this literally."

Burns winced.

Cusack answered quickly. "Inder was off at a" – he looked at Inder – "what do you call it?"

"Immersive roleplaying experience," Inder responded matter-of-factly, as if that explained why he was wearing a flowing white robe under his coat and was covered head to toe in gold body paint.

"It was supposed to last all weekend," said Cusack. "I promised him I'd have him back" – he glanced at his watch – "two hours ago. Sorry again, Inder."

Burns echoed the apology, both of which were waved away by Inder.

"What the bleedin' hell is he supposed to be?" asked Deccie Fadden.

Before anyone else could respond, Phil Nellis piped up at the far end of the table. "Isn't it obvious, ye ignoramus? He's Hermes, herald of the gods." He then addressed Inder directly. "Nice costume. Are you doing *Fall of Olympia*?"

Inder's face lit up, as much as it was possible for an already-golden face to do so. "It's actually a crossover with *Halls of Valhalla* that a friend of mine has developed."

"Nice," said Phil with an appreciative nod of the head. "Sounds epic."

"It was for the two hours I was there."

"Hang on," said Deccie, and pointed down the table at Phil, "he doesn't get to call me an ignoramus."

Paul gave an exaggerated sigh. "Not. Now. Lads." He turned his attention to Burns, clearly keen to move things along. "So, Superintendent, what's the plan here?"

"Inder and Mick have been looking at what you gave us." She glanced at Mick, then said, "Inder?"

O'Riordan nodded. "Whoever the Whole Truth is, they knew enough to use a dark-web server to ensure the emails were untraceable. The picture and video they sent have similarly been stripped of all IP identifiers. There are, however, the four Twitter accounts you've identified as being possible related accounts, given the similar misspelling of imbecile with an E that appeared in one of the emails."

"Can we trace those accounts?" asked Burns.

"Technically," said Cusack, "yes. But it takes a lot of court orders for any social media company to share data with us, and even then, that's no guarantee of a result. Inder has an idea on that front. You remember his demonstration on security last year?"

She nodded. Everyone in Garda senior management remembered it. "The click thing?"

"The click thing," confirmed Cusack.

The point of the demonstration had been to show that the biggest weakness in any system came from people clicking on outside links or opening video or image attachments. Inder had embarrassed the Commissioner by showing how he'd gained total control of her desktop PC using that precise method. Burns knew for a fact that Mick hadn't known about that part of the demonstration ahead of time. It was like when a kid mentions that an adult's flies are open.

"My suggestion," said Inder, pointing at Deccie, "is that we follow these Twitter accounts back from your account, Mr Fadden, and then you send them a video via direct message. I have an IP logger worm of my own design, which, as far as I'm aware, is currently unknown to all virus software in the world. You record the message, I wrap it in that and we send it. If this the Whole Truth person opens it and, ideally, watches it for longer than forty seconds, it should give Roger …" He paused. "That's the worm – Roger Rabbit. It should give it enough time to give us a location."

"Right," said Burns, looking at Deccie for his thoughts. "It's worth a shot, don't you think?"

"Alright," said Deccie with a shrug. "I'm game."

"Excellent—" said Burns.

"As I said, though," interrupted Inder, "for the greatest chance of success, we would need the recipient to watch the clip for at least forty seconds and, if possible, re-watch it. Social engineering research has shown that the best guarantee of that is to rouse the recipient into as high a state of irritation as possible. Do you think it would be possible for you to record something that would wind this person up?"

Despite himself, Paul Mulchrone burst out laughing.

Inder turned to Mick. "Sorry, did I say something wrong?"

"No, no," said Paul, holding up a hand. "Sorry, sorry, sorry. Let's just say – you've come to the right place."

"Testify," added Phil Nellis, with feeling.

40

EQUIDISTANT TRIANGLES, FUCKNUGGETS!

Brigit was finding it weird being in a hospital as a patient. She kept feeling the urge to get up and do something. Doing nothing was not in her nature, even when she'd been instructed to do precisely that. She had surprised herself by conking out and sleeping through the night, too. Her body must have recognised the opportunity to catch up on all the sleep it had been missing out on and grabbed it with both hands.

Still, she was fully awake now and going a little stir crazy, not least because she didn't have her phone. The nurses had checked and she hadn't been admitted with it. Great, she'd somehow come out of the mêlée of saving Deccie from an assassin's bullet minus an iPhone. Depressingly, the problem with getting another one is that she doubted she'd pass the requisite credit check right now.

The door to her room opened and Paul entered, pushed in his wheelchair by Phil Nellis.

"Finally!" said Brigit.

"What?" said Paul. "We were told to let you sleep."

"Not by me. What's going on? Tell me everything. Absolutely everything."

Paul smiled as Phil manoeuvred him into position beside the bed, then locked the brakes, presumably to prevent him from rolling off down any nearby hillsides. "We'll get to the update in a minute. First things first ..." He looked pointedly at his companion, who was wearing the habitual blank expression he so excelled at.

Despite being aware of the futility of the gesture, Paul still felt obliged to leave Phil a long gap he didn't fill. It was like playing chicken with a mountain.

"The cake, Phil. The cake!"

"Oh, yeah – right. You should have said." He opened the special confectionary-carrying satchel he had designed himself (wider, longer strap, thick cardboard-enforced sides to prevent squishage) and pulled out a box, which he placed on the table in front of Bridget. "Da Xin done it specially."

"Thanks," said Brigit quickly, before looking back at Paul. "So, update?"

"Da Xin done it specially," repeated Paul with a knowing grin and a waggle of his eyebrows.

"OK, but ..." Brigit realised what he was angling for and opened the box. After a few seconds she described what she saw. "So, that would be me tackling Deccie to the ground as he's being shot at. It's wonderful, obviously, but I guess my first question would be: Why is the shooter here represented by Barney the Purple Dinosaur?"

"Well," said Phil, "Da Xin didn't know who the assassin was at the time, and she didn't want to make it scary, so she went with something fun."

"Right. And she got Fudgy in, I see."

"Oh, yeah – she was dead proud of that bit. She's made him out of actual fudge and the blood is strawberry jam."

Da Xin had even included Fudgy's large "NO" sign – the woman certainly had an eye for detail.

"Wow. It's very ... It's very ... Words fail me." She smiled at Phil as she closed the box. "Tell her I said thanks, though. I'm sure eating it will really help me through my PTSD." She immediately slapped the table next to the box. How could she be so slow? "Wait a sec, wait a sec – 'at the time'." She pointed excitedly at Phil. "He just said 'at the time'. She didn't know who the shooter was, so we do now?"

Paul gave her a little round of applause. "Look at my girl go. Always detecting."

"Don't patronise me. Tell me, or you two will feature on the cake they present at my murder trial."

"First," said Paul, fishing his phone out of his pocket, "I need you to watch a video."

"What?"

"Look, you got to work so much of this case without me while I was stuck in our apartment. Let me tell the story my way."

Brigit rolled her eyes. "Alright, fine. By the way, I don't know where my phone is."

"It got a bit cracked when you tackled Deccie but the Gardaí gave it to me when they decided it wasn't evidence."

"Brilliant." She looked at him expectantly.

"And I may have forgotten to bring it with me. I'll give it to Phil when he comes to pick you up later. Promise. In the meantime ..." He passed her his phone.

Deccie was frozen on the screen, glaring at the camera.

"Yay, more Deccie."

"Just play it."

She did. Deccie started talking, jabbing his finger as he delivered a diatribe with all the testosterone-drenched energy of a wrestler before a big match. Phil, of all people, stood silently behind him, arms folded, scowling.

"You think you can mess with me?" Deccie ranted. "You've no bleeding idea who you're dealing with. You're in a house of pain, in a world of hurt, and I'm going to take you to slap-down town. When you come for the king, you'd best not miss. Take a good look ye basic-arsed sack of numb nuts. I'm still here. Standing tall and representing. Stick this in your pipe and smoke it – me and my crew " – he pointed at Phil – "are going to find you, and when we do, the third generation of the marsupial mafia is going to bring you to the ninth dimension of Bibi Baskin and show you what it means to be an intransigent life form of incandescent light and transcendental speed. Equidistant triangles, fucknuggets! Your problem is, you've got no appreciation of the fundamentals of the game. Deccie out!"

When the clip had finished, Brigit watched it again, then looked at her two visitors. "So many questions. Has Deccie had some kind of breakdown?"

"No," said Paul cheerfully. "Although he has started taking advice from Phil."

"Those two things are pretty much interchangeable." She tilted her head up at Phil. "Hang on. Are you two finally talking again?"

"No," he replied, genuinely outraged by the suggestion.

She held up the phone. "But you're in the batshit crazy video?"

"Yeah. He needed a crew and Paulie can't stand up, so I agreed to stand behind him and be all menacing and that. He's me mate."

"One you've not spoken to in two years."

Phil looked at Brigit as if she was the one being odd. "He's still me mate."

Men.

Brigit turned back to Paul. "So what the hell is the marsupial mafia and all that other crap?"

"It's very confusing, isn't it?"

"Yes!"

He smiled at her again.

"You'd better start explaining stuff instead of being so infuriatingly enigmatic, or some of the things we've discussed happening when that cast comes off your leg will be off the table. Literally, in the case of one of them."

"Like what?" asked Phil.

"Never you mind, Phil Nellis."

Paul, clearly sensing that Brigit's patience for fun and games had run out, held up a hand and started talking. "You remember the Twitter accounts I found that all called Deccie an imbecile and misspelled it with an E at the start, just like in the note from the Whole Truth?"

"Yes."

"Well, the Gardaí found that very interesting. They've got this tech guru dude—"

"Inder," Phil interjected. "Me and him are Facebook friends now."

"Cool," said Brigit. "Hold on – you told me you didn't use Facebook?"

"I keep it to a select group," said Phil.

"Brig..." warned Paul.

"Right, yes – keep going." She pointed an accusatory finger at Phil. "Although we're coming back to the Facebook thing."

"Anyway," continued Paul, "they suggested the easiest way to track those accounts – rather than trying to get court orders, et cetera – was to DM them a video message. The person would then open the link and all this wormy virus stuff that Inder designed would go to work, identifying who they were. Ideally, they needed the person to watch the clip several times. They just wanted Deccie to say something to wind them up to start with, but Phil's idea was to couple that with loads of confusing stuff they'd have to listen back to in order to check. Like you just did."

"And did it work?"

"Like a dream. One recipient opened it a minute after we sent it at 2am then watched it fifteen times in a row. By which point, the Gardaí knew exactly who they were."

Brigit nearly jumped up and down in the bed. "So, we've got them?"

"The Gardaí raided their house an hour ago and the loon confessed before they had the sense to shut up and ask for a lawyer."

"Brilliant." Brigit drummed on the table excitedly. "Who was it?"

"Oh, you know them."

"What?"

"You've met them a few times, in fact."

"You're pulling my leg?"

"Phil," said Paul. "Drumroll, please?"

"I don't play drums."

"Just make the noise."

"PAUL!" Brigit's shout surprised even herself.

"Alright, alright. It was David Phillips. The Whole Truth is David Phillips."

Even allowing for her head injury, it took her a few seconds to compute. "Wait, what? Rhona's husband?"

"That's him."

"The traffic guy?"

Paul furrowed his brow. "Who?"

"All he talked about was the fecking traffic. He was the dullest bastard I've ever met. Him? He tried to assassinate Deccie?"

"Apparently."

"Jesus," said Brigit. "Now I think of it, he wasn't going to the awards with Rhona. She said he was busy. And he's confessed?"

Paul nodded. "As Wilson drove him in to Garda HQ he was ranting and raving in the back seat. Talking about how much he hated Deccie. How he wanted him dead. How he'd ruined his life." He lowered his voice. "I'm not officially supposed to know this, but seemingly, Rhona would only have sex with him if he wore a mask and they listened to a recording of her and Deccie talking on the radio throughout."

"Seriously?" asked Brigit, her voice going so high it hurt her throat. "Her too? Has every woman in Ireland lost their damn mind? All going gaga over Deccie? I mean, he's a tubby little fella from Dublin who's in love with the sound of his own voice. They're ten-a-penny."

"No offence taken," said Paul, all mock offended. "Am I right, Phil?"

"Speak for yourself," Phil responded, entirely deadpan. "I'm tall and skinny."

"But seriously," said Brigit, shaking her head so vigorously that she felt a little woozy, "what am I not seeing here?" As soon as she'd said that, she felt bad. "I mean ... Deccie's not the worst, but I'm just ... My mind is blown."

"I can see that," said Paul. "By the way, the Gardaí asked if they can come round to the flat for a proper formal interview once you get out."

"Sure. I'm just waiting to be cleared by a doctor and then I'll be free to go. It shouldn't be more than a couple of hours."

"Great," said Paul. "In the meantime, you should try to get some rest. Phil and I have to head back to Garda HQ. Deccie is still in protective custody, and we said we'd keep him company."

"But one of you isn't even talking to him," said Brigit, half-mockingly.

"And?" asked Phil. "Deccie doesn't need other people to talk. He does enough of that for everybody."

41

BUS LANE DIPLOMACY

This close, thought DSI Susan Burns. *I was this close.* She rested against her car, felt the sun on her face and the cooling summer breeze ruffle her hair, and then, with a heavy sigh, she answered her ringing phone.

"Wilson, for your sake this had better be another butt-dial due to you going to the loo with your phone in your pocket again, because I'm in the car park and I'm heading to my neighbour's barbecue where I will exchange listening to him blather on about Formula One for chicken wings."

"I'm afraid it's not a pocket-dial, boss. Although, sorry again about that."

"If I were you, I'd be sorrier about this. I was mentally already deciding on desserts. The woman from across the road who once asked me to babysit her tortoise does an incredible pecan pie. What is it?"

"It's David Phillips's brief. He wants to have a word."

"About what? We've got all the computer evidence you could want. We've got burned remnants of forged one-hundred euro notes out in his back garden. And if we didn't have all that, we have the screaming row he had with his wife during his arrest about how

Deccie Fadden ruined their marriage. All that, before he ranted to you and DS Bishop in the car on the way back here about how much he wished Deccie Fadden dead. He even told you that he installed the cameras when he dropped by the day after Deccie's flat-warming party, claiming he'd lost his wallet. I'm no expert, but that sounds like pretty solid evidence. Scratch that – I've just remembered I am an expert and David Phillips is the Whole sodding Truth – end of story."

"Yes, boss, only ..."

"Only what?"

"He now says, according to his brief, that while he was blackmailing Deccie Fadden, and he wanted him dead or gone, he didn't actually attempt to kill him."

"Bullshit."

"He says not only did he not do it, he also knows with one hundred percent certainty who did."

"And we're supposed to believe that as well as him blackmailing Deccie Fadden, an entirely different person was trying to kill him too? Nobody is that unpopular."

"Have you ever heard the show, boss?"

Burns gave another heavy sigh as she watched a young couple cycle by on a tandem bike. They looked sickeningly carefree. "I'll be there in a minute."

"Yes, boss."

"Oh, and Wilson – for no good reason, I've decided you are to blame for this, and I shall find a way of exacting my entirely unjustified revenge at a later date."

"I'd already assumed that, boss."

"Good lad. Pop the kettle on, please."

"Already done."

TWO HOURS LATER, DSI Burns was standing at the front of the incident room containing Deccie Fadden, Paul Mulchrone, Jimmy Stewart, Wilson and the no longer golden Inder O'Riordan. On the wall behind her was a large screen showing David Phillips and his solicitor sitting in an interrogation room. Paul watched Deccie's face tense into a taut mask of anger as he glowered at the man who had tried to destroy his life.

"Gentlemen, thank you all for coming in." Burns turned her attention to Inder. "Inder, I thought you'd gone? Is your role ... thing finished?"

"No," said Inder, matter-of-factly. "They wrote me out."

DSI Burns winced. "Oh, shit. Sorry."

Inder shrugged.

"I'll make this as quick as I can as I've sent my team down to the canteen, and I'm pretty sure they're about to find out that on a Saturday, there'll be two cheese sandwiches and a scone to fight over. David Phillips," she said, motioning at the screen, "during the course of his interview with my colleague Detective Wilson, has made the assertion that while he was behind the blackmail, he had nothing to do with the assassination attempt."

"What?" said Paul.

"I know, it's a bit of a twist. Thing is, we've been checking and, while we can't confirm he was actually at home at the time of the shooting, his car was picked up on a couple of traffic cameras heading in that direction. Strangely, he was able to tell us exactly which ones to check, which, I'll be honest, is a new one on me."

She looked at Wilson, who shrugged.

"The man has an enthusiastic interest in traffic-calming measures," he explained. "I made the mistake of asking. That's fourteen days of my life I'm not getting back."

"Wait. If he didn't shoot at me," said Deccie, leaning forward, "then who did?"

"I must emphasise," said Burns, holding out her hand, "that he is still very much a suspect in that investigation, but we would be remiss if we didn't at least check out what he's saying. He claims to have evidence of who was really behind it."

"You're kidding?" asked Jimmy Stewart.

"I'm not, but again – I'm not saying he isn't."

"So, why hasn't he shown you this evidence that would exonerate him?"

"He has demands."

"Demands?" repeated Jimmy, not even attempting to keep the incredulity from his voice. "Demands? Before he shows you evidence that would clear his own name?"

Burns tilted her head to one side. "Unofficially, Mr Phillips is …"

"A few chimps short of a tea party?" suggested Paul.

DSI Burns didn't say anything, in a way that left nothing unsaid.

"What are these demands, then?" Jimmy asked in an attempt to redirect the conversation.

"There are three. One – he wants to meet Deccie—"

"Hard no," interjected Paul, which prompted Jimmy to turn and give him a pointed look. "Sorry."

"He wants to meet Deccie," repeated Burns, "and he would like Deccie to" – she looked uncomfortable at having to say the next bit out loud – "apologise for seducing his wife."

The rest of the room turned as one to look at Deccie.

"I've done nothing," he protested, his eyes so wide they looked as if they were about to pop right out of his head. "The station has a very strict policy on fraternisation. All we did was work together."

"Is that what they're calling it now?" said Jimmy.

"On my granny's life," responded Deccie, with such venom in his voice that everyone in the room leaned back.

"Easy, fella," said Paul, who understood what those words meant to Deccie. He reached across to pat him on the arm. "It's alright. We believe you." He turned back to Burns. "What else?"

"He would like all charges dropped."

"He's got more chance of a free speedboat," said Jimmy.

"Agreed," said Burns. "And the third demand is a complete non-starter, too. I won't even waste your time with it."

A pregnant pause descended in the room before Burns spoke again. "But I'm sensing you all want to know what it was anyway." She folded her arms across her chest and leaned against the desk. "He would like the bus lane on the Crumlin Road removed."

"Did it seduce his wife too?" asked Paul.

"Is he trying to establish an insanity defence?" asked Jimmy.

"He's got me convinced."

At that moment, a few seconds of high-quality Scandi-influenced dance music reverberated around the room.

"Sorry," said Paul, pulling out his phone. He looked at the screen before rejecting the call. "It's Phil – probably just telling me he's picked up Brigit. I'll ring him back."

"Look," said Burns, turning back to the others, "I know. I get it. The demands are ludicrous. What we were thinking was, in order to get him to prove either way if he has something, we say no to demands two and three, and …"

"No way," said Deccie.

"You wouldn't have to say you—"

"Good, because I didn't."

"But if you …"

Deccie stood up. "Hang on. This" – his lips went white with rage as he pointed his finger at the figure sitting behind the desk on the screen in front of him – "scheming loony bag of pustulating bollocks" – *Worth waiting for*, thought Paul – "tries to destroy my life and then wants me to apologise for something I didn't do?"

Burns nodded. "Only so we can find out if someone else really was trying to kill you. Which we need to know for obvious reasons."

"No."

"Maybe if we—"

Deccie slammed himself back into his chair and folded his arms. "N-fecking-O – no. Some things you don't do. End. Of. Story. I've never seduced a married woman. I have a code. Bleeding coppers, asking me to lie about stuff I never did. Bunny wouldn't have it!"

His final words were met with a tense silence. Paul was familiar with Deccie's distrust of the police. It wasn't as if he was alone in that among the lads they'd grown up with. Theoretically, Bunny McGarry should have made a difference there, but it was almost as if Bunny was seen as an entirely separate – and equally fearsome, albeit for different reasons – force in his own right. Paul knew loads of fellas who would rather chew their own leg off than talk to a copper, and yet they had bawled their eyes out at Bunny's funeral.

Eventually, it was Jimmy Stewart who broke the silence. "Just ... Let's all take a breath," he said calmly. "Let's say, hypothetically, that Phillips has some evidence that proves it was someone else. What would that even look like?"

"As in?" prompted Wilson.

"As in, if he was at home at the time of the shooting, how would he have any evidence of who did it?"

Paul leaped out of his chair. "The death threat! The one written on Deccie's wall."

"He's right," said Jimmy. "He had cameras in there. They would've picked up whoever did that. If it wasn't him, that's what he's got."

Burns looked at Wilson. "Right. Go in there. Tell him we know what it is and he needs to give it to us now or I'm throwing in obstruction of justice."

Wilson left the room.

A few seconds later, Wilson appeared on the screen, entering the interview room, and everyone in the room gathered round to watch. Everyone except Inder O'Riordan, that is, who wandered off down the other end of the incident room.

On the screen, Wilson took his seat opposite Phillips and his solicitor, and pressed "record" on the tape recorder. "Recommencing interview of suspect David Phillips at 11:39am on the eighteenth of June. Present: Detective Donnacha Wilson, National Bureau of Criminal Investigation, and Anthony Gregan, Mr Phillips's legal representative."

"For the record," said David Phillips, leaning towards the recorder, "I still haven't got that cup of tea."

"Right. I'll sort that for you in five minutes. Before that, can you please confirm that you have in your possession a video recording of someone scrawling a death threat on the wall of Mr Declan Fadden's apartment last Sunday night?"

Phillips sank back into his chair. Direct hit.

"That's not—" started the solicitor before Phillips put out his hand to silence him.

"Maybe I do and maybe I don't," said Phillips, "but you'll never find it. I've hidden it far too well. Far too well."

"I should now inform you that failure to reveal evidence in an attempted murder case is a serious criminal offence."

"I'd like to talk to my—" said the solicitor.

"I don't care," hollered Phillips. "I'm already screwed. This way, that yapping little imbecile will have to spend the rest of his life looking over his shoulder." He laughed. Even in profile on-screen, he looked more than a little unhinged.

Paul shook his head. "Does this dipshit think he's the Riddler or something?"

"I've got it."

Inder O'Riordan was so quietly spoken that, at first, none of the others paid attention.

"He seems to be ..." Burns held her thought and snapped her head around. "Hang on – what did you say, Inder?"

Inder was standing at the far end of the room, holding up a laptop. "Phillips has an encrypted online digital storage account based in the Philippines, where we technically can't get to it. Thing is, I just ran a program that pulls all the stored passwords for other websites off his password management software and tried them. He uses the same one for the digital storage account that he uses for eFlow – y'know, for paying the toll on the M50. There's a video file here called 'June twelfth – someone else wants to kill Deccie Fadden'. Do you think that might be it?"

The other three people in the room looked at each other and then back at O'Riordan.

"I'm guessing," said Paul.

Burns shook her head. "You managed to do all that in what ..."

"A minute," supplied Jimmy.

"A minute," repeated Burns.

"Takes me longer than that to open a browser."

Inder put down the laptop. "So, do you want to see it?"

"Absolutely," said Burns. "Just one second."

She went over to the wall and pressed a button, which activated a link directly into the interview room. "Detective Wilson, you can inform Mr Phillips that his help will no longer be required in acquiring that recording, and that the Crumlin Road bus lane isn't going anywhere. The bad news is he really shouldn't reuse passwords. The good news is he's fully up to date on his M50 toll payments."

Paul watched the satisfied smile spread across Deccie's face as Phillips realised what this meant and looked at his solicitor. "They can't do that, can they?"

The solicitor nodded.

Phillips's scream came clearly through the flat-screen speakers. "What? No! NO!"

42

LA REVEAL MAGNIFICO (THIS IS A DAN HANZUS SHOUTOUT!)

In the end, given the number of people in the room who wanted to watch the big reveal, Inder offered to cast the video to the big screen. This meant they wouldn't get to see David Phillips's continuing meltdown, but everyone bar Deccie was fine with that.

Paul folded his arms and shoved his hands under his armpits to keep himself from fidgeting. They were finally going to find out what the hell was happening.

An infrared image of what was evidently Deccie's apartment appeared on the screen.

"If you don't mind me asking, why is there a life-sized gorilla in your front room?" asked Wilson.

Deccie shifted in his seat. "I may have picked it up while drunk."

Paul coughed pointedly.

"I mean," clarified Deccie, "it was given to me by somebody while I was drunk. Legally, like. I didn't nick it."

Burns shook her head. "We're the National Bureau of Criminal Investigation – you're fine. Stuffed gorillas are not our department."

"It's not actually a real gorilla," clarified Deccie.

"Is anyone else finding it weird how gorillas keep coming up this week?" asked Paul. He surveyed the silent room. "OK, just me on that."

"Sometimes," offered Jimmy, "a coincidence is just a coincidence."

A sharp intake of breath from Deccie accompanied a flood of light on the recording from down the end of the apartment hallway.

"That's someone coming in the front door."

They watched in silence as a figure in a hoodie walked carefully down the hall, glancing around as it did so. The intruder's face was obscured from view by the hood.

"Any ideas who that is?" asked Burns softly.

Deccie shook his head.

They watched on as the figure moved across the main room.

"That's my bedroom door," said Deccie. "Jesus, this is creepy."

"I'm guessing they're checking if you're asleep," said Burns.

Jimmy turned to Inder. "Can we enhance this or something? We still haven't seen a face here."

"Not really," said Inder. "It's a low-quality recording."

As the figure on the screen stood perfectly still outside Deccie's bedroom door, the incident room was similarly still, suspended in taut silence.

"Christ!" exclaimed Burns, as the self-composed ringtone on Paul's phone blundered through the tension.

"Sorry, sorry, sorry," he said as he went to accept the call. "Phil, I'll ring you back." And then he hung up.

The figure moved.

It sauntered across the room and then ... the picture cut out.

"What the ..." started Jimmy.

Inder held up a finger. "Give it a ..." As he spoke, the screen changed again, and now showed the room illuminated as normal. "Readjusting," he explained, "from infrared to normal imaging. The intruder just turned on a light."

In the new image, Paul could see a lot more of the living area. "Are those your clothes thrown about the place, Deccie?"

"Not just his," observed Burns, as the figure on the screen picked up a black lace bra draped over the back of the sofa and stared at it.

"Deccie?" said Paul, raising his eyebrows.

Deccie's face was fully red now. "As it happens, I had a female friend over that night."

"And you never told us this?" asked Jimmy.

"Or us," added Burns.

"A gentleman never tells," he replied stiffly.

Paul was aware of Jimmy muttering something to himself but he remained transfixed by the screen, where the figure had pulled a can of spray paint out of its pocket and was now scrawling on the wall in letters three feet high: *DECCIE MUST DIE.*

Once the threat was finished, they turned towards the front door.

"Ah, for …" said Wilson, exasperated. "We've still not seen his face."

The figure moved back towards the light switch then stopped and looked down at the floor.

After a second, it bent down to pick something up.

"Those are my boxer shorts," said Deccie.

As one, the room urghed in disgust as the figure held the boxers up to its face and took a long, deep breath.

"That is nasty," said Burns with genuine feeling.

"But we still haven't …" started Wilson again, then stopped as the figure tilted its head and the hood fell back for a moment.

"Pause it!" yelled Paul.

Inder did as instructed.

"Jesus!" exclaimed Deccie, his face as white as a sheet. Burns stepped forward and pointed at the screen. "Do you recognise that woman?"

"He should do," said Jimmy. "She's his PA. That's Shauna Walsh!"

43

AN EERIE SILENCE

Paul, Jimmy and Deccie moved themselves into the corner of the incident room without being asked. The entire place was now a hive of activity, none of which required their participation. Twenty or so people surrounded them, all busy doing something. The realisation that the Gardaí had a blackmailer in custody but not an attempted killer, and that the latter was still very much at large, had sent the place into overdrive. Cars were being sent to various locations, alerts were being put out, all in an attempt to find Shauna Walsh.

Deccie wore a dazed expression. Paul couldn't blame him. Being "the victim" in an incident room was probably a lot like being the father in a delivery room. Everyone said you were important but really your bit was long over and now you were, at best, an encouragement and, at worst, a distraction.

Paul couldn't take Deccie's silence any longer. The last five minutes had been the longest he'd ever seen him with his mouth closed during their entire friendship, and that included time spent sleeping. "How are you feeling, Deccie?"

"My personal assistant tried to kill me."

"If it's any consolation, my girlfriend dropped me off a ladder and broke my leg. It happens."

Jimmy laughed, which earned him a look of admonishment from the other two. "Sorry, but to say the least, you boys have interesting love lives."

"What are you on about?" said Deccie. "Love life?" He snorted derisively.

Jimmy furrowed his brow. "Do you really not understand what this is?"

"What?" asked Deccie, suspicious now.

"All that stuff with sniffing your undies. The woman is mad, and mad about you."

"She tried to shoot me!"

"Yes," said Jimmy. "Some people have a hard time expressing their emotions."

Paul's phone rang again.

"Jesus," said Deccie, "would you ever change that awful ringtone?"

"Please," Jimmy said in agreement. "It's doing my head in."

"It's one of my songs," protested Paul, wounded by their reaction.

"Ahhhh, right," said Deccie. "It's shit. Has nobody told you that yet?"

Paul responded with a furious glare. "It's hard to believe someone tried to kill you," he muttered as he answered the phone. "Phil, sorry about that. It's all gone a bit mental here."

"That's why I've been ringing ye."

"Yeah, there's been some incredible developments. Put me on speaker so Brigit can hear too."

"That's what I've been trying to tell you – she's not here."

Paul felt an icy shiver run down his spine. His mouth went dry as his eyes met Jimmy's. "What do you mean, she's not there?"

"I came into the hospital to pick her up and they said somebody already had."

"Who?"

DSI Burns was in her office, on the phone with a station in Kildare, asking them to position a car outside Shauna Walsh's parents' house until her officers could get there.

"To be clear, she's to be considered armed and dangerous. Do not approach until my detectives are present. We may need armed response. Observe and report only."

"DSI BURNS!"

Her name was roared so loudly in the incident room that she nearly dropped the phone.

"I'll call you back. Thanks."

"DSI BURNS!"

She threw open the door. "I'm here. What? What?"

Paul Mulchrone was attempting to propel himself across the office in his wheelchair. His face was pale – a picture of distress.

"She's got Brigit. She's got Brigit."

"What?"

"Shauna," supplied Jimmy Stewart. "She picked Brigit up from the hospital about twenty minutes ago."

"Christ. Has Brigit got a phone?"

"No," said Paul. "Phil was in the process of returning it to her."

"Crap." Burns ran her fingers through her hair. "OK. Don't worry, they can't have got far." She raised her voice. "Listen up, everyone – your attention now. Our suspect is in the company of Brigit Conroy, who may or may not be a hostage. They left the Mater Hospital twenty minutes ago. I want teams at the hospital, taxi firms checked. Did she have a car? Was she on foot? Did anyone see where they went? Let's move!"

Deccie walked up to the group, his phone in his hand. "C'mere to me, Superintendent."

"Moira?" asked Burns, ignoring him. "Can you please chase the phone company? I want that trace." She glanced at Paul, not wanting to say the words "threat to life".

From the look Moira Clarke gave her boss, it was clear she already understood. She snatched up her phone.

"DSI Burns." insisted Deccie.

"Wilson?"

Donnacha Wilson looked up from his desk. "You know Brigit. Get her picture out. She's been in the paper. Use that."

"DSI BURNS!"

She stopped and looked at Deccie. "What?"

He held up his phone. "I just realised I've got Shauna on that Find My Friends thing. Do you think that might be useful?"

The room went quiet. DSI Burns blinked a couple of times. "Yeah, that'd be handy. Thanks for finally mentioning it."

44

SURPRISE!

Something felt off. *It was probably the meds*, Brigit thought. Shauna had just appeared at her bedside with a wheelchair, told her she was good to go and off they'd gone. Brigit had needed to explain that she had to get changed back into her clothes first. She felt incredibly over-dressed putting on the summery peach dress she'd worn on her way to the awards ceremony, which felt like a lifetime ago now, but it beat the alternative. Shauna would have been happy to take her out of there in just a hospital gown. The girl was all nervous energy. She was on a schedule and seemed hellbent on keeping to it. Brigit was surprised that she was there at all, but Shauna had explained that Phil had been delayed by "investigation stuff" and she'd offered to help. It also meant that, annoyingly, Brigit still didn't have her phone.

While delighted to be out of the hospital, Brigit still felt a little woozy and tender. On that front, Shauna's driving style wasn't helping – she had a tendency to hurl the rather nice SUV she'd picked Brigit up in around the road. It was like Shauna's new mohawk was inhabiting her being and encouraging her to go full Mad Max behind the wheel. Brigit was the last person to criticise someone else's driving, but still. That and the fact that since she'd picked her up, Shauna Walsh hadn't stopped talking. From the moment she'd put her into the wheelchair to push her out to the car park, she'd been rambling on a mile a minute. It was better than the terse silence that had existed between them the last time they'd met in St Stephen's Green, but it was all a little much.

Speaking of a little much, Brigit had been looking forward to going home, sleeping in her own bed and spending some quality time with Paul. With that in mind, she'd been less than thrilled when she realised they were heading back to Deccie's apartment.

"But I thought Paul said that Deccie was going to be under Garda protection for a while?" she asked Shauna. "Have they not put him somewhere else?"

"Oh," said Shauna with a wave of her hand, "no need for that any more. Did you not hear? They caught the guy. It was all over the news this morning. As were you, by the way. There's been non-stop talk about how you saved Deccie's life. Non-stop!" She let out a high-pitched giggle, took both hands off the steering wheel and wiggled them jazz-hands style to emphasise her point. "'Deccie Fadden saved by girlfriend' – that was a headline in one of the papers this morning."

"Oh, brilliant," said Brigit, exhausted at the mere thought of it all. "It'll take me ages to explain that nonsense – whoa!"

The SUV skidded to an abrupt halt in the bus lane outside of Lansdowne Towers.

"And we're here!" announced Shauna.

"Don't you need to put this into the underground car park?"

"No time. I mean, no need. I'll get you upstairs and then come back for it."

"You'll get a ticket."

Shauna slapped her on the arm playfully. "Don't worry about it, silly. This won't take long."

"But ..."

Before Brigit could say anything else, Shauna was out of the SUV and opening her door for her. "Quickly, quickly, slowpoke. Lots to do."

Shauna took Brigit by the elbow as she got out of the car and started hurrying her towards the door. Brigit was beginning to think that Shauna might have had too much coffee, or some other form of stimulant.

As they entered reception, a security guard she didn't recognise behind the concierge desk stood up and held up a newspaper. "Oh, wow – are you Brigit Conroy?"

"I used to be," she said as Shauna rushed her past.

"You're a hero."

"I'm really not."

"Could I get a selfie?"

"No time," said Shauna, all but pushing Brigit into the waiting lift. "See, you're famous now!"

"Hang on," said Brigit, shaking Shauna's hand off her. "What do you mean, no time?"

Shauna sighed theatrically. "Alright, I wasn't supposed to tell you this – we're having a surprise thing for you."

Brigit self-consciously raised her hands to the bandages on her head. "Oh. I'm not a big fan of surprises."

"Trust me – you'll love this one."

45

THE TRAFFIC REALLY IS MURDER

Deccie was seated in the back of the unmarked car, Jimmy beside him, as Detective Wilson drove and DSI Burns occupied the passenger seat, her phone glued to her ear. They were travelling down the Quays as fast as they could, siren on, but, it being a Saturday, their journey was still slow-going.

It had felt weird leaving Paulie behind, but he had told them to. Getting him in and out of a car with the wheelchair would be a time-consuming affair, and time was one thing they didn't have.

"And they've confirmed that?" asked Burns. "Right." She hung up the phone. "Wilson, get us across the Quays onto the Southside. Hopefully there'll be more room to manoeuvre there."

She turned to address the duo in the back seat, ignoring the honking that Wilson attracted by pulling across two lanes of traffic.

"OK, here's what we know. The gun recovered yesterday was an old hunting rifle that we were having trouble tracing. Turns out Shauna's daddy is quite the firearms collector, a lot of which aren't legally held. He confirmed the rifle sounds like one he's just discovered is missing, along with a handgun ..."

"Christ," said Jimmy. "So she's definitely armed?"

"We have to work on that assumption. The concierge has

confirmed that Brigit and Shauna are back at Lansdowne Towers. We're expecting a possible hostage situation."

"Cameras," said Jimmy. "We have cameras in Deccie's apartment. I'll ring Phil."

Jimmy fished his phone out of his trouser pocket and started dialling.

"OK," said Burns, "good." She turned to face Deccie and focused her eyes intently on his. "Now, I'm only going to ask this once, and I will remind you that Brigit's life might be on the line here. Did anything happen between you and Shauna?"

"No," said Deccie.

"A one-time thing? You made a pass? She made a pass? A misunderstanding?"

"Absolutely not. She was my PA."

"I'm pretty sure people have screwed their PAs before."

"Not me," he said firmly. "The station has a very strict no-fraternisation policy."

"Did she ever do anything weird? Anything that gave you cause for concern?"

"No. I mean, I never had a PA before, so I don't have a great frame of reference."

The car jolted as Wilson hit a kerb. "Sorry," he said, either to the occupants or the irate people on the footpath.

Burns bit her lip and looked out the car's rear window. "Sunday – when this threat was written on the wall" – her eyes refocused on Deccie – "did you have somebody with you?"

"A woman, yes."

"What was her name?"

"I ..."

Burns gave him a look as he floundered. "Never mind. Do you often have one-night stands?"

"No. That was my first."

"I see. Have you been in a relationship with anyone since Shauna started working for you?"

"No. I mean – I met this Dr Megan Wright woman on Monday

night and she came back to mine." Deccie cringed. "I am going to ring her but I've not yet. Y'know, with the blackmail and everything."

"Yeah, quite the week you're having. Two one-night stands back to back, a blackmail plot and death threats. Pretty clearly it was Sunday that triggered Shauna. How would she have known?"

"She was at the thing – the event on Sunday."

"I see. And she's normally at these things with you?"

"Yeah. Telling me where to go and that."

"And she did nothing to arouse your suspicions before this?"

Before Deccie could respond to that, Jimmy interrupted. "Sorry, but Phil's just checked the cameras in the apartment. He can't see anything and he says they haven't detected any motion since yesterday."

"Then where the hell are they?"

Nobody answered. Instead, Deccie asked the question that nobody seemed willing to address. "What do you think Shauna is going to do?"

DSI Burns paused for a second then turned back around in her seat. "Nothing. We're going to stop her."

46

TOLD YOU – IT REALLY IS THE QUIET ONES YOU HAVE TO WATCH

Are there really good and bad ways to die?

Brigit wasn't sure about that, but she was sure that there were annoying ways to die, and this would be one of them. Yes, she wasn't in top form thanks to the concussion and the meds and whatever else, but still.

The bad feeling had really kicked in in the lift. That was when she considered that Shauna being so wired really was odd. Even so, she'd chalked it up to her own paranoia and had allowed herself to be led blindly up to the roof. Perhaps the girl just really loved the prospect of a surprise party?

Embarrassingly, Brigit had allowed the chance of some more of Da Xin's cake to distract her a little. The one depicting the assassination attempt, which she'd shared with the nurses this morning, had been incredible. It had resulted in a room full of people just chewing in quiet, worshipful ecstasy with the occasional 'mmmm, moist' thrown in. The world really needed more words to describe good cake. Most people didn't eat cake at ten in the morning, but then nurses better than anyone knew that you had to take the chance when you could, as you didn't know which way your day might end up going. Case in point.

Despite the gnawing bad feeling, Brigit had still been daft enough to expect a gaggle of people waiting to shout "surprise!" when the door opened. Instead, as she'd emerged onto the roof, shielding her eyes from the dazzling sun, a hand had roughly pushed her forward, causing her to stumble.

When she turned around, Shauna was drawing her hand out of her handbag, and it was holding a gun.

"Oh, for Christ's sake," said Brigit. "You have got to be joking?"

Shauna's little face turned into an alarming snarl. "Do I look like I'm joking? Put your hands in the air."

Brigit did as she was instructed. The two women stood there for a couple of seconds, Shauna in front of the door, Brigit about a dozen feet from the railing that was all that stood between her and a whole lot of gravity. She looked around. "So, am I right in thinking there isn't going to be cake?"

Shauna jabbed the gun in her direction. "Is this funny to you?"

"No," said Brigit, "it really isn't. Do I get to know what the hell is going on?"

"You know!" Shauna spat, her eyes wide.

"I honestly don't."

"You took Deccie from me!"

"Oh, for ..." Brigit looked up to the heavens. "You're kidding me! You as well?"

"As well as who?"

"The rest of women in Ireland, apparently. Ironically, all of us apart from me."

Shauna hesitated, a shake of rage visibly passing through her. "He. Is. MINE."

"OK," said Brigit, trying to sound placatory. "I'm marrying someone else. I mean, I was. Obviously, getting murdered might put a serious crimp in that plan."

"You don't understand him like I do. Nobody does."

"I can believe that. I mean, he's alright underneath all the ... sheer Deccie-ness, but he's not my type."

"You're lying!"

"I'm not."

"The paper said—"

"Oh, fuck me," howled Brigit. "No, sorry to interrupt your little rant, but am I here right now because of that shitty tabloid story? I shoved a lowlife into a bin and he printed that to get his own back." She shook her head. "I'm annoyed I turned down the opportunity to feed him his stupid little porkpie hat now. It's true what they say – you regret the chances you didn't take."

Shauna looked unsure for a moment then hissed at Brigit, "You're lying!"

"About which bit? Ah, never mind. Think what you like. Hang on a sec – what about you and the hunky guy in the nightclub?"

Shauna waved her free hand dismissively. "He was just some nobody I hired off a website to make Declan jealous."

"Right. If you've got a number, I've got a friend called Nora who is tricky to shop for and she's got a birthday coming up."

"Silence!"

"D'you know what? No. It's been a very long week and I'm done being pushed around. Also, my arms are getting heavy. I'm taking them down."

"Don't!"

Brigit shrugged. "What are you going to do – shoot me? Isn't that already the plan?" She lowered her arms slowly. "There we go. Feel free to put the gun down if you're getting tired."

"Stop making fun of me!"

"I'm too tired to try. Can I ask, though," said Brigit, having calmed down enough to look properly at the gun that was pointed at her, "what's the deal with the gun?"

"This is a Walther P38 9mm semi-automatic pistol that belonged to an officer in the Luftwaffe. Daddy has quite the collection."

"It's an antique?"

Shauna looked oddly defensive. "A working one, I assure you. Lots of people died in the Second World War, you know?"

"Yeah, I think I read something about that." Brigit looked around her. She'd not managed to form any sort of plan, but so far, she'd hit on the idea that keeping Shauna talking was a better option than anything else happening. In the distance, she heard a police siren. Might be nothing to do with them, but any hope was hope. "So, if you don't mind me asking, you're in love with Deccie?"

Shauna blinked. "Yes."

"Was it you who scrawled 'Deccie must die' on his wall?"

"I was angry. He was making bad choices. I wanted him to see that. I ... I was there when he let that awful woman invite herself into his ... He didn't want her. He just doesn't know what he wants. He needs to be" – she paused, as if looking for the right word, and a smile spread across her face – "protected. Yes, that's it. He needs to be protected."

"I know the feeling. And why did you try to shoot him yesterday?"

Brigit already knew the answer as Shauna's mouth formed into an O of outrage. "I would never hurt Declan. I was shooting at you!"

47

A BAD DAY TO DIE

DSI Burns felt like throwing her phone against the wall of the stairwell. They had taken up position on the top floor of Lansdowne Towers. She had officers quietly clearing residents off the next two floors down at that very moment.

"It turns out this is happening on a bad day resource-wise," she explained. "Armed response is coming in from Kildare, where they were on standby due to some foreign dignitaries playing a round of golf. Our on-call negotiator is an hour away and, even when armed response get here, our subjects are on top of the tallest building in the area. There's no shot unless Shauna positions herself in a very convenient location for us. Are you sure that there's only one way onto the roof?"

That question was directed at Deccie. As luck would have it, today was literally the on-duty concierge's second day on the job, and he had never even been to the roof. Wilson was currently downstairs trying to ring the building manager or contact any other member of staff. In the absence of anything better, Deccie was her local knowledge.

"As far as I know," he replied. "What are you going to do?"

Burns hesitated. "That's what I'm trying to figure out."

"Brigit might not have long," said Jimmy Stewart.

"That has occurred to me." Her phone vibrated in her hand. "Commissioner, thank you for getting back to me."

Over the course of the next minute, Burns laid out the situation as efficiently as possible while her boss listened and assessed. Hostage situation. Mentally unstable person with a gun. Imminent threat to life. Possibly only one viable point of entry.

"I see," the Commissioner said, when Burns had finally finished. "Have you attempted to ring this Walsh girl's mobile?"

"Yes. She isn't answering. The only option for communication is to go up onto the roof. I'm happy to do so."

"That is not your job."

"Respectfully, Commissioner, it needs to be someone's job."

"You are a DSI, Susan. Your job is command. Given the information to hand, I feel the only option is to wait for the negotiator to arrive."

"But—"

"We are not sending an unqualified person up there and we cannot risk any form of assault. That is my decision. We have to play this by the book."

"Respectfully, again, ma'am, I don't think the book was written with this particular situation in mind."

"Stand ready and contact me if things change. Good luck."

As the call disconnected, Burns held her phone in her hand and looked at it.

"She won't go?" asked Jimmy.

"Bloody politics. That thing in Cork three years ago is in her head. She's not saying it, but it is."

"So, what do we—" Jimmy Stewart stopped abruptly. "Oh."

Burns turned to look at him. "What?"

"Would now be a good time to point out that Deccie isn't here any more?

48

FRATERNISATION WITH THE CRIMINALLY INSANE

Hard as it was to believe, given the circumstances, Brigit found herself running out of conversation. And to think that old bag Mrs Hickey, who had taught her in third class, had told her chatting would be the death of her. It had turned out to be the opposite.

It looked a lot like Shauna was gearing herself up to do something, and there was only one thing that seemed to be on the agenda.

Think fast. Think fast. Think fast.

Oddly, the urge to tell Shauna that rumour had it Deccie was great in bed popped into her head. She decided now wasn't the time for that. As last words go ...

Shauna pointed at one of the gates in the railings around the roof. "Move over there."

"Why?"

Shauna's face scrunched up. "Because I said so."

"Yeah, but I'm not a fan of heights."

"Move over there. NOW!"

Brigit kept trying to sound infinitely reasonable. "Why, though? What's the plan here, Shauna?"

"If you must know, you are going to take your own life."

"Seriously?"

"Yes. And Deccie will be upset … and I will comfort him and …"

Shauna didn't explain beyond that. Brigit guessed her mind wasn't exactly thinking logically as clearly that plan was batshit insane and ran out of road really fast after that particular "and …".

"How about you put the gun down and we think this through?"

Shauna shot at the ground just to the left of Brigit's feet, and the bullet pinged off the concrete before it ricocheted into the blue sky.

"Christ!" yelled Brigit.

"Move."

"You're a fruit loop. Gaga. Away with the fairies!"

Shauna stamped her foot. "Don't call me that. You don't get to say that."

"No, I do," said Brigit, thoroughly sick of trying to meet the unreasonable with reason. "I don't know what's caused you to be like this, but I think it predates Deccie by quite some margin. You need to stop. Put the gun down, let's talk, and we'll see if we can't get you some help."

"Move or I will shoot you," screeched Shauna.

"What's the other option here, Shauna? Move and you'll push me off the building? I think if it's a choice of how to die, I'll take the gunshot wound, please. At least it'll leave something they can bury."

Shauna jumped up and down this time, and the gun in her hand veered about wildly. "That. Isn't. The. Plan."

For the briefest moment Brigit thought about rushing her, but as soon as she took a step, Shauna fired another bullet into the ground, this one just inches away from Brigit's right foot.

"Fuck me!"

Shauna was the worst combo imaginable – unbalanced and yet somehow in control of the bit you really didn't want her to be.

"Stop trying to trick me."

Shauna was advancing towards Brigit now, the gun unwavering as it pointed at Brigit's chest. A dive to the left or right and Brigit would just die lying down instead of standing up.

Then, as if Shauna was reading her mind, a sly smile of pride broke out across her face. "I'm good at shooting. Daddy taught me."

As Brigit's slim selection of options fell away, the thought struck her that she'd really like to meet Daddy as she'd a strong idea he might hold some of the blame for this. She clenched her eyes shut and tried to summon a nice thought. None came.

"Ah, fuck it. Fuck this and fuck you."

As last words went ...

"Shauna?"

His voice was so quiet that Brigit thought she'd imagined it.

There was a pause.

"Shauna, it's me – Deccie."

Brigit opened one eye. Deccie was crouching in the doorway.

Shauna had half turned to look at him. "Declan ..."

"How's it going?" he asked.

Her voice came out bizarrely peppy. "Great, thanks."

"I just wanted to let you know some big news. I've left Caint FM."

"Oh no," said Shauna, sounding horrified.

Deccie put out a hand. "No, no. That's a good thing. It means I'm no longer subject to the fraternisation policy."

"They do have a very strict no-fraternisation policy."

Brigit had now opened both her eyes, but her brain seemed incapable of kicking into gear. Oh God, was this hell? Had she already died and gone to hell? It sure as shit couldn't be heaven. She looked around. Nobody had a ukulele, so there was a chance it wasn't hell either.

"Yes," admitted Deccie, "they do have a strict policy, but, seeing as we no longer work together, would you be free to go out for a curry this evening?"

Shauna left a very long pause before saying, "I've actually got plans for this evening."

Deccie looked stumped by this, and Brigit couldn't blame him. She was generally in favour of playing a bit hard to get, but this didn't seem the time for it.

"Right," Deccie said with a nod.

"I'm free tomorrow, though?" Shauna added quickly, because you don't want to overplay your hand.

"That'd be grand."

Another pause followed. People asking each other out was often awkward, but this particular situation might have broken new ground. Maybe, dream achieved, Shauna was about to drop the gun and go home to dye her mohawk a new colour, but Brigit decided her current run of luck wasn't something she wanted to put a lot of faith in, so ... she charged.

Shauna glanced in her direction and her beatific smile dropped away and was replaced by an angry snarl.

Deccie hit the floor.

Shauna swung her gun-wielding hand up and around. Brigit collided with it and a bullet was sent into the roof. Once you got past the gun, Shauna was a pretty small woman with not a pick on her. Brigit lifted her off her feet and took visceral delight in the expulsion of air as she body slammed her onto the ground.

The gun skittered across the rooftop and came to a stop near the edge. Brigit pulled herself up, sat astride Shauna, and pinned her hands behind her back.

"Ha!" she shouted, a part of her dimly aware that she might be losing it a tad. "There are some definite advantages to being what a national newspaper recently referred to as, and I'm quoting, 'plump'."

Almost immediately came the sounds of running feet and the feeling of hands taking her away while others held Shauna down.

Brigit looked up at the sky, not really hearing the voices of whoever was talking to her. "I tell you what, it's a bloody nice day."

49

AH, MIGHT AS WELL JUMP!

Shauna was whisked away quickly, shouting about how she was going to sue Brigit as Daddy had excellent lawyers.

They'd have to be really excellent.

DSI Susan Burns was incredibly annoyed with Deccie, but Brigit was long past caring why. She started to giggle when it came to her that she was now in a position to no longer have to care why people were angry at Deccie.

Gardaí were running about the place, talking about cordons and forensics. Because nobody told her she couldn't, Brigit started walking slowly back down the stairs. She'd had enough of roofs for quite some time.

Deccie followed her. "You alright, Brig?"

"Super, Deccie. Thanks for asking. Yourself?"

"I'm alright. That was intense, wasn't it?"

"Ah," said Brigit, "not my first armed stand-off."

"Mine neither, as it happens."

Brigit looked at the lift. "I think I'm going to take the stairs all the way down."

"It's eighteen floors," said Deccie.

"I know, but my lasting memory of that lift is going to be standing in it with a woman who was about to kill me."

"Fair enough," said Deccie, pushing open the door to the stairwell. "I could do with the walk. Besides – I've got terrible memories of that lift too. I was once in it and the bloke from the fifteenth floor with the poodle let out a fart that'd strip paint."

They started walking down the stairs, side by side. "That sounds very traumatic for you, Deccie."

"Ah, it's the dog I feel sorry for. Poor sod has to live with that twenty-four-seven."

They descended in silence until the eleventh floor, then Deccie spoke again. "I don't want it to be weird."

"What?"

"Between you and me."

"For the last time, Deccie – I may be the only woman in Ireland who feels this way, and congratulations on that, by the way, but my interest in you is entirely platonic."

"Is that something to do with plants?" asked Deccie with a grin.

"Y'know, I have no idea when you're joking."

"Actually," said Deccie, "I don't think anybody does. People are always laughing when I'm being dead serious and taking me seriously when I'm having a laugh."

"That must be annoying."

"It is. Still, I've sort of built a career on it."

"Have you made any decisions on that front?"

"I'm going to stay where I am. Besides, did you hear? I won an award last night. Only found out this morning."

"Congratulations," said Brigit, punching him lightly on the shoulder.

"Yeah. Apparently, Oliver Dandridge picked it up on my behalf."

"Christ, good luck getting that back."

"I might need to hire you to strong-arm him for me."

"Oh, I'll do that for free."

They walked down another couple of flights before either of them spoke again.

"Wait," said Brigit, "what were you saying before? About it not being weird?"

"Oh, because I saved your life and that."

Brigit stopped walking. "What?"

"Ye know, like, I don't want it to be like in one of them Japanese films where I save your life and now you feel like you owe me a life debt or something? That you've to be my faithful servant, following me wherever I go, trying to repay a debt that cannot be repaid." He looked around to see that Brigit had started walking back up the stairs. "Where are you going?"

"I've changed my mind," she said, without looking back. "I'm going to throw myself off the building."

50

PARTNERS IN CRIME

Brigit stood up in the centre of the room. "Right, thank you all for coming. I would like to welcome you to the first MCM Investigations owners meeting."

The other four attendees applauded.

"I mean, technically," began Paul, "we've had these meetings before, but they always happened in bed."

Brigit picked up a cushion and tossed it at him. "Shut up."

"Yes," agreed Jimmy Stewart. "There are some things a man of my advanced years does not need to know."

Brigit looked at Cynthia. "Before I forget, I would like to officially welcome Cynthia as a full-time employee of MCM Investigations." This was roundly applauded, and Cynthia gave an embarrassed nod and wave. "And also, while I appreciate your professionalism in taking minutes, I would like my idiot boyfriend's remark about meetings in bed to be struck from the record."

Cynthia nodded and duly scratched out something on her notepad.

"In fact," said Brigit, snatching the pad from her and deftly replacing it with a glass of mid-price sparkling wine, "I'm giving you the night off."

"Hear, hear," said Paul.

"Hey," said Phil, who was standing at the doors to the balcony. "There's a bloke over there with a garden on his roof. I've been saying we all should do that."

"Yeah, that's Mr Thorwald who owns the Last Drop."

Phil nodded approvingly. "The man is a forward thinker."

"Yeah," agreed Paul. "Oh, and good news, Brig – Mrs Thorwald came back. They're back together."

"Ah, that's nice."

"Is she a redhead?" asked Phil.

"She is," confirmed Brigit.

"She's out there with him now. They're having a snog as the sun sets."

"G'wan the Thorwalds!" cheered Paul.

"And now they're … Blimey," said Phil, turning away from the balcony, "that escalated quickly."

"Oh," said Brigit. "Well, OK. Not wild about that. Then again, I'm staying off the balcony for a while. Really lost my taste for heights. Can't think why. Anyway, I just wanted to say, for the record, which come to think of it is no longer being taken, but anyway, big thanks to our two angel investors."

"No problem," said Jimmy. "It's a brilliant investment. Well, *we* are. I surveyed my four kids before putting money in as, well, it's their inheritance. Turns out it is a small price to pay if it means I'm not hanging around the place like a wet weekend."

"Absolutely," agreed Phil. "And Da Xin said it was worth it just to get me off deliveries for the Little Cake Lady. Apparently," – his face scrunched up as he tried to recall the exact words – "I have received consistently negative feedback from the customers for being both miserable and weird."

"That doesn't sound like you," said Paul loyally.

"No. It was me, alright. Some of the customers sent in pictures." Phil held up his bottle of beer. "So this has worked out well for all of us."

Jimmy raised his glass of orange juice. "That it has. To us!"

They started to clink glasses, then remembered Paul still couldn't stand up, and so gathered around his wheelchair to do it again.

"Now," said Brigit, "we've got that out of the way. Who fancies a curry?"

"Nice one," said Phil. "By the way, how's Maggie getting on in her fat camp?"

Brigit and Paul looked at each other.

"Well," said Paul, "we're due to collect her tomorrow, but we've not heard anything."

Brigit nodded. "I did try to ring them yesterday, but there was no answer. Still, though – I'm sure it's fine. They're professionals."

Phil pointedly raised his eyebrows.

"I mean," offered Paul, "what's the worst that could happen?"

51

DOGGED DETERMINATION

"The person you have called is unavailable. If you'd like to leave a message, please do so after the tone."

Beep.

"Hi, Mr Mulchrone, it's Ben here from the Fido Fit for Life camp. I think this is the right number – as long as that's a seven and not a two. Can't read my own handwriting!" *Laughs.* "Anyway, just wanted to let you know your partner dropped Maggie off without any problem and she's settling in great."

Beep.

"Hi, Mr Mulchrone, Ben here from Fido Fit for Life. Just wanted a quick word. Nothing is wrong, but we just want to double-check a couple of things after Maggie's first day. Give me a shout when you get this."

Beep.

"Hɪ, Mr Mulchrone, Ben from Fido Fit for Life again. Just following up after my message yesterday as I've not heard back. It'd be great to have a chat. Maggie is having some issues. She doesn't like the food and, well, yeah ... Our behaviourist Tony is going to do a couple of sessions with her to deal with the aggression, but we needed to make you aware."

Beep.

"Mr Mulchrone, Ben from Fido Fit for Life. I need to speak to you urgently. Maggie broke down a door last night and ate the staff's food. We don't know how she got out, but ... yeah. Tony is having a look into things, but we really need to talk."

Beep.

"Mr Mulchrone, Ben from, y'know. Maggie took Tony hostage for a while there and he's quit. The poor guy swallowed his whistle. We finally got Maggie into solitary, but you need to come pick her up. We can't deal with this."

Beep.

"Mr Mulchrone, if you don't pick up your dog, we will have to call the authorities."

Beep.

"The authorities are on their way."

Beep.

"The authorities have left. Apparently, the guy knew your dog and refused to touch her. I didn't even know that was possible. Please. Ring. Me."

Beep.

"Things have escalated! She has broken free and is now leading the other dogs in a revolt! WHAT THE FECK IS HAPPENING?"

Beep.

"Ehm ... Mr, whatever. All the dogs have gone. Maggie has led them off. We don't know where. We're closing the camp down. Good luck."

Beep.

"They're back! We're surrounded! I ... What do we do? WHAT DO WE DO?!"

Beep.

End of messages.

EPILOGUE – IN CASE YOU WERE WONDERING

Paul stared at his laptop screen.

It was 3am.

Brigit was in the bedroom, happily snoring away, but he couldn't sleep. Maybe it was because she'd been a nurse for so long, working shifts at odd hours, but Brigit could conk out at the drop of a hat. Paul was incredibly jealous. He'd always been an amateur insomniac, but the last couple of months with the cast and the confinement to the apartment had really taken things to the next level. The accursed cast was finally coming off later that day and he couldn't wait. He intended to spend the first few days just enjoying being able to scratch any bits of himself he felt like. It was the little things that made life worth living.

He'd been downloading a piece of video-editing software, which Phil told him they needed for editing footage together, when he'd run out of storage. The discovery had escalated to a full digital spring clean. Gone was all the music he'd created. While he hadn't admitted as much to anyone, it had gradually dawned on him that it was, in fact, terrible. In hindsight, seeing as he wasn't a fan of dance music, maybe he shouldn't have tried to create it.

He'd then got rid of some software he wasn't using, some files from old cases that were all backed up online, and then all the random crap that had built up in his downloads folder. The endeavour had left him sitting there, looking at one particular file that remained on his desktop, staring at him. He'd put it out of his mind but there it was, almost winking at him.

Thankfully, as part of David Phillips's plea deal, all remaining copies of the file had been destroyed. The world would never know what the Whole Truth had to hold over Deccie Fadden.

Paul had only ever watched the clip twice; once in the company of Deccie and then again with DSI Burns. Both had been utterly excruciating experiences. He was going to delete it. Then he would run a load of things to make sure it was impossible for anyone to retrieve it.

To her credit, Brigit, despite undoubtedly dying to know, had never asked him what was on the video.

He put on his headphones.

Just one more time. He'd watch it one more time and then it would be gone from the world for ever.

With a final glance around, he pressed "play".

An old title sequence from the *Oprah* show played – a little flourish David Phillips had added to proceedings.

When it had finished, it cut to a shot of Deccie, wearing just his underpants and sitting in one of two chairs positioned facing each other. Paul distinctly remembered looking over at Deccie when the image had first appeared on screen, concerned by the lack of clothing. While he had been grateful that what subsequently transpired wasn't anything sexual, at least that might have been slightly easier to brush off. It was one of those irrefutable facts of life that, deep down, everyone was weird about sex.

This, though ...

"Deccie Fadden," said Deccie, pulling a serious face but thankfully not doing the voice, "thank you so much for joining us."

Deccie moved across to the other chair. "It's my pleasure, Oprah."

Back to the first chair. "You have just become the first person in history to win an Oscar, a Tony, a Grammy, an Emmy, an Irish radio award and the All-Ireland Hurling Final as a player-coach. How on Earth did you manage all that?"

He moved back to the second chair and gave his best humble look. "Well, Oprah, I don't know what to tell you. It's all about having an appreciation for the fundamentals of the—"

Paul hit "stop". His flesh was crawling with embarrassment, and he was only thirty seconds in. There were several more minutes of this stuff and it only got worse. After the Oprah interview, Deccie had had "chats" with Graham Norton, Ryan Tubridy and the Dalai Lama. Among all the cringeworthy moments, which were plentiful, the worst was the point when it had become blindingly obvious that Deccie didn't know who the Dalai Lama was, and somehow believed him to be an actual llama. The thing was eleven minutes of memeable moments that would have made Deccie ridiculously famous while at the same time utterly destroying his career.

Paul grabbed the file with his mouse, dragged it across to the special mushroom-cloud logo to access the software Phil had installed for him, and dropped it in.

A box appeared on the screen: "Are you sure you want to destroy this file for ever?"

Yes.

He wheeled himself over to the balcony to enjoy the view. It was late summer now and unexpectedly warm, so they'd left the doors open to let in some air. Paul looked out across the city – at the bits of it that he could see, at least. Dublin was his town and he, together with Brigit, Phil and Jimmy, could look forward to many more exciting adventures in it. They would dig themselves out of the hole they were in and become not just a successful business, but the finest bloody detective agency going. He felt his chest swell with pride. Tomorrow was the first day of the rest of his life and he couldn't wait.

They were going to make a difference. Right wrongs, fight for justice and ...

A snatch of movement out of the corner of his eye caught his attention and derailed his train of thought.

Paul grimaced.

For Christ's sake. Enough is enough.

"Oi! Mr and Mrs Thorwald, any chance you could do that indoors? Why are you waving at me? Stop waving and ... Oh God, seriously? I'd prefer you put clothes on rather than taking them ... Don't move any nearer to the edge – that's very unsafe and ... Ah, forget it. Ye freaks. You've totally ruined a moment here."

Paul awkwardly wheeled himself back inside and closed the doors.

That did it. Tomorrow, he was buying a high-powered hose.

FREE BOOK

Hello again reader-person,

I hope you enjoyed Deccie Must Die. Thanks for buying it and taking the time to read it. There'll be more Bunny in 2023 and something else may emerge out of Dublin or the States later in 2022. If you need a Caimh fix before then make sure you've signed up for my monthly newsletter for free short stories, audio, and the latest goings on in the Bunnyverse.

You'll also get a copy of my short fiction collection called *How To Send A Message*, which features several stories featuring characters from my books. To sign up go to my website:

www.WhiteHairedIrishman.com

The paperback costs $10.99/£7.99/€8.99 in the shops but you can get the e-book for free just by signing up to my newsletter.

Cheers muchly and thanks for reading,
Caimh

ALSO BY CAIMH MCDONNELL

Visit www.WhiteHairedIrishman.com to find out more.

Printed in Great Britain
by Amazon

85399784R00176